Brexit Comes
To
Bedwell Ash

S.A. LAMA

DEDICATION

Thank you to those who inspired me to write this book, especially our politicians whose incompetence knows no bounds. Without you this novel would never have been written.

Also, a special thank-you to my cats who sit and stare at me typing while waiting patiently for their next meal.

CONTENTS

FOREWARD

If you want to write a novel write about what you know they said. So, I set my first novel 'A Dedicated Professional' in an office and plotted the murderous goings on. When the extraordinary events of 2016 happened I stopped writing 'A Dedicated Professional' and put pen to paper (or more precisely fingers to keyboard!) and started work on this novel 'Brexit Comes to Bedwell Ash'.

I have my own ideas as to why the UK voted to leave the EU and I needed to tell that story. There are so many people angry at what has happened (and what is still happening) for so many different reasons. The situation is not helped by our politicians who (in my opinion) behave like mental Munchkins skipping along the yellow brick road to Westminster pretending to represent us while squabbling amongst themselves in their self-serving efforts to build their own Emerald Castles.

Brexit Comes to Bedwell Ash takes a sideways look at the issues surrounding Brexit. It uses examples and scenarios which interweave into the lives of the characters to explain the reasons for the choices they make. It discusses bullying and how the strong take advantage of the weak and vulnerable in an effort to accumulate wealth. It also questions why somebody on minimum wage and struggling to pay their rent would go through the same thought processes as a person with a second home abroad when casting their referendum vote.

My hope is that my novel is informative, entertaining and funny although that is of course for the reader to decide. I ask that should you read my novel and decide to leave feedback that any negative comments are pitched in a constructive way as it is only through understanding my weak points that I will grow as a writer.

It's my first published novel, it's a controversial topic. I welcome feedback:

Instagram: salama_author
Facebook Page: S.A.Lama_Author

PART 1

ELIZABETH

It was a full moon, not a super moon or a blood moon but a full moon, a glorious full moon, controlling the tides and – some say – manipulating malleable individuals to commit acts of inexplicable behaviour by exercising a gravitational pull on their bodily fluids.

The night was playful, stars teasing, disappearing and then reappearing in glitter circles, a sky-scape of wonderment, all visible to the naked eye. On such an evening Elizabeth Rossi would often sit in the conservatory of their home to view the astral party, but on this April night she was instead in the local French Restaurant celebrating the eighteenth birthday of her only son. It could be said that the mood in the restaurant was just as playful as the skies that night: one minute laughter, the next a silent respect when the party boy requested a hearing and the audience hushed to digest every word he uttered. But that was only until Elizabeth rose to the fore and sucked the spirit from the occasion as her words transformed the evening from one of celebration to an active crime scene.

"You racist!" The birthday boy was the first to voice his opinion.

"You bigot!" his elder sister screamed so loudly it almost bump-started the birth of her first child.

"What's a bigot?" asked the youngest sibling.

The mother of the two disgruntled adults and one curious child looked along the table. All eyes were on her. She lowered her head and sat down.

The evening had been going so well. The venue had been selected for its superb food and attentive service. The freshly minted waiters listened, fetched and carried with the minimum of fuss, shimmying around tables with their stuck-on smiles and suited livery. There was champagne on arrival and wine with every course. Each main meal was conceived, sculpted and served as if it were a work of art being presented to its benefactor. A brief interlude, another glass of wine and the dessert trolley rolled in like a merchant ship arriving at port ready to jettison its cargo.

There was no shortage of other drinks either. On offer were cocktails, beer and shots: everything a liquor lover could wish for. In reality the birthday boy had already tippled most of what was on offer. He'd discovered alcohol at the age of twelve and on his journey to adulthood had frequently climbed onto a virtual wagon so that he could fall off into alcoholic oblivion. In fact, on two occasions a toxic mix of vodka and bad company had brought him to the attention of the local law who contacted the Rossi household to request the attendance of a responsible adult. On both occasions it was his father who attended to liberate his son.

Tonight was the first night he had tasted champagne, though, and he was on his third glass drinking in his honour. There was chatter, laughter and jokes, and then a voice shouted...

"Speech!"

Rory was at the head of the long wooden table. He stared down the parallel lines of family and friends - all eyes were upon him. The lack of chatter signalled an attentive audience, sharpened ears - waiting for him to say something. He placed his wine glass down and stood up like an Oscar winner, bemused and grateful.

"First of all, thank you all for coming (cheer). I would especially like to thank my parents for arranging this party (cheer) for steering me along life's footpath and pulling me from the undergrowth when needed (cheer). I know it's not always been easy for them – on many occasions I've rung them up in the middle of the night because I was drunk or lost or the car had broken down... sometimes all three!"

Amid the cheers and laughter his mother shouted.

"Don't remind me..."

"And those times when I needed a responsible adult - my dad was there for me..." Rory continued.

"Enough, enough..." His father laughed along with the guests.

"Mum, Dad..." He turned to face his parents sitting to his right and raised his near full glass. "Thank you, and remember I'm a responsible adult now if ever you need one."

Rafael took his wife's hand and held it up, nodding at his son as he did so. Elizabeth blushed and smiled.

More cheers and laughter and as they faded the focus of attention was back to Rory. He turned to his gran sitting beside his mother.

"I would also like to thank Granny Demelza for being there for me..."

"Hey, less of the Granny..." Demelza laughed.

"Especially after school when I was younger... oh, and for the olive bread you bake. I've heard some parents send their kids food when they go to uni. So if you're still baking, I'm only a food parcel away."

Demelza laughed, as did friends and family.

"And Grandpa Freddy, what a surprise." Rory put his hand above his eyes in a mock search down the table. He spotted his grandpa down the other end and waved. "Thank you for turning up. Be good to catch up on what you've been up to these last six years."

More laughter: this time friends, not family.

Rory held his glass up towards his gran.

"Thank you, Gran, for all you've done for me." Then he pointed his glass in the direction of his grandfather, winked and drained it.

"And now..." Rory placed his glass down and looked along the table, seeking the faces of his godparents. He spotted them sitting at the other end of the table, opposite his grandfather. "To my godparents, Crispin and Ava."

"Oh no..." Crispin laughed. "We've not really done anything."

"You've been great! Always got me fantastic presents for Christmases and birthdays."

"That was Ava..." said Crispin.

Rory picked up his replenished glass and was about to take a sip but then stopped, pointing it at Crispin.

"And you gave me my first proper sex talk..."

"Did he?" Elizabeth shouted. "I thought you did that!" She turned and looked at her husband, almost spilling her full glass of wine.

"But I did!" Rafael shouted towards Rory. "I distinctly remember..."

"Dad, you just told me stuff we learn at school..."

Rafael rubbernecked across the table, trying to look down and speak directly to Crispin. Crispin – not wanting to be the centre of attention - sat back in his chair.

"It was nothing, just a chat really, you know, when he was going through a phase."

"A phase?" Rafael was still staring along the table.

"You know, when he fancied Ava."

"When he what?" Elizabeth butted in.

Ava sat and smiled to herself throughout the exchange.

"I can only say in my defence that I was thirteen years old." Rory quickly turned his attention back to his parents. "And one more thing, Mum, thanks for having me when you did – and thanks Dad, obvs! I can vote now! And just in time!"

He paused, his audience cheered. He smiled and waited until he had their attention once more.

"We cannot allow bigotry and racism to lead us from the path of unity and cooperation."

Most people cheered. One person did not.

"Well said, son," his father shouted.

His grandmother cheered and clapped and so did his siblings. Elizabeth reddened, drained her glass of red wine and picked up the nearest bottle of champagne.

"It's up to us – all of us – young and old, to enlighten the small-minded people who live amongst us, people who shy away from change, who judge others based on their race, who do not want integration or progress. We must help them to see the bigger picture. We must of course remain in the EU."

8

At that precise moment Elizabeth was pouring champagne into her glass. Mid-pour, she stopped, stood up, swayed a little, regained her balance and then, holding the champagne bottle aloft like a nautical figurehead on the front of a galleon en route to the choppy seas, she hollered.

"I'm voting leave."

RORY

The village of Bedwell Ash had a chequered history. It was rumoured amongst the locals that in the seventeenth century coin clippers worked the area and that bandits lived in the woods. Over the years, as the desire for change took hold, trees were felled, land was reclaimed for farming and the woods matured into a shrunken area of bush-land with a conservation order and managed footpaths.

When Rory was a child, the woods were a playground for him and his friends. Sometimes they would search for evidence of highwaymen – a cave or dugout, anything that might have been a place where robber thieves rested to count their takings.

"I wish there were highwaymen now," an eight-year-old Rory said one day at tea-time after spending an afternoon in the woods playing hide-and-seek and climbing trees.

"That wouldn't be very nice," said Elizabeth. "They'd stop you playing and steal your things."

"Thieves don't live in the woods anymore," said Grandpa Freddy. "They live here, amongst us, with their smiles, their suits and their briefcases."

"Anybody fancy ice cream?" Elizabeth glared at her father.

Over the years as convenience shops closed and land was sold off for housing, families, eccentrics and rascals were enticed to the area to set down roots and live their lives within parish boundaries. Not all shops were demolished, though. In the 1980s a writer by the name of Markus Mark retired to the village. He bought what had been the local haberdashery and converted it into a second-hand bookshop. Every day he would sit in the window tapping away on his typewriter, only giving his fingers a rest when a customer came in – most often for a chat and a cup of coffee. Three years later another bookshop opened, six months after that another and then another, and another.

When Rory was eleven years old, his class at school were given a project to write about their village. Rory didn't pay it much attention. He was more interested in the alcohol content of flat cider than he was at quantifying class structure in the UK.

When he was twelve, Grandpa Freddy disappeared. Rafael and Elizabeth told their son that he had gone back to Poland for a while and were puzzled because Rory didn't seem to be at all upset.

"Okay," was Rory's only response. He did not ask questions about his vanishing grandad because he knew his mother and father were lying to him.

"It's like this, son," his grandpa had said one day while out walking in the woods. "Me and your Gran... well, we've drifted apart... and... you see... I've met someone else."

"What? Why?"

"It's adult stuff. You'll understand when you're older."

"Gran's gonna kill you."

"Your Gran doesn't know... yet..."

"And her... where does she live?"

"Scotland."

"Scotland! How'd you meet her?"

"On that internet thing..."

"No! She's gonna kill me for showing you how to use it."

"Don't you worry yourself... she's not going to find out from me."

When they got back to the house, he gave Rory a worn canvas bag.

"Here, these are for you. Will you take care of them for me?"

"I'll look after them until you get back," said Rory.

His grandpa did not reply.

Rory peeked into the bag. It contained a battered photo album and four diaries. The twelve-year-old Rory put the bag into a rarely opened box which he kept under his bed and promptly forgot about it. It was the near sixteen-year-old Rory who – wanting to hide his cannabis stash - opened the box one Saturday morning and picked up the bag from under his porn magazines. He looked inside, took out the photo album and flicked through it. Inside the faded cover, between the worn edged pages, were seven faded black-and-white photographs. Each photograph was stuck with photo corners in the centre of its own page:

Page 1, a man
Page 2, a man and a woman
Page 3, a man, a woman and a baby
Page 4, a man, a woman, a two-year-old boy and a baby
Page 5, a man in an army uniform
Page 6, a headstone
Page 7, a woman, a boy of about eight and a girl of about six.

He didn't recognise any of the faces but he did know that their blood ran through his veins.

On that Saturday Rory was meant to be meeting friends, the plan being to get lunch and then go on to see a film. Instead he texted them to say he couldn't make it. He stayed in his room, got the four diaries out of the box and read each of them in turn. Alongside the sometimes scrawled text there would often be a short poem, or a pencil drawing of a flower or a dog or a boat or an airplane. He was reading the 1942–1945 war diaries of Jakob Aleksander Kocel, his great-grandfather.

"You know it's my birthday soon?" he said at breakfast the following Monday.

"We hadn't forgotten," Elizabeth replied.

"There's something I need…"

"What's that?" asked his father.

"I'd like a book on politics, and one on the war."

Rafael stopped making Sydney's sandwiches and turned to his son.

"Any particular war?"

"The Second World War."

"Are they for school? If so I'll get them for you anyway," said Rafael.

After Rory left for school Elizabeth turned to her husband.

"Do you think he's okay?"

"Course he's okay. He's growing up, finding out about life."

"I'm worried about him."

"Oh, get a grip. He asked for books on politics and the war, not drugs and porn…"

So they bought Rory the books he asked for. They were pleased when his reading habits developed and – as he absorbed new life-information - were relieved when his drunken antics reduced to an intoxicated full stop at the end of a studious week when he would also attempt to remedy the ache in his loins by seeking out female company. Their only cause for concern was one day when Elizabeth got back home from work just after 6:30pm to an empty house. She checked her phone; there was a text:

'Taken Sydney & friends 2 cinema then meeting Crispin 4 pint. Be back about 8:30pm. Rory not home from school, he said going 2 be late. R x'

Rory turned up at 8:20pm. Elizabeth met him in the hallway.

"Where the hell have you been?"

"Chill, Mum. I phoned Dad to say I'd be late."

"A 'bit' late, you said a 'bit' late!"

"For fuck's sake, I'm nearly sixteen! I'm not a kid."

"Don't swear. I tried to call you."

"The battery went flat. If I had a decent phone we wouldn't have this problem." He dumped his bag in the corner and headed for the kitchen. "I'm starving."

"Where's your blazer?" Elizabeth shouted after him.

Rory had left the house that morning in his school uniform. Now he was heading towards the kitchen without it.

"And your jumper?" She looked and spotted he was barefoot. "Where are your shoes… and your socks? Have you been mugged?"

"Fucking hell, I'm hardly gonna be mugged for my school blazer and shoes, am I?"

"I said don't swear! So where are they?"

There was a sound at the front door.

"We're home!" It was Rafael.

Sydney arrived in the kitchen first.

"Can I sleep over at Charlotte's tomorrow?"

"Hello to you too. No."

"I knew you'd say no!" She turned and shouted to her father. "The witch said no."

Rafael appeared.

"What's up?"

"Well first, my daughter just called me a witch, second I bet you've already said yes to her and third our son has only just arrived home and he's minus his school blazer, jumper, socks and shoes."

Rafael turned to Sydney.

"I'll talk to her, go get washed up." Then he turned to Rory. "What's going on? Where're your things?"

Rory sat down at the kitchen table.

"It's just stuff," he said.

"Stuff that we paid for," said Rafael. "Where?"

"I gave them to someone."

"Any particular reason?" asked Elizabeth.

"He needed them…"

"Did it occur to you that you also need them?" asked Rafael.

"He needed them more."

"I see," said Elizabeth.

"I don't," said Rafael.

"Dad, I've got another blazer and jumper and loads of socks and shoes. He didn't have any of that stuff."

"So he stopped you and asked you for yours?"

"No. He was sitting in an alley, next to the bins. He was trying to sleep; he looked freezing so I gave him some of my stuff…"

"You gave him your stuff…" said Rafael.

"…and a bit of cash."

"…oh, and money… so he was begging?" said Rafael.

"He wasn't begging. He was just sitting there, trying to sleep, like someone had put him out with the rubbish. I sat with him, we chatted, then I went with him to the homeless shelter."

"So some homeless guy is wandering around in your school blazer," said Rafael. "I'm sure the school will be delighted! Whatever possessed you?"

"Hold on… now hold on a minute…" Elizabeth turned to her husband. "Our son has given a few of his belongings to somebody who needed them more than he does. That's a good thing."

"Thanks, Mum - he couldn't have been much older than me."

"Well, I'm proud of you. That was a very kind gesture," said Elizabeth, glaring at Rafael.

"His father died, his mother's an alcoholic, he's got nothing… no-one…" Rory continued.

"Everyone has a story nowadays," said Rafael. "You do realise it's probably all lies."

"But so what! So what if some of it is lies?" Rory replied. "He's obviously had a terrible start in life. He needs help. Besides it was obvious he was homeless, he was trying to sleep."

"What?" said Rafael.

"He was trying to sleep. The proper homeless, they have to sleep in the daytime because it's too dangerous for them to sleep at night."

Good intentions in place, Rory started to volunteer at the homeless shelter one day a week. Initially he got teased by some of his mates but it wasn't long before he managed to enlist their help.

"Could you sort out any clothes you don't need, I'll take them to the homeless shelter."

And several weeks later:

"I'm gonna be in town collecting money for the homeless shelter on Saturday. It'll be a laugh, why don't you come?"

It was a start. When he was older he would do more, much more. It had been his intention to say as much during his birthday speech.

"It's up to us – all of us – young and old, to enlighten the small-minded people who live amongst us, people who shy away from change, who judge others based on their race, who do not want integration or progress. We must help them to see the bigger picture. We must of course remain in the EU."

His next line was going to be…

"We are not all born equal but we must all be treated equally…"

But his mother had put a stop to that with her:

"I'm voting leave!"

She did apologise in hissed whispers almost straight afterwards.

"I'm so sorry I said that, I didn't mean to say it, not like this, not here... not now, in the middle of your lovely speech..."

But the shock had sobered him like black coffee and shortly afterwards he left his party to go clubbing with friends. At the club they did drunk dancing, chatted to a number of girls and then regrouped and left at 3am. Outside, a busker was strumming his guitar and singing The Beatles.

"We all live in a yellow submarine, a yellow submarine, a yellow submarine..."

They stayed to listen and then one by one joined in.

"Yesterday all my troubles seemed so far away..."

Song after song they sang.

"Blackbird singing in the dead of night..."

It wasn't long before an appreciative group gathered to collaborate in their sing-song resurrecting The Beatles' back catalogue...

"Hey Jude, don't make it bad, take a sad song and make it better..."

...and enlivening The Square with a pre-dawn chorus.

"Imagine there's no heaven, it's easy if you try, no hell below us, above us only sky..."

As their throats dried, they valiantly attempted their final chorus...

"Imagine no possessions, I wonder if you can, no need for greed or hunger..."

Each took a note or two or three from their wallets and chucked them into their song-master's guitar case. Then they split from the crowd and went for a stroll along the river, heading to a hotel for breakfast.

They were the five survivors. Rory had grown up with Archie, Moses, Ahmet and George. They were at school together; they had played together and shared secret experiences of alcohol, girls and drugs. That was the past. On this morning, the day after Rory became an adult, and talk was of the future.

"You do realise we're not going to see each other for ages?" said Moses.

They were each at the start-line of their own human highway, following the signposts to their elected life-choices. Rory was preparing to go and study European Law at Edinburgh University with a longer-term ambition to continue his studies 'somewhere in Europe'.

Archie was going to study in America, George was going to Germany, Ahmet was going to study at the University of Oxford and Moses hadn't quite decided on his route to adulthood. Even with the advent of social media they knew any future alliance would not be the same.

After talk they ate. Then tiredness took its place around their table. There was some discussion about where they should bunk but Rory wanted to go home. He wanted to sleep in his own bed. He wanted to wake up in his own room. He wanted to speak to his mother.

He arrived home in a taxi as the sun was starting to peek above our earth's contour. As the vehicle pulled up outside his house, he opened the door and fell out, landing with a yell on the pavement. His ankle hurt but he managed to limp to the front door and after a six-minute search for his keys he entered the house and sought the sanctuary of his bedroom. Sleep came quickly. He dreamt of the previous evening, the fun, the laughter and the shock.

He woke with a start just after midday. His unwashed body felt sticky, his mouth felt as stale as a used duster and the words 'I'm voting leave' rang in his ears. He got up but his ankle gave way when he put his foot to the floor and he relived his fall from the taxi. He limped to the en suite to make things better.

Three-quarters of an hour later the grime was washed away, his hair was lathered clean and his mouth was refreshed. His head still hurt, though, and so did his ankle. He wrapped himself in his new navy jacquard dressing gown - a birthday present from his gran - limped downstairs and headed for the dining room. It was the room he'd been born in eighteen years and one day ago.

The tale of Rory's birth was frequently told at family gatherings. Rafael was painting the main bedroom in the house when he was informed by Elizabeth to scrub up and change as their second child was about to make an appearance. The boy was delivered by a midwife and a somewhat stunned Rafael on the rug by the fireplace as the dining room was the only room that did not smell of paint.

The building had once been a pub going by the name of 'The Maid's Head'. The pub closed in the 1950s and the place was left empty until it was bought by a horse trader in the 1960s who converted it into a house and lived there until his death in 1996. Rory's parents bought the house in 1997 and transformed it into the Rossi family home. They fixed the roof, added two extra bedrooms with en suite bathrooms, a study and a conservatory, and restored the traditional open fireplaces around which the locals once supped their ale and told their tales.

On this day the fire was not lit; instead the hearth contained a large copper vase full of dried flowers. Rory's father sat on the oversized tan leather settee, staring at the flowers.

"Is she up yet?" Rory asked.

Rafael turned to look at his son.

"Good morning, son. Good night last night?"

"What do you think?" Rory sat down next to his father. "Did you sleep down here?" He looked at the duvet and pillows stacked in a neat pile on the floor.

Rafael nodded.

"It was my choice," he said. "We didn't have a row or anything."

"So what are you going to do about it?"

"About what...?"

"For fuck's sake! Last night. What she said."

"Language!" Rafael paused. "I'm not going to do anything."

"What?"

"And neither are you. Toast?" His father got up and went over to the table which had the bare breakfast essentials laid out. Rory accepted the offered plate of two buttered granary slices and watched as his father poured tea from a Mad Hatter teapot into an Alice in Wonderland mug.

"Have you gone bonkers as well?"

"Your mother didn't actually mean what she said. It was the drink and her hormones talking." He placed the teapot down, added milk and handed the mug over with the hint of a smile. "Don't you worry, she won't vote leave – she's just at that funny age."

"You had better be bloody well right."

"Trust me, son. Voting leave would be against everything she believes in. She is going to be so embarrassed when she wakes up..."

"So she should be!"

"Of course she might have forgotten… so best not mention it."

"What! But I can't not say anything!"

Rafael shook his head and winced at the double negative.

"You know one day you… we… all of us will look back on last night and laugh, you'll see."

Rory took a bite from his toast and turned and stared at the fireplace. The open hearth was edged with blue and white picture tiles which had been salvaged from the original pub. He remembered how, as a child, he had helped his father dismantle them, clean them and match them up before retiling the surround. Tile by tile, they told a gruesome story. The original name of the pub had been 'The Maid's Head in Hand'. The Maid in question had supposedly enchanted a local Squire and he - in an apparent fit of madness - had severed her head from her body and walked down the street, waving it about by her long red hair. The Squire had been saved from the gallows by his well-to-do connections who pleaded his innocence on the grounds that she had bewitched him.

Elizabeth entered the room; she wore a purple dressing gown, ruffled hair and a pained look. She dragged a wooden chair from the table, pushing off the two family cats huddled on the seat.

"Shove off."

Dingle and Toc jumped off the chair and headed for the sofa. Rafael leant over to call his pets.

"Here, Dingle, here, Toc, did naughty Mummy wake you up?"

Elizabeth wiped the seat with her hand in a pointless attempt to remove Dingle's black and Toc's tabby hair.

"Christ, my head hurts." She sat down at the table, placed her head in her hands and groaned. "Get me some tea and painkillers, will you?"

"…please," said Rory. "And not until I get an apology."

Rafael glared at him.

Elizabeth turned to her son. It was a few seconds before her first puzzled expression changed to one of recollection and then embarrassment. She returned her attention to the table, to the breakfast items laid out in front of her. She leant over, picked up a slice of dry toast and sat with it poised in front of her open mouth. She was about to take a bite but instead turned again to her son.

"Oh, okay, about that... what I said... did... last night... sorry."

"Is that it?"

"You see, didn't I tell you your mother was just being stupid," said Rafael.

"Stupid?" Elizabeth placed the toast down onto the table and turned around fully to look at her husband. "Excuse me?"

"Let's put it down to a temporary lack of judgement and say no more about it." Rafael paused before adding, "We'll all be laughing about this next week, you'll see."

"What?" Elizabeth turned to Rafael. "What?"

"I was just telling Rory – just before you came in - how you obviously didn't mean what you said."

"Really?"

"I mean, how on earth could you? It was so ridiculous."

"Mum, it's okay. Dad explained it to me. How stressed you've been and how... you know, your age, your hormones..."

Elizabeth turned to her husband.

"How dare you call me ridiculous!" Then she turned back to her son. "And what exactly did your father say?"

"Just that... well... it wasn't actually you talking..."

"So if it wasn't me doing the bloody talking, who the bloody hell was it?" She reddened further as she spoke.

"Mum!"

"Who?"

Rafael sat in silence, not daring to look at his wife. Rory stood up and went over to where his mother was sitting.

"He hasn't the guts to tell you but I bloody well will. It was some fucking racist, that's who..."

Rafael and Elizabeth turned on their son.

"That's enough! How dare you swear like that," said Rafael.

"How dare you call me a racist," said Elizabeth. She paused and then looked at each in turn. "And for the record, of course I bloody well meant it."

"But you just fucking apologised!"

"I said that's enough!" Rafael shouted this time.

"I only said sorry because I had no right announcing it like that at your party. It was your night." She paused. "But do not be in any doubt that me and my hormones - every single one of them – will be voting leave." She looked at her son, picked up her toast and snatched a bite. Then she stretched over to pick up the teapot and began to pour herself a cup.

Rory looked to his father to say or do something but, with Dingle ensconced on his lap, he was gazing at the fireplace. He turned to his mother. She had put down the teapot; the Mad Hatter lid was off and she was peering inside, searching for tea which had long been drunk.

RAFAEL

The room at the back of the Rossi house had changed use several times over the years. It had started out as a playroom, a messy place filled with toys and laughter, and then it had become the room where the children would have their parties and sleepovers and where they would often do their homework. It was during this period that Rafael constructed a seven-shelved bookcase along each of the long walls to house the family library and provide a healthy source of reading material, most books having been gathered before the days of the Internet. In recent years it was the room used by family members searching for peace, quiet, reflective tranquillity, and a great view of the garden, and it was for this reason it was now known as the 'Garden Room'.

It was the room where, just over one month before the referendum, Rafael chose to read his latest novel with Toc sitting on his lap purring quietly. Elizabeth entered, her own book in hand, ready to do the same. She spotted Rafael and turned to walk back out.

"Hold on, don't go." Rafael looked up.

Elizabeth stopped and turned to face him.

"Are you okay?" he asked her.

"Not really."

"Anything I can do to help?"

Elizabeth closed the door and turned to her husband.

"Not unless you fancy going and sorting out Peter Dawson."

"What's he done this time?"

"It's Kevin, I can't believe the way he's treated him... how he's got away with it..."

"Nobody can... but really, it's for Kevin to sort out. He should get himself a good solicitor."

"But he's got no money... and mental health problems... I saw him sitting on the bench by the post box this morning. He looked so lonely."

"People like Peter Dawson prey on the weak and vulnerable... Kevin's unlucky because he's got that excuse for a human being as his brother..."

"I know, it just seems so unfair... all that money his parents had... he's got the lot."

"It's will fraud and it's not your problem. Kevin needs to sort himself out and do something about it."

"Don't you get it? He can't, he's too mentally weak."

"You're not his mother, you need to realise you can't solve everyone's problems."

"Do I? But isn't that why you fell in love with me in the first place?"

"It is, but quite frankly you need to be looking closer to home and paying attention to your own children."

"Ouch!"

"Ouch indeed!"

Relations in the house had been strained. Not that there had been any arguments; there hadn't. In fact, there had been no discussions at all. Not about the incident at the party, nor the referendum. There was some talk, but it was the bare bones of communication such as 'where are my pants?' or 'pass the milk'.

"Look, I'll talk to Rory," said Elizabeth.

"And Sydney. She needs reassurance that you've not completely lost it."

Rafael looked at his wife and smiled.

"What are you reading?" he asked, placing his own book face-down on the floor.

"A biography."

"Whose?"

"Emile Zola."

"Interesting book." Rafael paused. "Look, I bought you a present... a peace offering. It's on the dresser."

Elizabeth looked toward the dresser and spotted a book-shaped package. Her curiosity got the better of her and she went over and picked it up. It was wrapped in orange tissue paper and tied with green hessian ribbon. She undid the ribbon and unfolded the tissue paper to reveal a poetry book, 'The Complete Poems of Emily Dickinson'. Before opening the book, she refolded the tissue paper and placed it and the ribbon in the dresser drawer.

"I was going to buy this." She looked at her husband and for the first time in several days smiled. "Thank you."

"I know you were. I saw you'd been…"

"You saw I'd been what? What?"

"Looking at it… on the computer…"

"So you're checking my browser history now?"

"No, of course not… not checking exactly…"

"Exactly?"

"I noticed it by accident… The page popped up… It obviously wasn't one of the kids."

"Oh very good Sherlock…"

"Don't be sarcastic, dear, it doesn't become you."

"I wasn't aware we were at war," Elizabeth said, flipping through the pages of her present.

"Pardon?"

"You said it was a peace offering."

There was a short silence. Rafael spoke first.

"We need to… sort out this nonsense." He lifted Toc from his lap and placed her on the floor. The disgruntled cat stopped purring and headed for the door. Rafael got up and went and stood in front of the fireplace, legs apart and hands behind his back as if absorbing heated energy from the unlit hearth. "I can't help thinking you're not seeing the bigger picture here."

He spotted her shiver.

"Are you cold?" he asked. "I could light the fire?"

"Don't bother." She replaced the poetry book on the dresser and went and sat in her husband's chair.

Rafael hid his surprise; it was something she had never done before – it was, after all, his chair. He watched as she manoeuvred herself into it as if to make it fit snugly to her bottom.

"Okay," she said. "I'm ready, so go ahead, break the ice."

Unmoving, Rafael took a deep breath.

"What on earth is going on with you?" His voice was quiet but confident. "What's with the whole 'I'm voting leave' thing, and why on earth did you have the audacity, the nerve, the bloody cheek, to announce it at Rory's party?"

Elizabeth spoke without looking at him.

"I shouldn't have. I know that," she said.

"So why?"

"Look, all I can say in my defence is that I was tired... I'd had too much to drink, and listening to our son preaching..."

"Now that's hardly fair. You should be proud of him. He's a fine lad."

"I know he is. And I am proud of him..."

"But?"

"But his views are so blinkered. So narrow-minded."

"Don't be ridiculous. His views are those of an educated young person. They're generous. They show kindness, they demonstrate compassion for other people. Look how he helped out at the homeless shelter..."

"I know... but..."

At that moment the door opened, and as it did Toc dashed out and Sydney entered, nearly tripping over her. Sydney stood there open-mouthed as if to speak but instead froze and looked at each of her parents in turn.

"You're having a row, aren't you?"

"No, as a matter of fact we're not," said Rafael.

"We're just talking," said Elizabeth.

"What about?" asked Sydney.

"About Friday night," said Rafael. "We've been invited over to Ava and Crispin's."

"Can I come?"

"Adults only, I'm afraid," said Rafael, turning to his wife. "So are we still going?"

"Are you happy to be seen out with me?"

"If you behave yourself...." he said with a half-smile.

"Huuh! Fat chance!" said Sydney. She turned to her mother. "You know it's all round school how you got drunk and ruined Rory's party. It's so embarrassing."

"Thank you..." Elizabeth turned to her husband. "Yes, let's go. I'll phone Mum to come over and babysit."

"I'm twelve, I don't need a babysitter." Sydney glared at her mother.

"What did you want?" asked Rafael. "Is everything okay?"

"Please can I go over to Charlotte's? She's going to let me ride her pony."

"As long as you're back by six o'clock," said Elizabeth.

Sydney looked at her mother and then turned to her father.

"Seven o'clock... please?"

"No later," he said. "And no falling off," he shouted as she left the room.

"Course I won't," she yelled back.

"Don't contradict me like that again," said Elizabeth. "She's rude enough to me as it is."

"I'd noticed. I don't think she likes you very much at the moment..."

"Why, thank you."

"To be honest none of us do. You haven't even apologised properly to Rory yet."

"I bloody have."

"You bloody well have not."

His hands were behind his back, thumbs twiddling around each other – a child-like gesture of nervous behaviour he had never grown out of.

"Why are you being like this?" he asked.

"Like what?"

"So... so... bloody impossible?"

"Which particular impossible act are you referring to?" Elizabeth asked. "The announcement at Rory's eighteenth birthday party where I ruined his evening... sorry, no, his life apparently – or the one I haven't done yet?"

"What one you haven't done yet?"

"When I actually go and cast my vote."

"No! Please no!" Rafael spoke louder than he intended. He paused before adding, "Look, the party thing, I get that... You were tired, you'd been drinking. You weren't thinking straight."

"Wasn't I?"

"But to actually do it. To actually vote leave. You can't..."

"Oh, can't I?"

The room returned to silence. Rafael watched as his wife got up out of his chair, went to the dresser and picked up the book he had bought her. Then she returned, settled back down again and began flicking through it, granting it exaggerated focus. He stood there mentally struggling, attempting to select and sequence words to express his views and explain how he felt without offending her.

It was Elizabeth who broke the silence, reciting from his gift to her in whispered words…

"Hope is the thing with feathers,
That perches in the soul,
And sings the tune without the words,
And never…"

"Have you had a knock on the head or something?" he asked. She stopped and looked up at him.

"No…"

"I thought maybe you'd fallen off your bike…"

"No, I haven't fallen off my bike but with all the flaming potholes on the roads it's a bloody miracle."

Rafael watched as she closed the book and placed it on her lap.

"Look… I know things in the EU aren't perfect but actually intending to vote leave? Why? I just don't understand." He paused before adding, "And I want to, really I do."

"Okay," she said. "Look at it this way. When most people go to vote they are going to ask themselves one question."

"What question?"

"'Do I like my life as it is?' If they do they'll vote remain and if they don't they'll vote to leave. It's as simple as that."

"So you're saying you don't like your life?" Rafael walked over to the ornate French windows and looked out across the garden before turning to look at his wife. "Well, thank you. Thank you very much."

"I didn't mean…"

"A remain vote is the only path to prosperity and long-term peace in Europe."

"Aaah, yes, the United States of Europe. Winston Churchill would be so proud."

"I'm sure he would be, he was pro the EU. So what's wrong with that exactly?"

"Winston Churchill didn't care about the poor, he didn't support the welfare state. Why do you think they booted him out after the war?"

"Now you are being ridiculous."

"His vision was one where the rich get richer – you do realise that many of his business practices would be illegal in government today."

"Maybe so, but you have to view his actions in the context of the times they took place in. We live in enlightened times, we need to move forward…"

"I know, I know," said Elizabeth.

"Look, the better the economy is doing the more there is for everybody. Can I have my chair back, please?"

"No, the sofa's over there."

"I don't like the sofa. I like my chair."

"Well, I like it too, and possession is nine tenths of the law."

Rafael sighed and went and sat on the sofa.

"And as for government cuts, austerity, decisions being made based solely on finance with no thought of the social consequences…" said Elizabeth.

"I think you've got a bit confused."

"I'm not the one who's confused."

"Austerity has nothing to do with the EU."

"I know that, but…"

"Your anger, your rage, it's not about the EU at all, it's a rage against this government, isn't it?"

"I suppose."

"Lizzie, love, don't blame the cleaner for the cooking…"

Rafael's phone rang. It was sitting on the floor next to his armchair by Elizabeth's right foot. She bent to pick it up, glancing at it before holding it out to her husband.

"It's Rory."

Rafael leant over to take it from her.

"Hi, son."

Short pause.

"She's here with me, we're talking."

Short pause.

"I'm doing my best."

Long pause.

"That sounds jolly. How long for?"

Short pause.

"Sounds brilliant. What an opportunity."

Long pause.

"No problem. We may be out on Friday night. If we are, I'll need to be back for about seven."

Short pause.

"Who do you think? Your mother, of course. We're going to Ava and Crispin's."

Short pause.

"Three o'clock Friday, I'll make a note."

The conversation ended. He turned to his wife.

"Rory and a few of his friends are going to Brussels for a few days, some sort of EU lecture."

"I'm sure they'll have a wonderful time," said Elizabeth.

"Do I detect a hint of sarcasm?" Rafael waited for a response but none came. "He's writing an article about positive and negative factors of the EU."

Elizabeth smiled.

"What's so funny?"

"Don't you think that it might be just a teensy bit biased?"

"Don't be daft. He's quite capable of seeing both sides."

"Don't call me daft!" Elizabeth was quick to reply.

"So don't say bloody daft things then!"

"He's so for the EU he's hardly going to be objective, is he?"

"How dare you say that about your own son."

"Oh, I'm sure he'll gather and present the facts… or at least some of them. It's how he interprets them I'd question."

"Will you listen to yourself… you're talking rubbish."

"I'm just saying…"

"No! I've had enough of your… your nonsense. Give it a rest."

An uncomfortable silence encompassed the room. After a couple of minutes, books in hand, Elizabeth stood up and turned to her husband.

"Don't you ever talk to me like that again."

"Well, don't you ever question our son's integrity again."

"I wasn't questioning his integrity."

Rafael went and sat down in his armchair, forcing Elizabeth aside. She glared at him.

"It's like the government, let's face it, when they commission a report they know the outcome they want and they'll put people in place to deliver that outcome!"

"Where did that come from?"

"I'm just saying…"

"Now you're just being bloody paranoid…" He picked up his book and started to read again. "Get a grip…"

Grasping her books Elizabeth headed for the door. Once there she turned to her husband.

"Anyway, I don't get why you're so flaming worried. After all, it won't be a leave result. Everyone knows that."

"So why are you voting leave, exactly?" Rafael asked without looking up.

"Because it'll make me feel bloody better knowing I have voted against all of the bloody bullshit."

"So it's a protest vote."

"I suppose."

"So roll out the protest songs… I'll go get my Pete Seeger and Bob Dylan albums. We can all join in."

"Oh, don't take the piss."

Rafael placed his book back onto the floor, got up, went to the window and stared out at the garden. It had a higgledy piggledy splattered paint look that had taken years of toil to perfect. At the bottom of the garden was his workshop where he spent most of his daytime hours making and restoring wooden furniture. He spoke, still staring out of the window.

"Who the hell are you?"

Elizabeth winced.

"We have a wonderful home, great kids - who you don't appreciate. Why are you being so… so…?"

"Don't say another word," said Elizabeth.

"Fucking awkward. There, I've said it. Why are you being so fucking awkward?"

"I've never heard you swear before!"

"That's because you've never been so fucking awkward before."

"How dare you!" Elizabeth headed for the door.

Rafael shouted after her.

"How dare I? Hold on a minute, let's get a bit of perspective here. You're outraged by the fact that I'm swearing and we - all of us - are outraged because you intend to vote leave in the referendum. BUT not only do you intend to vote leave, you announce the fact in a drunken stupor at your son's birthday in a public restaurant! Let's face it, when it comes to being daring, you trump me. You win hands down!"

Elizabeth glared at her husband then turned and left the room slamming the door behind her. The bang of the door shutting transported Rafael back to his thirteen-year-old self when a friend had dared him to light a banger and throw it to see how far it would go. As soon as it was lit there was a bang as the firework exploded in his hand. The lesson he'd learnt on that day was that once the blue touch paper was lit, anything could happen.

KEVIN AND PEETURD

K evin Dawson, or 'Kevin the Kilt' as he was known in the village, was asleep on the grass next to the bottle bank behind the village newsagents. Splayed out beside him, looking like a dead animal, were his bagpipes, bought for him by his father for his fourteenth birthday. To the casual onlooker he looked like a drunk sleeping off a night's liquor.

Around him a bird assembly chorused their dawn approval as light overtook shadow. The bird-choir got louder and as it did so Kevin started to awake from his dream world, tossing and turning in the dew as if to try and escape his inevitable return to planet earth.

"Mum said to bring this for you." It was a child's voice but it woke him proper. Re-entry complete.

Nine-year-old Oliver Goodchild stood in front of him, offering a paper cup of milky tea in one hand and a serviette wrapped around a buttered crumpet in the other. Kevin rubbed his eyes.

"Oh, thanks Ollie. Kind of you…" He accepted the offerings, stuffing the crumpet in his pocket.

"Go on… eat…"

"I'd best go. Your dad won't want to see me here."

"But I want to see you eat it… the crumpet… and drink your tea…"

"But your dad'll go mad if he sees me."

John Goodchild owned the village general store. He had worked in an insurance firm until he was sacked for book-keeping irregularities. On the same day he was sacked, his girlfriend informed him she was pregnant. A week after their son was born they moved into the village store. They named their son Oliver and renamed the store 'Olivers' (until then the sign just said 'General Store') to herald the birth of their first-born. Oliver Goodchild was generally anything but a good child. He was a mean-spirited spiteful boy who, when asked by his kindly mother to take a cup of tea and a crumpet out to Kevin, took the offerings from her and on his way out to deliver them spit in the cup and dropped the crumpet on the ground butter-side down before handing them over with a kindly word and a secret smile.

Kevin took a sip from the cup, retrieved the crumpet from his pocket and was about to bite into it when a cheery voice interrupted.

"Morning, Kevin."

He looked up as a familiar face peeked around the container.

"Hello, Mrs Rossi…" He paused. "Fancy seeing you here."

"I… I guessed you might be here."

"Nice one! I'm a tourist attraction, me…"

Elizabeth looked at the bottles not placed in the over-full bottle bank. "Are they yours?"

"No, no, they're not, honest Mrs Rossi, they're not…" He looked at Elizabeth. "Smell me breath, I've not been drinking, honest."

He opened his mouth and exhaled in Elizabeth's direction. She winced, not because his breath smelt of alcohol – it didn't – but because he was missing his two front teeth.

"Look," he said. "I know you were me mum's friend and all but you don't have to look out for me… honest… I'm okay."

"You don't look it. Besides, I'm not here in a professional capacity, I'm here as a friend."

"I'm just going through a bit of a rough patch at the mo… I just need to get me head sorted."

Kevin was twenty-six, six years younger than his brother Peter. Born into a dysfunctional family - the main cause of the dysfunction being his older brother - it surprised no one in the village when, after the boys' mother died, Kevin took to the bottle and lost his footing on the alleyway of his life.

He was twenty-two when she died. Elizabeth had tried to help him, both in her professional capacity as a social worker and in a personal capacity as a friend of both of his parents – but he did not make it easy for her. He could often be found outside the pub where many of the locals - aware of his family issues - would take pity on him and buy him a half pint of lager. Once he'd had a belly-full his humble disposition would take temporary leave of absence to be replaced by a Pied Bagpiper who expressed the contents of his emotional suitcase through his music. It was not so bad during daylight hours. In spite of his personal issues he played his instrument well and kindly villagers would often throw a coin or two at him. But after dark he would take to marching up and down the High Street performing to the planets and stars, which would often prompt a call to the boys in blue from a vexed local. If it was a quiet night, the police would send somebody to arrest him for a breach of the peace and lock him up for the night. If it was not a quiet night, his older brother would be contacted and told to sort out the situation.

There was some physical resemblance between Kevin and his older brother but that was where any similarity ended. Without a drink inside him Kevin was a kind and humble man; with a drink inside him he was an angry nuisance with mental health problems. The villagers either liked or pitied Kevin. They did not feel the same about his brother Peter. At the mention of his name many a villager would shake their head and mutter there was '*something seriously wrong with that one*'.

Elizabeth had heard many rumours about Peter, about how he'd had a girlfriend and had beaten her when she was pregnant so that she lost the baby, about how he got a builder in to do work on his house and then refused to pay him citing shoddy work, about how he had threatened his own father with a knife. Until their father's death she had always given the lad the benefit of the doubt. She changed her views on the day his father died. She was out walking Nutter in the woods and she found Kevin sitting on a bench, sobbing like a child. She sat down next to him.

"*What's wrong, Kevin?*"

"*It's me dad, he died last night.*"

"I'm so sorry. Is your mum okay? Here, let me take you home."

"No!"

Elizabeth was surprised at the response.

"Sorry, Mrs Rossi. It's just that he's still there."

"He?"

"Me brother."

"I see. How has he taken it?"

"He barged into my bedroom yesterday morning and said 'Dad's had a heart attack. He hasn't died but hopefully he will soon,' so he's taken it well, I think."

The conversation confirmed to Elizabeth that the villagers were correct in their assessment of the first-born Dawson. There was *'something seriously wrong'* with that one.

Elizabeth turned to the near toothless young man and took his hand.

"Come on, let's get you to the café and I'll buy you a proper breakfast," she said. "Then I'm going to take you to see a dentist."

******

A hundred years ago there were three hundred and eleven cottages, eighteen farms, a number of factories and shops, a hospital, a train station, a police station, two manor houses and a slaughterhouse in Bedwell Ash. After the Second World War each new decade gave birth to new housing and infrastructure policies while simultaneously signing the death warrant for local amenities. Houses were built on previously farmed land. Factories and shops closed so people had to travel to the city for work. The hospital merged with one in the city and the slaughterhouse put its last animal to death. The train station was closed in the 1960s after the Beeching enquiry, and the police station closed in the 1970s after no enquiry. A once reliable bus service was reduced to a 'take your chances' once-an-hour service as people were encouraged to go out and buy cars. The two manor houses were still intact, though. One was 'Bedwell House', a working farm owned by an eccentric lady of middling years known locally as Farmer Garlic. The other was 'Bedwell Hall', which - after a series of dubious owners, 2 murders and a fire in the 1960s - was bought in the 1980s by one Anne Chever who completely renovated the property. A woman of questionable background, she held lavish parties for a host of different men and her drunken ill-informed rants on life in Bedwell Ash ensured she soon became the talk of the village. However, her reign of notoriety came to an end in 2007 when she was murdered in her bed by a disgruntled client who then cut up her wrinkled body and buried it around the estate. The building stayed empty after that - many said it was haunted - but that pleased Peter Dawson who bought it at a knockdown price with the money plundered from his parent's estate and renamed it 'Plutus Manor' after the Greek god of wealth.

Peter's birth hadn't been easy for his mother. He was dragged out of her with forceps; some said this was the reason he had such rosy cheeks. Once out of confinement he screamed for attention. It was the blueprint for his life to follow. A natural narcissist, he grew to intimidate all those around him. By the age of six he dominated the Dawson household. His father Loucas tried to persuade his wife that she was spoiling the child but so obsessed was she with her baby it made no difference. Even when her second child arrived, Briony Dawson's focus of attention remained with her first-born son.

At primary school Peter was initially known as 'Pete Third' because there were two other Peters in his class. By the second year of secondary school his nickname had changed to 'Pete Turd' because, during his effort to rule the classroom with the same manipulating force that he ruled his parents, he went and shat on the doorstep of a boy who stood up to him. His tyrannical efforts were deflected one day when three elder brothers of bullying victims in his class dragged him into the woods, threatened him, stripped him and left him there. He was found by a walker who covered him with his jacket and took him home to a mother so distressed it pleased the young Peter to see her hurt so. The incident changed the lad inasmuch as it reaffirmed in his mind what he already knew. Every person on the planet was out to get him and must therefore be treated with manipulative contempt. The immediate focus of his bullying was his younger brother Kevin, who was frequently threatened and beaten by him.

Pete Turd studied hard, scraped through to university to study business and accountancy and then returned to the village, much to his mother's delight and his father's dismay. On his return he set up shop using his new-found qualification in financial matters to do accounts for small businesses and advise those vulnerable enough to listen 'off the record' on how they should invest their money. He was a man who interpreted trust as a business opportunity and kindness as weakness and he became very rich very quickly - mostly at the expense of his parents' friends. Within five years of returning home his nickname was once again adjusted - this time to PeeTurD.

When his father died, Elizabeth was at his funeral. Few villagers showed. The once popular man was now tainted as an accomplice to the smiling swindler who robbed many of his friends of their life savings. PeeTurD stood beside his mother, confident and smug, while she gazed only at her son for strength. Kevin cried. He was the only one who did.

Five days after his father's funeral PeeTurD took his mother along to the bank in charge of executing the will and paid them a fee to allow him and his mother to execute it instead. The estate consisted of two houses, a garage and a shop. He sold the lot and then bought Bedwell Hall in his name, renamed it Plutus Manor and moved his mother in.

Elizabeth rarely saw her friend after that. She did try to keep in contact but access was now controlled by her friend's first-born. She turned up at Plutus Manor - bunch of yellow and white roses in hand - one week after they moved in. She pressed the doorbell but no sound came so she banged on the door.

"Hi! Anyone there? It's only me… Elizabeth."

The door opened. PeeTurD was standing there, wearing a dressing gown and a smug look.

"What do you want?" he asked.

"Morning," said Elizabeth. "I've come to see your mother."

"She's busy cooking."

"I've brought these for her… for you both." Elizabeth thrust the bunch of roses forward. "A moving-in present…"

"I'll give them to her," he said, snatching them and shutting the door.

On the few other occasions that Elizabeth did see her friend the woman spoke only of her first-born son, how proud she was of him and how close they were. He made sure he was all she had in her life and when she died two and a half years later Elizabeth was the only villager who attended her funeral. Kevin looked stunned but there were no tears for the mother who had let him down.

When she died she owned nothing. With the help of a solicitor paid not to ask questions, PeeTurD had painted Kevin out of the family picture.

On several occasions Elizabeth had tried to speak to PeeTurD about his treatment of Kevin but she got nowhere. PeeTurD slept well in his bed; it was never his conscience that woke him.

On this morning it was the 'Rule Britannia' doorbell that stirred him.

"What the fuck…" He rubbed his eyes then scratched his balls awake. It was nearly midday but the previous night's interplay with a bottle of scotch and 'The Walking Dead' DVD meant he hadn't interacted with his bed until after 4am. He got up, groped his way around the room, fumbled his way into his dressing gown and stumbled down the stairs.

"It's only me." He heard a female voice on the other side of the hardwood double doors.

"Who the fuck's me?" he shouted back.

"Elizabeth, Elizabeth Rossi…" PeeTurD opened the door and looked at the smiling figure in front of him.

"I was a friend of your mother's."

"I remember you. What do you want?"

"I'm here about Kevin."

"Fucking hell… What's he done now?"

"It's a damn thing… he's gone and made himself homeless…"

PeeTurD totally failed to recognise the sarcasm in her voice.

"Can I come in?"

"If you must." He stood back to let her in.

"So what is it you want?" he asked.

They stood in the hallway facing each other.

"First of all, I'm not here in an official capacity," said Elizabeth. "I'm here as a friend of your parents'."

"In case you've forgotten, they're both dead."

"I am aware," said Elizabeth, deliberating her response. "Young Kevin, he's going through a really difficult time, you know."

"So what do you expect me to do about it?"

"He is your brother…"

"So what? I'm not my brother's fucking keeper…"

"Okay, so how can I put this…?"

"Just spit it out."

Elizabeth took a deep breath. Her voice trembled as she spoke.

"I know it's not actually my business but everybody knows he lost his inheritance because of you."

"You're fucking right there…"

He leant forward as he spoke. Elizabeth stepped back.

"It ain't any of your fucking business, so piss off."

"But your father… your mother wouldn't want to see him like this."

"He brought it on himself. He's a nutter… you know he tried to kill himself when he was eleven. He's unstable. He should be locked up."

Elizabeth was aware of Kevin's suicide attempt. It was how she had got involved with the family in an official capacity. At the time no reason for the suicide attempt was offered other than he was 'highly strung' but as PeeTurD grew and his bullying tactics became public knowledge and his barely legal activities burned the lives of villagers, she understood. All of the villagers did.

'If you were my brother I'd top my bloody self,' thought Elizabeth. *'You're the nutter who should be locked up.'* She gulped, forced a smile, took a deep breath and turned to him again.

"Look, can't you just give him his share… give him something? To help him get on his feet?"

"He won't fucking need it." PeeTurD laughed. "He'll probably try and top himself again soon. And when he does, let's hope he fucking succeeds this time."

Elizabeth stepped back, and almost in unison he stepped towards her.

"Besides, it was me who looked after me Mum after Dad died - he didn't."

"You looked after her money. That was all, don't deny it." She paused before adding, "Can't you just do the right thing for once in your life?"

PeeTurD stared at her; she could feel herself start to tremble so she turned and headed for the door. Then he opened his mouth and bellowed.

"Fuck off and leave me alone!"

CRISPIN

Crispin Quentin Bore looked out of the kitchen window down the garden. The space was a mix of shape and colour; everything planned, plucked, pruned, trimmed and weeded. Every sown seed and buried bulb had been graphed and plotted. A manicured lawn abutted by daffodils and other spring country-garden flowers splattering shape and colour. The attempt was to give the appearance of random but the linear aspect of the bloom parade gave away the human intervention. At the far end of the garden was a vegetable patch where the furrows of earth and newly sprouted seeds gave only an expert eye any clue as to what was taking root. Crispin did not have an expert eye, but he had enough money to buy the time of somebody who did. He had instructed the gardener to plant potatoes, tomatoes, beans, onions, beetroot and marrow, and so that is what he expected to grow.

Crispin worked as an IT consultant in maritime insurance. He had an ego onboard and a company offshore. He lived with his wife Ava. She was flighty, self-centred and beautiful; she did not like babies and had managed to convince her husband that he didn't either. When they first got married - if the baby topic was raised - she would point out that if they ever did have one it would have to be delivered with a fully trained-up nanny. Crispin always likened the advent of a new-born to the situation going on in their vegetable patch. Other than the occasional glance at the work in progress, neither he nor Ava were particularly interested in what was being coddled and nurtured until it was grown enough to be cooked and eaten or - in the case of a child - old enough to be reasoned with.

At the end of the garden was the writer's hut which he had bought for Ava for her birthday three weeks earlier. He had sent her to a spa for a couple of days so that it could be craned over their Victorian terrace house. When she arrived home and saw it, she was overwhelmed. She hugged and kissed her husband and told him she loved him, and then he felt overwhelmed too. To please her further he instructed the gardener to plant mint and sage and rosemary and thyme alongside the pathway to the hut so that when she was working away at her latest novel she could inhale the bouquet.

A knock on the front door alerted Crispin to the present day and the arrival of his guests.

He turned and there, standing in the kitchen doorway in a flowing white linen dress, her hair tied into a single plait and draped over her left shoulder down to her breast, was Ava, his friend, his wife, his lover, holding his second love, their silver point Siamese cat Clementine.

"They're here," she said.

Crispin watched her lips as she spoke, ensuring he caught every word. Clementine jumped down from her arms and headed towards him.

"Clemmy, Clemmy..." Crispin bent down and put out his hand as if to offer a morsel. Clementine walked up and sniffed the fingers of his human, then turned away to head for the dining room.

"You answer the door, darling. I'll take the plates through," said Ava.

Crispin wiped his hands on his red gingham apron, untied it at the waist, folded it in two and placed it on the worktop. Then he turned on his party smile and went to meet and greet his guests.

"Lovely to see you," he smiled as Elizabeth and Rafael entered the house. "Elizabeth, so glad you decided to come after all," he said, approaching her arms outstretched.

"Yes, sorry to have messed you about," she said.

"It was a last-minute decision," said Rafael. "But we are talking again…"

"For now…" said Elizabeth. "Joke, I'm joking!" she said when she saw the look he cast her.

"I don't mind acting as referee if you two need to punch it out," said Crispin with a grin. "Coats?"

"Sorry we're a bit late, I had to take Rory to the station," said Rafael, taking off his jacket. "I got stuck in traffic."

"Where's he gone?"

"Off to Brussels, some sort of EU lecture taking place."

"He's a fine boy," said Crispin, adding in a whisper, "The sex thing, you know, him fancying Ava, you're okay with it?"

"Of course…" said Rafael.

"We're glad you could help out," said Elizabeth.

At that moment Ava appeared from the dining room.

"Raffy!" She approached Rafael, arms outstretched. "Wonderful to see you, darling."

Crispin saw Elizabeth wince. He knew she hated Ava calling her husband 'Raffy' but it was what she had always called him. He looked on as his wife first hugged Rafael, then squeezed his bottom, then kissed him. It was a proper snog, as if they were back at university. To Crispin their touchy feely relationship was never a problem. He knew Raffy was her first love and he knew his wife was a flirt.

"I'm glad you decided to come." Crispin turned to Elizabeth.

"I couldn't let him come on his own…" she said, still staring at her husband. Then she turned to Ava. "Now then, put my husband down."

"But darling, we were just having a quick grope," said Ava. "For old times' sake."

Crispin sighed with relief as Ava withdrew from Raffy and headed for Elizabeth, who got a polite hug and an air kiss on each cheek.

The four of them had met at university. Ava had known Raffy long before Elizabeth came along. When they broke up and Elizabeth appeared on the scene, Ava continued to treat Raffy as a good friend with benefits.

"Please follow me," said Crispin, turning and heading for the dining room.

"We're on a strict eating timeline. We don't want the deconstructed lobster to spoil now, do we?"

"The what?" asked Elizabeth.

"The deconstructed lobster." Crispin turned to her. "And don't worry, I've cooked you a special veggie dish. I'm so glad you decided to come along."

"So am I…" said Elizabeth.

"You're always such good company," said Crispin.

"Not always, apparently," said Elizabeth.

"Entertaining, you're always entertaining, now come…" He turned to include Raffy and Ava in his address. "Unless you want to sup cold soup, you'd best go sit your arses down."

"Husband, you always spoil my fun!" Ava turned and winked at him.

The eye movement reset the rhythm of Crispin's heart. He watched as she let go of her ex-lover.

"After dessert," Raffy said, patting her on the bottom as she headed for the dining room.

"We've had it remodelled since your last visit," Crispin shouted to him. "And look, here's Clementine."

The Siamese cat wandered towards them, having come to investigate the intruders into her home. Crispin bent down and picked her up. She immediately started to purr.

The cat looked at Rafael and Elizabeth as if daring them to stroke her. Rafael put his hand out; the purr stopped and the cat hissed at him and lashed out.

Crispin laughed.

"She doesn't like intruders," he said. "She'll be fine once I've introduced you."

"What, she can't remember me from my last visit?"

"Of course she does, she just needs to be reassured that you are still a friend." Crispin stopped and turned around. He lifted Clementine up. "She's clever, you see." He pointed Clementine towards Rafael. "Now my darling, this is Rafael." Then he turned her around and pointed her to Elizabeth. "And that is Elizabeth." Then he turned his cat to face him. "You know them. They are our friends. You understand me, friends." He turned to Rafael and Elizabeth. "She'll be fine now."

The dining room was painted in pale cream, with minimal furniture and few personal possessions other than a bookshelf full of books unread.

"Very nice," said Rafael.

The cream paintwork perfectly matched the curtains. The curtains perfectly matched the seat pads. The seat pads perfectly matched the rug, which was positioned at a precise angle to the stone fireplace. The only hint of discord was the Dewey catalogued books with the spines presenting a random pattern of letters, shapes and colours across each shelf.

Crispin nodded towards the table.

"Sit down," he said. "You've met Bob. He's over at the moment so we invited him along."

Crispin spotted the look that passed between Elizabeth and Rafael but chose to ignore it. He had long ago resigned himself to the fact that his university friends would never be close to his oldest school friend. Bob stood up and held out a podgy arm. Elizabeth's was the nearest so he grabbed her hand and shook it vigorously.

"Good to meet you again..." he said. "You can ask me anything, anything at all, brain the size of a planet, me."

"Which planet?" asked Elizabeth with a feigned yawn.

"Pardon?" said Bob, making static eye contact.

"Which planet, you know... which planet is your brain the size of? Is it Saturn? Or Mars? Or Pluto?"

Bob let go of her hand and looked at her.

"...or is it Uranus?"

"Haha funny..." he said. "Very funny..."

Bob Windass was Crispin's accountant. He was forty-five years old but looked fifty-five. He was a man with a wealthy belly, thick glasses, thinning hair, few redeeming personal traits and Crispin loved him like a kinsman.

"You're sitting between Bob and me," said Crispin, pointing Elizabeth to her seat. He then nodded Raffy to the chair next to Ava. "You're sitting next to each other so you can play footsy under the table if you like."

"Of course I planned it that way," Ava said with a wink to Raffy as he took his place. She then turned and headed to the kitchen. When she got to the door she wiggled her bottom confident all eyes would be on her. They were.

"You know I look forward to the day when I come around here and at least one of you has grown up even just a little bit," said Elizabeth.

"I don't," Ava shouted from the hallway.

"Nor me, I'll stop coming round," Raffy said, then he turned to his wife. "God, you sound so old…"

"For your information, we're all getting older," Elizabeth said. She looked up as Ava re-entered carrying a vase of white roses which she placed centre table. "Whether we accept it or not."

"Well, I would like to state here and now that I have no intention whatsoever of ever acting my age," said Ava. "And neither has he," she added, nodding towards Crispin who was apportioning the recently deceased lobster at the hostess trolley.

"Can't 'he' speak for himself?" Elizabeth asked.

Crispin had his back to her so Elizabeth could not see him redden up. She turned to Ava again.

"Oh, by the way, I bought you flowers and wine but I'm sorry, I left them at home on the hall dresser."

"Darling, I'm afraid that is the start of mental decline."

"Excuse me? It was just flowers and wine. I simply forgot them."

"Short-term memory loss. You must not accept it. You must fight it." She thrust a clenched fist forward, smiled, and then turned and headed for the kitchen again reappearing a couple of minutes later with a tray of square white soup bowls, prompting Crispin to return to his seat.

"Homemade vegetable soup," Ava said, handing the bowls round.

When the soup had been politely supped by all, Crispin jumped up and with expert care replaced the empty bowls with plates of lobster dressed in a thick creamy sauce with asparagus floating alongside looking like logs about to hit white water.

"Mmmm, looks good," said Rafael.

"Here, vegetable lasagne for you," said Crispin, putting a plate in front of Elizabeth.

Without waiting for the others Bob piled his fork high and stuffed it into his mouth.

"A superbly cooked repast," he said, as the food was being masticated by his spoken words.

"So Bob, how is France... do you like living over there?" asked Rafael.

"Love it; it's much better than here. I hate the weather here, it's always bollocking raining."

"Oh, I like the change in the seasons," said Elizabeth, trying not to look at him.

"I far prefer the Spanish climate," said Ava.

"Me too," said Crispin. "You know you really must come over to our villa. Best thing I ever did – buy that place."

He was referring to the holiday villa he had bought two years previously.

"When we were last over there," said Ava, "it never rained at all. Not for one single day."

"It was pure glorious sunshine, we went out every day," said Crispin.

"We went to a bullfight..." said Ava, choosing not to look at Elizabeth. "And we went to one of the villages during their Pero Palo festival. It was horrible though - they beat a donkey half to death."

"Excuse me but please can we not talk about animal cruelty during our meal," said Elizabeth. "Or at any other time."

"It was research for Ava's novel." Crispin glared at Elizabeth.

"It's bloody barbaric," said Elizabeth.

"Bullfighting and that donkey festival are a traditional part of Spanish culture." Bob spoke through a newly stuffed mouthful. "Who do you think you are calling the Spanish barbaric?"

"Not the Spanish, not as a race, I just think some of their traditions... their culture, if you like, is bloody barbaric." Elizabeth looked at her husband. "Literally."

"It did seem a bit cruel," said Crispin. "Poor little donkey."

"I couldn't sleep for three nights afterwards," said Ava.

"It's called suffering for your art," said Rafael.

"It's horrific," said Elizabeth. "And it highlights the difference in our cultures, particularly relating to the treatment of animals."

"Of course it does darling," said Ava. "But it also shows how arrogant we are that we condemn them for it."

"We have fox hunting," said Crispin. "It's no different."

"I agree, that's abhorrent as well," said Elizabeth. "But we actually don't have fox hunting, we've banned it."

"Of course we have." Bob didn't attempt to disguise the sarcasm in his voice.

"Animal cruelty is a huge global problem," Elizabeth continued.

"Here we go," said Rafael.

"Now don't be like that," said Elizabeth. "It wasn't me who raised the question of cultural differences."

"Well, I'm raising the question of dessert." Crispin stood up. "I have a wonderful surprise for you all." He started to gather up the plates before heading to the kitchen.

"More wine, darling?" Ava asked Raffy, tilting a bottle of red above his glass.

After replenishing glasses Ava cleared the plates, put them onto the hostess trolley and replaced each with a dessert bowl. As she placed the last bowl in front of Bob, Crispin reappeared carrying a large scallop-edged glass bowl filled with Eton Mess. He planted the bowl next to Ava and then sat back down and watched and listened as she put out a call for fulfilment and the dessert bowls were thrust towards her, filled and returned.

"You beauty," shouted Bob. "I love this stuff. So reminds me of our school days."

"Me too," said Crispin. "We had some laughs, didn't we?"

"Remember that day I had five helpings?" Bob said, patting his stomach and leaning towards Elizabeth, eager for her to share the warmth of his belly along with the joke.

"Lumpy mash potato reminds me of mine," said Rafael. "School days," he added with a wink towards his wife.

"Obviously a school way ahead of its time." Ava smiled and leaned towards him. "They're called crushed potatoes now."

"Is that it then?" Elizabeth asked.

"Is what what?" Ava turned to her.

Elizabeth nodded towards the garden.

"The blue and yellow thing at the end of your garden, is that your new summerhouse?"

"Yes, that is it, and it's a writer's hut, darling, not a summerhouse," Ava said.

"Isn't it wonderful?" said Crispin. "My birthday present to my beloved." He smiled towards her.

"Looks like a summerhouse to me," said Elizabeth.

"There's a lot of difference you know." Ava turned on Elizabeth.

"About six thousand pounds' worth of difference, to be precise," Crispin interrupted.

"Oh, I see," said Elizabeth. "Well, it's very colourful."

"It looks very nice," said Raffy. "Are you going to take us down there? You know, show us around."

"Of course darling," said Ava.

"Brandy, anyone?" Crispin asked. There were more nods. Brandy glasses were handed out and generous shots poured. Elizabeth abstained and opted for a glass of water.

"You not drinking?" said Crispin. "Worried about what you might say?" he added with a wink.

"Not at all," said Elizabeth.

"You must admit you did let rip a bit the other week." Crispin smiled at her. "What on earth possessed you?"

"Is Rory talking to you yet, dear?" asked Ava.

"Rory's just fine," Rafael interrupted eager to deflect the conversation. "More importantly how are things with you?"

"Oh, nightmare." Crispin was quick to respond.

"Fucking nightmare." Bob voluntarily backed him up. "It's all this referendum nonsense. It's left everyone feeling vulnerable."

"Everyone?" asked Elizabeth.

"You know, us Brits living abroad. What if it's leave?" Bob continued. "What'll I do? I don't want to come back here. It's too flipping cold for a start."

"It's got to be a remain vote," said Ava. "Surely..." She turned to Elizabeth. "And for the record, dear, I know you didn't mean what you said the other day... at Rory's party."

"I heard about your announcement!" said Bob. "Vote leave? Were you on the wacky baccy or something?"

Elizabeth looked at him and then at her husband.

"Look, we all know this referendum was just a ploy by the Tories to help get them elected," Rafael said.

"Oh, I agree," said Crispin. "Waste of taxpayers' money."

Elizabeth laughed out loud.

"Are you joking?" she said.

"Well, it is. In fact I should say it's another waste of taxpayers' money!"

"But you don't pay your taxes."

"I do," said Crispin. "I pay my fair share. Not that it's any of your business – no offence."

"None taken," said Elizabeth. "Except I feel it is my business when I have to listen to you knowing you don't pay your fair share - no disrespect."

Crispin felt himself redden.

"I'll have you know my tax affairs are both up-to-date and legal," he said. "Aren't they, Bob?"

"I can vouch for that." The fat man nodded as he spoke.

"But that's part of the problem. What you do," Elizabeth responded. "It shouldn't be legal."

There was a short silence. Bob opened his mouth to speak but Crispin got in first.

"I've a good idea," he said, looking at Ava. "Why don't you show everybody your writer's hut?"

AVA

Ava was born of a Swedish father and French mother. They met and married while studying in Oxford. She was an only child of a happy marriage where her creative spirit was nurtured and her whims indulged. As a teenager she wanted to paint and so she was sent to The Sorbonne to study art at summer school. She was fed up with painting by her fifteenth summer and she shifted her enthusiasm to singing. She was bought the best singing teacher money could buy and for eight months she bored her friends and rattled her neighbours with her monotone voice. She then turned her creative spirit to writing poetry. After several favourable reviews from her English teacher she decided her future was to walk the Writer's pathway.

At eighteen she was accepted to Durham University to study English Literature and Creative Writing. On her first day – travelling up by train - she met a young and slightly nervous lad called Rafael Rossi. She christened him Raffy. He became her lover and then her friend.

She was tall, model-thin, and fell in love every time she looked in the mirror. She was satisfied with her facial features, her cheekbones, her slender neck and pert breasts. Her positive body image helped her grow into a confident teenager who subsequently grew into an over confident adult. It was only in recent years that her self-assurance had taken a body blow as novel after novel was rejected because it was 'no specific genre', it was 'not what they were looking for', it was 'too long' or 'not long enough' or – on several occasions – she emailed her manuscript off and got nothing at all back, not even a tactfully worded standard reply thanking her for sending it in and telling her to send it somewhere else.

Thanks to her darling of a husband, she had found a publisher for her latest effort. It was he who funded her desire to write and indulged her vision of a Bohemian lifestyle. He did it by buying into the capitalist culture of financial greed and she totally failed to see the irony.

"Come on," said Crispin, eyes on her. "Let's show them your creative space."

Ava was only really comfortable when she was the focus of attention and she welcomed her husband's intervention.

"What a wonderful idea," she beamed. She placed her wine glass down and got up. "Please everyone, follow me."

She led the way to the double doors, opening them outward in unison. A breeze wafted into the room. She tooted her virtual flute and like mice trailing after their very own Pied Piper they got up, one by one, and followed her in single file out into the garden and along the herbal pathway.

She stood at the entrance to her writer's hut and waited for everyone to assemble in a semi-circle around her. Suitably positioned, she pushed the door open.

"Ta da!" She stepped aside to allow entry.

She watched as first Elizabeth, then Bob and then Raffy entered her space. When all were safely inside, she and Crispin entered, standing in the doorway, cutting them off from the exit.

The walls were shelved, the ceiling was painted pink and pink veiled curtains were draped over the two windows - one either side of the door.

"Very nice." Elizabeth turned to Raffy. "Will you build me one?"

"No," he said in a voice suggesting no further discussion was required.

Elizabeth turned back to Ava.

"So does that mean you can write now?"

"Actually my novel is all but finished," Ava replied. "I'll be sending it to my publisher at the end of the month."

She watched as Elizabeth went around the room fiddling with the drapes, then running her fingers along the wooden desk and then going over to the bookcase and bending sideways as if scrutinising every title.

"Do they meet with your satisfaction?" asked Ava.

Elizabeth did not reply, but instead turned her attention to the photo-print hanging on the wall beside the window. Ava watched as her friend examined it.

"Is that the Toffs and Toughs?" Elizabeth asked.

The print was of a photo taken outside Lords cricket ground in 1937. It was of five schoolboys. Two of the boys wore Harrow school uniforms while the other three were obviously from a poor background.

"Very well spotted," said Crispin. "You win the banana."

"It's the inspiration for my novel," said Ava.

"Tell us more, I'm intrigued," said Raffy.

"Oh, Raffy darling, I thought you'd never ask!" said Ava, back in her comfort zone. "It's a fictional account of five boys who - quite by chance - have their photo taken together." She paused and looked around to ensure all eyes were upon her. "You see, each boy has his own story. I provide a dramatic account of each of their lives as they intertwine, sometimes knowingly, sometimes not. Five fictional tales bound together by that single photographic event."

"Sounds great," said Raffy. "But I seem to remember both the Toffs in that photograph came to a somewhat sticky end. The Toughs did far better."

"Not in my novel, darling. It's going to be a study of wealth versus poverty. How the rich became rich at the expense of the poor."

"I must say it does sound very ambitious for a first novel – you know, telling five stories when you've not even told one before," said Elizabeth.

"She has. She's written loads." Crispin was quick to jump to his wife's defence.

"Sorry, published, I meant published one before." Elizabeth was even quicker.

"She can do it. She's a brilliant writer," Crispin added, glaring at Elizabeth.

"You should get it made into a film – you'll get loads of tax breaks," said Bob.

"Well, it's already paid for our trips to Spain," said Crispin. He turned to Bob. "Which reminds me, I've got the receipts indoors. Don't let me forget to give them to you."

"If you do turn it into a film, can I be in it?" asked Bob. "I've always wanted to be a film star."

"Darling, of course you can," said Ava. "We can all be in it."

"Have you got a title?" asked Raffy.

"It's going to be called 'The Rich and the Wretched' and its strap-line will be 'A story about people, about class divides and about the apportionment of wealth."

"And you know all about that, do you?" asked Elizabeth.

"Of course she does, my wife is extremely knowledgeable about life," said Crispin.

"Darling." Ava turned to Elizabeth. "I've done hours and hours of research."

"We're going to have a party when it's published," Crispin said.

"That's tax deductible," Bob interrupted.

Crispin turned to Elizabeth.

"You can come if you behave yourself."

"A big huge party," Ava added, smiling at Elizabeth. "Of course you must all be there."

"Will you publish it under your own name?" asked Elizabeth.

"Of course I will, why would I not, dear?"

"Ava Bore doesn't sound right for a serious novel to me."

"I'll probably just use my first initial then," she replied. "That seems to be the thing nowadays so readers don't know if the book has been written by a man or woman."

"Apparently a lot of men won't read books written by women," said Crispin.

"The Rich and the Wretched by A. Bore... seriously?" said Elizabeth.

Ava stood for a moment, vacant of any expression. Then inspiration struck.

"I know. I could have a pseudonym! How wonderfully mysterious!"

"How about Sue Donym?" said Elizabeth. She spelled out the letters. "S U E and D O N…"

"That's enough," said Crispin.

"Let me know the date and I'll book flights back," said Bob. "You know, the party…."

"When are you going back to France?" Raffy turned to Bob.

"Day after tomorrow, then I'm coming back for the big vote," he replied. "Gotta get mine in."

"Have you still got your house here?"

"Yes, it's rented out at the moment. Glad I kept it – if it all goes tits up I'll have to come back."

"That would be so unfair, darling," said Ava. "If you had to do that." She turned to Elizabeth. "Look, I know it was a blip the other week. You know, you and your 'I'm voting leave' thing… I know what I'm like… I say all sorts of daft things when I'm pissed."

"Thanks for that," said Elizabeth.

"We all know you didn't mean it. You had so much to drink, darling, so much pressure organising it all. Believe me; I know what it's like at our age, hormones raging…"

"We all say silly things when we're drunk," said Crispin. "I once told…"

"It wasn't the drink," said Elizabeth.

"What was it, dear? The change?" Ava asked.

"I meant it," said Elizabeth.

"Now you really are being silly, dear," said Ava. "How much have you had to drink?"

"Elizabeth!" Raffy yelled out.

"Not a drop, I'm driving." Elizabeth replied, staring at Ava. Then she turned to Bob. "Have you any idea, the number of people who don't have a home to live in?"

"Don't know, don't care," he replied.

"Why doesn't that surprise me?"

"Elizabeth," said Rafael. "Enough!"

"Blimey, your missus is a feisty one," said Bob, looking at Rafael.

"And not even a house to buy," Elizabeth continued. "Just a house to live in, at a rent they can afford."

"Yeah, with half a dozen bedrooms for all their flaming kids," Bob said. "Kids that you and I end up having to pay for."

"I know," said Ava. "They have so many sprogs." She paused and looked at Raffy. "No offence, darling your children are adorable, especially Sydney – she is the cutest child ever."

"None of you lot, *none* of you, has any idea how lucky you've been in life," said Elizabeth.

"Lucky!" said Bob. "It's hard bloody work got me where I am today."

"I mean lucky because you've had parents who gave a damn. Who supported you, guided you, helped you make the right decisions."

Ava turned to Elizabeth.

"Darling, I do think you're being a teensy weensy bit melodramatic…"

"Look at Kevin…" said Elizabeth.

"Kevin?" Ava looked at her.

"Who's Kevin?" asked Bob.

"One of Elizabeth's projects," said Rafael.

"Kevin is a lad who lives in our village. His mother never cared about him…"

"Now I do think you're wrong there…" said Raffy. "I think that she probably did care, but she was just overwhelmed by PeeTurD."

"PeeTurD? Great name," said Bob. "How'd he get that nickname?"

"Long story," said Elizabeth. "Anyway, he… Kevin that is, has lost everything."

"Bit careless of him…" said Crispin.

"When I say lost, I mean had it stolen from him, by that bullying brother of his."

"So why doesn't he take him to court?" asked Bob.

"Because he's weak, and he's vulnerable."

"More fool him," said Bob.

"When the strong take advantage of the weak and vulnerable it is not the weak and vulnerable who are at fault."

"Course it is, survival of the fittest, everyone knows that."

"Your views show no compassion," said Rafael.

"And let's face it," said Elizabeth. "If someone sees nothing wrong with stealing from their own family then what else are they stealing? Are they fiddling their taxes?"

"But so what if they are?" said Bob.

"You can't blame people for that," said Crispin.

"So at what point do we say 'no', what you are doing is unacceptable?" Elizabeth looked at Bob and then Crispin. "Too many people condemn the weak and vulnerable for receiving handouts yet think tax evasion is a white-collar privilege. It's a disgrace!"

"Are you unwell again, dear?" Ava paused and looked at Elizabeth. "I don't understand why you're saying such mean things."

"But what most of them do is a little thing known as fraud," said Bob.

"If falsifying figures on a document is fraud…" said Elizabeth, "then…"

"Please, enough. Stop this! Crispy! Raffy! Make her stop," Ava shouted. "She's ruining my evening."

BOB

Crispin grabbed hold of his wife's hand, then turned and glared at Elizabeth.

"If you want coffee before you go home then come back to the house."

Elizabeth flinched as his eyes moved down her body, taking in her yellow blouse, dark green trousers and new yellow sandals as if for the first time. Then he shook his head ever so slightly and turned and left the hut with his wife.

Bob, Rafael and Elizabeth watched as, hand in hand, they strolled back to the house. Halfway along the herbal pathway Crispin let go Ava's hand and pulled her towards him, letting her rest her head on his shoulder.

"Satisfied?" Bob said to Elizabeth as he left the hut to follow them.

Rafael glared at his wife and then he too turned and followed them.

Elizabeth stood in the centre of the hut. She thought about going back to the house, slipping out of the front door and going home, but then she thought of her husband and how angry he would be.

It was dusk as she left the hut and the fairy lights along the herbal pathway popped open to light her way back.

She found everybody in the lounge.

"My, it's chilly," said Ava, looking up as she entered.

"Look, I'm sorry," said Elizabeth. "I didn't mean to…"

"Already forgotten." Ava smiled as she spoke. "So who wants to play a game?"

"A short game," Crispin said as he entered pushing the hostess trolley. "Remember Elizabeth and Rafael have to drive home. Coffee anyone?"

Ava got up and went over to a wooden chest placed in front of the window. She knelt down and opened it.

"We've got 'The Game of Life', 'Who Wants to Be a Millionaire', 'Monopoly', and 'Scrabble'."

"Monopoly," Bob shouted. "And wine, more wine, my friend." He held his glass out to Crispin.

"Not Monopoly," said Crispin, replenishing the glass with a quality red. "We'll be here all night. Let's play Scrabble."

So the board was set out and letters distributed.

"I was brilliant at Monopoly…" said Bob. "It was my life plan."

"Why doesn't that surprise me," said Elizabeth, approaching the table to pick up her letters.

"Elizabeth," Rafael hissed at his wife. "Why don't you come and sit here next to me." He patted the cushion next to him.

The room had recently been repainted apple-white to match the bleached theme of the rest of the house. Two oversize burgundy sofas placed diametrically opposite each other in the middle of the room added colour; with a coffee table in between, a bookcase empty of books on one side of the fireplace and a cabinet on the other side.

Elizabeth took the place next to her husband, sitting opposite Ava and Bob.

"I'll keep score." Crispin went and got a pen and paper from the top drawer of the cabinet then sat down between Ava and Bob.

Ava went first, placing her letters down slowly, deliberately.

"Yacht… there" she said. "Thirteen, no, twenty-six points for me!"

Conversation dulled as they concentrated on their letters and how they could jig-saw them into the emerging pattern of Scrabble tiles on the board. Ava was in the lead, then Crispin, then Rafael.

"Aha! Here's one to remind those people who are only half alive. Remain!" said Bob. "Triple word score, thirty points for me!" He turned to Elizabeth. "You know, some people just want to suck what they can from society. They don't contribute anything."

"Wanker," said Elizabeth, placing down her tiles and refusing to make eye contact with anyone. "That's seventeen points."

Bob glared at her and then turned to Crispin.

"Do you mind if I have a ciggie?" He took a packet of cigarettes from his jacket pocket.

Crispin and Ava looked at each other.

"We'd rather you didn't smoke in here," said Crispin. "It makes the place smell so bad. You can go out the front if you must have one." He placed his letters onto the board. "Money: twelve points. I'm in the lead."

Elizabeth watched as Bob fiddled with his cigarette.

"So, Bob, let us say – hypothetically – that you were to have a heart attack," she said.

"Me? A heart attack? That'll never happen, strong as an ox, me."

"I said hypothetically… and let's just say you couldn't work anymore," Elizabeth continued.

"Not ever?" said Bob, putting the cigarette back into the box.

"Nope," said Elizabeth. "Your heart has worn out. Oh, and you can't have a new one because there are younger people not as fat as you who don't smoke so they're in front of you in the handing out a new heart queue."

"That's stupid…" said Bob. "I'd get a new heart, I'd go private."

"Oh, sorry, I forgot to mention," said Elizabeth.

"Elizabeth," said Rafael.

"You lost all your money," she continued, ignoring her husband. "When you went bankrupt."

"Bankrupt? How did I manage to do that?"

"Some sort of banking fraud," Elizabeth replied. "You lost your pension as well, in a pension scam."

Bob placed his letters down on the board.

"B I N T, bint." He turned to Elizabeth and smiled. "Well, first of all I wouldn't be so bloody stupid as to lose my money to fraudsters or scammers and second…"

"Not allowed… slang."

"Rubbish," said Bob. "It's a proper fucking word." He picked up his phone and started to fiddle with it.

"I think you'll find it is a proper word," said Crispin.

"Here we go," said Bob. "Bint - a contemptuous term used to refer to a woman."

"Thank you. We all know what it means," said Elizabeth. "You've never been married, have you?"

"What's it to you?" said Bob, adding under his breath, "You daft bint…"

"How dare you talk to my wife like that!" said Rafael.

"Excuse me, I am here, you know." Elizabeth turned to her husband. "And I'm quite capable of fighting my own battles, thank you."

"And don't we all know it…" said Ava almost – but not quite - to herself. She turned to her husband. "Crispy, do something."

"Will everyone please just shut the fuck up!" shouted Crispin.

"Charming," said Elizabeth.

"It's my turn," Crispin said. He placed four of his letters down on the board. "C A L M, calm, get it?"

Rafael was still glaring at Bob. He placed his coffee cup onto the table and stood up. As he did he jolted the Scrabble board.

"Oh, Raffy!" Ava shouted.

"Oh, shit! Sorry, I'm really sorry." Rafael attempted to gather the pieces and place them back into their jig-sawed positions.

"Look," Crispin said. "I think we need to call it a night."

"Sorry, sorry," said Rafael, "I got a bit carried away."

"Would you like another coffee before you go?"

Rafael nodded.

"I'll go get some," said Crispin. "It'll have to be instant."

"Any brandy?" asked Bob.

"On the trolley, help yourself," Crispin shouted back.

Bob got up and went over to the trolley.

"Anyone else?" he asked.

"Yes please," said Ava.

He picked up the brandy bottle and two balloon glasses and went and sat back down. He placed one of the glasses in front of Ava and poured her a single shot.

"I'm sorry," Rafael said again.

"Me too, mate. Glad I didn't have to hit you."

Crispin returned with the final tray of the night.

"Good, I'm glad we're all friends again," said Ava. She turned to Elizabeth. "And for the record, darling, we do pay our fair share of taxes. Honestly."

"I think people on the dole shouldn't be allowed to vote," said Bob leaning over and pouring himself a triple brandy.

"It's a little thing called democracy," said Elizabeth. "You know, one person, one vote."

"Well, I'm with Winston Churchill on this one: 'The best argument against democracy is a five-minute conversation with the average voter'," said Bob.

"Oh, give me strength," said Elizabeth. "You're just a heartless…"

Rafael sank into the armchair and put his hand over his face.

"Excuse me!" said Ava. "You've come into my house…"

"…our," Crispin interrupted.

"Eating my…"

"Our."

"Food." Ava glared at Crispin then turned to Elizabeth. "Being all judgemental about us… who the hell do you think you are, judging us?"

"And who the hell do you think you are, judging people you know absolutely nothing about?" said Elizabeth.

"I think we'd better be going," said Rafael. "Elizabeth?"

"There is an old Indian saying, do not judge a man until you've walked three moons in his shoes," said Elizabeth.

"Have you had a stroke or something?" Bob asked.

"I think it's the change." Ava looked around at each of the men as she spoke.

"My auntie killed herself," Bob interrupted, "when she went through the change, she went and hanged herself in her barn, she did."

They all turned and looked at him.

"I remember," said Crispin. "A terrible time for you."

"It was," he paused, then turned to Elizabeth. "You know what you were saying about luck? Well, when I think about it I suppose I was kinda lucky - she left me all her stuff."

"Okay," said Elizabeth, looking at Rafael. "I'm ready to leave."

"Yeah, we all know you're a leaver," said Bob.

"She's not going to vote leave," said Rafael, looking at Bob.

"I beg your pardon?" Elizabeth turned on her husband. His gaze shifted from Bob's face to the brandy glass in his hand.

"Rest assured on that." Rafael spoke quietly, as if the words were rebel thoughts, for his ears alone.

"Common sense at last," said Bob.

"Excuse me?" Elizabeth could not disguise the surprise in her voice.

His courage returning, Rafael looked up at his wife and spoke again; louder this time.

"I said you will not be voting leave."

"You look like you need a brandy, love," said Bob, smiling at her. "It'll settle down those hormones." He leant forward, offering her his glass.

Elizabeth accepted the glass. Bob watched as she put it to her lips as if in readiness to down the contents in one. She paused. Bob knew what was going to happen next – or he thought he did. He ducked as if to avoid a soaking, but there was no need, Elizabeth turned around, looked at her husband and chucked the brandy directly at him.

KIRSTY

The room was shabby but not chic. The furniture was functional: a well-worn two-person settee, a square wooden table and two worn ladder-back chairs. The stone walls, covered in pale green paint, were unadorned apart from a single Jackson Pollock print 'Lucifer' hanging above the settee. It was a large abstract, a riot of colour and shapes intertwining and melting into each other, making sense to some but no sense to others.

Kirsty sat on one of the chairs with her baby on her knee. Her two older children were there with her. Leo, her seven-year-old, sat on the chair at the opposite side of the table playing with wax crayons and a well-thumbed colouring book. Sitting in the corner on the uncarpeted wooden floor was her eldest, thirteen-year-old Miriam. For the first twenty minutes after their arrival Kirsty had paced the room with the baby – swaddled in a grubby blanket - in her arms. Eight paces turn, eight paces turn.

"You're driving me nuts!" said Miriam.

So Kirsty took a place at the table. The act of sitting down served to calm her and the baby who fell asleep within minutes. Over an hour after their arrival a man in his early twenties bought them tea and biscuits. Leo ate the biscuits and Kirsty drank the tea from a chipped mug. When she placed it back down onto the table she sat with her gaze turned to the painting, and her eyes got lost in its wash. Half an hour later she was reminded again of their predicament by a tap at the door. Elizabeth entered.

"About bloody time too." Kirsty, baby drawn tight to her, stood up and shouted at the woman who had come to help her.

Miriam struggled to her feet. Elizabeth turned to the undernourished child: tatty dress, worn shoes, hair not brushed.

"Mrs Rossi, they chucked us out. Mum tried to talk with them but they chucked all our stuff on the pavement." The child burst into tears.

"I know, I heard, I am so sorry," Elizabeth said. "Look, we're trying to find somewhere for you to stay." She turned to Kirsty. "You knew this was going to happen... have you been looking for somewhere else?"

"Course! But no one will rent to us. We can't pay what they want. Eight years we've lived in that little house and now we're out. Just like that!"

"Have you tried the papers?"

"Course I bloody have!"

"What about Facebook? Sometimes people advertise property to rent on there..."

"Do you think I'm bloody stupid? I've looked! Trouble is, rents have shot up. Landlord says he's got some Poles for my house! How's that right?! Bloody foreigners!"

"That's not a very helpful comment, Kirsty. I'm going to pretend I didn't hear it."

"She doesn't mean it, Mrs Rossi, Mum's not a racist."

"But come on, you tell me. I was born here. I've lived here all me life. I paid me rent and now I'm out! Just like that!"

"Your landlord gave you due warning." She paused before adding, "And it is his house..."

"But it's my... our... home!" Kirsty spoke so loudly that the baby woke and started to cry. "I always paid me rent on time, always." Kirsty attempted to soothe the baby but the infant's screams continued. "Now the baby's woke," she said. A tear appeared and then another. Miriam went over and took hold of her baby sister.

"Mum, Mum, don't cry. Mrs Rossi's going to sort it." The child turned to Elizabeth. "Aren't you? You'll find us somewhere to go."

Elizabeth turned to the thirteen-going-on-thirty-year-old child. She could hear the fear in her voice and for a second she saw panic in her eyes, then the image of Miriam blurred, Elizabeth swayed and tried to stand straight, placing her hand on the table to steady herself.

Kirsty didn't notice, neither did Miriam, but Leo did.

"Are you okay?" he said. "You look like you're gonna fall over."

"I'm fine thanks," she said, taking several deep breaths.

"You will help us, won't you?" Miriam asked again.

"Of course. Now, where are all your things?"

"Outside, they got soaked," said Miriam. "Is there anywhere my mum can get some sleep? She's not been sleeping."

'I know the feeling,' thought Elizabeth.

"Trouble is, there's more people than houses, so someone's gonna be out on the streets, aren't they?" Kirsty said between sobs.

"That's us, isn't it?" said Miriam. "No one cares about us..." She burst into tears. Leo looked up, unsure if he should be crying too. Elizabeth went over and knelt down next to him.

"What is it you're colouring?"

"It's a house and a garden, and look, that there's a shed."

"It's very good..."

"You know there's a shed in the woods..." He settled back down to his colouring-in. "We could go live there..."

Elizabeth got up and approached Kirsty.

"Here, let me take her."

Kirsty handed the baby to Elizabeth. She looked at the screwed features, only five months old, already homeless. *'No wonder you're screaming,'* she thought to herself. She swayed gently to and fro; the motion soothed the child.

"I think we should get you something to eat and then get you off to school," she said to Miriam.

"No! Not today. Please don't make me. I've not done me homework and I've no clean clothes..."

"I've got no clean clothes for her..." Kirsty looked up and sobbed again. "They call her scruffy cos I get the kids' clothes from charity shops."

Leo stopped colouring.

"They call me smelly, they say I don't wash," he said. "But I do…" He paused before adding, "But I haven't yet… today…"

"I told you, if anyone calls you that you gotta tell me," said Miriam.

She got up, went over to her little brother and knelt beside him.

"Let them say it to me and see what happens."

"I don't care," said Leo with a sigh. "I'm used to it."

Kirsty looked over to Elizabeth.

"Mrs Rossi, what's gonna happen to us?"

"Well, first we are going to get you cleaned up, then we are going to get you something to eat, then I am going to call the school."

"Okay, okay, but where we gonna live?" Kirsty asked.

DEMELZA

emelza was born in a traditional Cornish cottage, the youngest child of Jowan and Hope Hammett. She and her four older brothers enjoyed a rowdy but happy childhood. From an early age she learned to work hard, stand up for herself, and act as peacemaker when her brothers fought.

She studied history at university and then left the UK to travel the world. A trip which should have taken eighteen months lasted over three years due to an extended stay in India. On her return she followed a boyfriend to London and although they broke up within a month she stayed on in the city, working as a secretary for a children's charity. It was there she met Frederic Kocel, a Polish Jew who had come to the UK after the war. In 1970 she bore him a daughter, Isobel, and in 1972 another, Elizabeth. In the long hot summer of 1976 she gave birth to a son, Henry, who died in his crib at four months old. Overcome with grief she continued through the motions of motherhood for several months before kissing her girls goodbye one evening, walking out of the house and getting on a train to Cardiff. A place she had never visited and where she knew nobody.

It was nearly eighteen months before she saw her daughters again. She was in the institution for six months before one of her brothers took her in. It was another year before the fog lifted and she was able to return to her home and when she did she swore that she would never again neglect her girls. At home, hanging on the back of the door in the toilet, was her hand-written citation:

'Before diagnosing myself with depression I must look around and remove the aggressive, negative and spiteful people from my life.'

It was a philosophy that had served her well. Other life-rules hanging in a variety of places around her house included *'take plenty of exercise'*, which she hung in her kitchen above the fridge, and *'always get a good night's sleep'*, which hung in a gilt frame above her bed. Being a working parent of two lively daughters tired her so most nights she dropped off to sleep quickly.

During the years that her daughters were growing up, Freddy's work as an Encyclopaedia salesman often took him away from home. When she knew he was returning she would go to her bedroom, take the sign down and place it in a tin at the bottom of her wardrobe in case he looked upon it as an excuse to withdraw conjugal benefits.

Age had brought peace to Demelza. She now lived on her own in a cottage two villages along from Bedwell Ash. Her home was small, as was her bedroom and her undersize double bed which she had pushed next to the window so that - on those nights when sleep was not immediately forthcoming – she could gaze skyward, place herself amongst the stars and contextualise herself as a single dot in the picture universe of life.

"Perspective is everything," she would whisper.

Recently she had been tossing and turning and staring to the skies. She wondered at a shooting star. Where had it come from? Where was it going? What the hell was going on? Her picture universe was painting an unsettled image.

She had heard about the recent incident at the dinner party and she was troubled. Things had not been right between Rafael and her daughter since Rory's eighteenth. She knew they were barely speaking and that Sydney was not herself and spent most of the time in her room. There was no laughter - it was no longer a happy house. She decided she must do something.

In Demelza's experience, if you gathered the right people in a room to talk about their problems while supplying them with copious amounts of tea and cake, then any problem could be resolved. It was why – exactly three weeks before the referendum

– she spent the afternoon in her daughter's kitchen baking cakes and discussing tactics.

"Crispin and Ava are coming," said Rafael.

"Must they?" said Demelza. "Can't we just keep it as family?"

"They are family... of sorts. Besides, they're Rory's godparents."

So they rearranged the furniture in the front room into a semi-circle – the three-seat Chesterfield was placed between the two-seat settee on the right and two tub armchairs on the left.

"I'll tell them to keep their mouths shut," said Rafael, sensing his mother-in-law's displeasure.

"So why invite them?" she asked.

"Why not?"

In the centre of the room confronting the semi-circle and facing them all was a wooden chair. Rafael had carried it through from the dining room and placed it underneath the light, giving it an air of torturous intimidation. Demelza looked at the chair and then at Rafael.

"Couldn't we give her one of the comfy chairs to sit on?" she asked.

"That chair's just fine."

"But it looks... well... rather intimidating."

"Don't you get it?" Rafael turned to face Demelza. "I want her to feel intimidated. I want her to understand that her life, my life, the kids' lives and everything we've worked for is under threat because of her ridiculous behaviour."

Demelza shivered.

So with the rain beating down, carving its way through the landscape, the front room of the Rossi home was host to a select few, drinking tea, eating cake and waiting for Elizabeth to arrive home.

"She went to see Kevin and then went to the dentist," said Demelza. "She went on her bike."

"But it's pouring with rain," said Ruby.

"It wasn't when she left," she replied.

Demelza sat with Ruby and Lars. Rory sat in one of the chairs, fiddling with his phone; the other was taken by Rafael's cardigan. Rafael was in the kitchen checking the cook status of an upside-down apple cake. Ava and Crispin sat on the other side, holding hands.

Sydney burst through the door.

"She's coming!"

The group hushed and looked at each other while Sydney headed back to the hallway. Demelza got up and followed her, then went and opened the front door. She watched as Elizabeth got off her bike and removed the panniers. Demelza noticed as she approached that she wasn't just wet, she was muddy too.

"Hi," said Sydney. "Yuk! Did you faceplant?"

"Good grief, what on earth happened to you?" asked Demelza.

Elizabeth took off her duffle coat.

"I fell off my bloody bike..."

"So 'yes', then," said Sydney.

"Bloody potholes," said Elizabeth, pushing past Sydney. "There's a bloody great big one on the corner. Fell off into a massive puddle, then got soaked by a passing van."

"Oh dear, are you okay?"

"Just about, those bloody Goodchild kids saw me - you know, Oliver and Olivia – the pair of them couldn't stop laughing – little sods."

"Language, mother," said Sydney.

"And why aren't you at your piano lesson?"

"Not going." Sydney stood aside, still gazing at her mother. "Oh no – Ollie probably videoed it, it'll be all round school! How embarrassing!"

"Little buggers!" Elizabeth turned to her mother. "So what are you doing here?"

"Oh dear," said Demelza. "Look at the state of you, you'd best go and get yourself changed."

"Why, thank you, Mother." Elizabeth took off her duffle coat, folded it and pushed it towards her. "I'm guessing this is something to do with why Ruby's and Crispin's cars are outside?" She sat down on the carpeted floor and attempted to pull off her boots.

"Pull this off for me," she said, pointing her muddy boot towards her mother. "It's stuck."

Demelza tugged off one boot then the other and placed them side by side next to the stand; then she took herself and the muddy duffle coat off to the utility room. She dropped the coat into the dry cleaning, washed her hands, went to the kitchen and picked up a Victoria sponge which had been cooling on the tray. Then she returned to the lounge.

"Where is she?" asked Rory, looking up from his phone.

"She went to get cleaned up," Demelza replied, placing the Victoria sponge onto the coffee table next to the Alice in Wonderland mugs. She sat down and an awkward silence followed before she added. "She had a fall… from her bike."

"Is she okay?" asked Ruby.

"Karma…" said Lars.

"I heard that," said Elizabeth, appearing at the door. "Oh my, a surprise party, I should have put my party dress on." She paused. "Ava, Crispin, how wonderful to see you."

"No need to be sarcastic," said Rafael.

"We… we were invited," said Ava.

"Thought we'd best come along," Crispin added. "You know, for moral support."

"Darling, we just want to support you during this troubled time," said Ava. "Help you to see the bigger picture."

"For God's sake, if someone says that to me one more time I'll scream." Elizabeth went and sat down on the wooden chair in the centre of the room. "I suppose this is where I'm meant to sit?"

"No need to be narky darling," said Ava. "We're here to help you."

Demelza sighed. She had played her cameo in this theatre; now it was down to everybody to play their part.

"Tea, anyone?" Rafael asked, Mad Hatter teapot in hand. "Or coffee?"

"I suppose this was all your idea." Elizabeth turned to Demelza before turning on Rafael. "You wouldn't have the balls."

"Uncalled for," said Rafael.

"It was a joint decision," said Demelza. "Cut yourself a slice of cake, dear, it might put you in a better mood."

"You cut it," Elizabeth said, glaring at her mother. "I don't trust myself with a knife right now."

Demelza went over to the coffee table and picked up a knife.

"How is Kevin, dear?" she asked.

"Not good."

"Are you helping him as part of your job or is he one of your personal projects?"

"He's one of her personal projects," said Rafael.

"He won't accept help officially…" said Elizabeth. "Not that there is anything I could do officially."

"How was the dentist, dear?"

"Bloody awful," Elizabeth replied. She stood up and went over to the framed photograph hanging by the window. It was a photo of Bedwell Ash in Victorian times. It had hung unmolested in the same spot for years but tonight – for an unknown reason - it had tilted to the left. She straightened the picture, went over to the coffee table and poured herself a glass of water, then went and sat back down.

"Did they fill the hole, dear?" Demelza handed her a slice of Victoria sponge in a serviette. "In your tooth."

"I think they might bar me."

"Why doesn't that surprise me?" said Rory without looking up from his phone. "What did you do?"

"They tried to charge me for a full check-up when all they did was replace a filling."

"Oh dear" Demelza said. "Did you pay?"

"I did in the end. They said that they did give me a check-up. Apparently it involved looking at my cheek and my tongue to see if the hole had damaged it… bloody bullshitting cheek."

"So you haven't got us all banned," said Rory.

"Not yet," she paused. "Now come on, get on with it… whatever 'it' is." She took a bite from her cake. At that moment Dingle padded into the room. He stood and looked at everybody.

"Dingle, here Dingle…" Sydney shouted to him but he ignored her and instead headed for the jumbo cushion in the corner where Toc was asleep. Without warning, he leapt onto the cushion while at the same time hissing at his cat mate. The smaller cat startled awake and jumped away and although she hissed back she knew her place had been taken.

"Dingle!" Sydney shouted. She got up, retrieved the disgruntled displaced Toc, and picked her up to cuddle her.

"Well, dear…" said Demelza, turning to her daughter.

"We need to talk about..." Rafael paused as if struggling to find the right words. "The situation we're in."

"I'm guessing one situation in particular," said Elizabeth between mouthfuls.

"Since my eighteenth you've been so weird," said Rory.

"And there was me thinking one person one vote was a personal thing."

"It is. It was, until you made yours public," said Rory. "And humiliated me in front of the world."

"Oh, don't be so dramatic." Elizabeth's response was instant, and short-tempered.

"If you'd just kept your mouth shut, not told anybody what you intended to do, we wouldn't be here," said Rafael.

"We would never have known what you are really like," Lars added.

At that moment Elizabeth's phone alarm went off. The tune *'the sun has got its hat on... hip hip hip hooray... the sun has got its hat on and is...'* stopped the talking.

"Sorry," she said, shutting it off.

"Even your phone alarm's bloody racist." Lars looked at her accusingly.

"Oh, stop it Lars," said Demelza. She watched as her daughter looked around the room as if appealing to each of them in turn for some sort of back up.

"You all know I'm not racist," Elizabeth said.

"Come on then," said Rafael, turning to his wife. "Explain yourself."

"First of all," said Elizabeth, "do any of you know what racism actually means?"

"Duuuhhh!" said Rory.

"Please be sensible, dear," Demelza pleaded. "This is serious."

Elizabeth turned on her.

"I am being bloody serious." She got up and left the room, returning a couple of minutes later with a dictionary. She sat down again and, with the book on her lap, flicked through it until she was satisfied she was at the correct page, then ran her finger down it.

"Racism; hatred or intolerance of another race or races."

She turned to face her family and friends once more.

"Now, I challenge any one of you to tell me when I have ever shown any intolerance to anybody based on their race?"

"You told off Mrs Ionescu, she's from Rumania," said Sydney.

"She nearly ran over Nutter…"

"But it was Nutter's fault he ran into the road," said Rory. "Daft bloody dog."

"I know, I panicked a bit." Elizabeth paused before adding, "And anyway, I did apologise…"

Sydney spoke again. "You had a go at that man at the petrol station the other day. He was a foreign person."

"I thought he'd short-changed me," said Elizabeth.

"But he hadn't."

"So you jumped to conclusions because he was foreign," said Lars.

"Yes," said Elizabeth, "I did jump to the wrong conclusion and again I apologised for it."

"Racist." Lars turned to his wife. "Ouch, don't punch me."

"He was from bloody Liverpool," said Elizabeth.

"Enough!" shouted Rafael.

An ear-splitting silence followed, broken by a buzz from Sydney's phone. She looked at it.

"Can I go over to Daniela's?"

"Who?" asked Elizabeth.

"Daniela Esposito, you know, they run the Italian," said Rafael.

"We're going to help in the restaurant."

"You're what?" said Elizabeth.

"Help in the restaurant. Not properly, just do odd jobs. Her dad's going to pay us."

"No," said Elizabeth.

"You can," Rafael said, just after his wife had spoken.

Sydney got up and headed for the door.

"Thanks, Dad. And he lets us watch the pizzas being made. It's great fun."

"I want you back by eight," he shouted after her as she disappeared.

"Well, it's good to see you're putting on a united front for your daughter," said Ruby.

"I might as well not bloody well be here these days," said Elizabeth.

"You can say that again," Rory muttered.

"I thought it best she not be here," said Rafael.

Demelza could see the hurt in her daughter's eyes.

"Elizabeth, dear… we know you are not an actual racist," she said.

"Why, thank you, Mother."

"But there is a lot at stake here," Demelza continued. "Voting leave – it would have huge implications for so many people."

"As would voting remain," said Elizabeth.

"No it wouldn't," said Rory. "Things would just carry on."

"Exactly," said Elizabeth. "A remain vote will say to the EU and this government that everything is okay. Continue with austerity. Continue neglecting the NHS, it's okay that there are not enough homes for people to live in, continue to reduce the police force, it doesn't matter that crime will rise, carry on saving money and dismantling our infrastructure, it's all okay. As you were."

"Oh, what complete nonsense you are talking," said Lars.

"You would think that, because you've got a house, you've got a fancy car and private health insurance. None of this impacts you."

"It impacts the losers," said Lars.

"Oh, don't be so patronising," said Elizabeth. "You can be an arrogant arse sometimes."

"Mum, don't," said Ruby. "That's the father of your grandchild you're talking to."

"Shut up, Lars," said Rafael.

"Would anybody like another cup of tea?" asked Demelza.

"I would like to point out," said Rory, looking up from his phone, "that austerity has nothing to do with the EU."

"I know," said Elizabeth. "But allowing uncontrolled immigration at the same time as making savage cuts to our infrastructure is wrong. Surely you can see that?"

"I know there are issues but they are problems that can be resolved," said Rafael.

"Not if we vote remain. Why would the government address any issues if it gets approval from its electorate to carry on?" Elizabeth got up, went over to the coffee table, picked up her Queen of Hearts mug and slowly, deliberately, poured herself tea. Then she sat down again, placing the mug on the floor beside her foot.

"I get what you're saying, Mum, but Dad's right – they are issues that can be resolved," said Ruby.

"I'm not sure I want a friend who is a leaver," said Crispin.

Ava nodded in agreement.

"It would just be too weird, darling. You really must think again," she said.

"I'm voting with my conscience," said Elizabeth.

"Bollocks!" Lars shouted.

"Lars! Shut up!" Rafael shouted across at him, making everyone jump. "How dare you swear like that in my house."

"Sorry, I got carried away," said Lars. He turned to Elizabeth. "Look, supposing we vote to come out of the EU."

"I'm sure the banking industry will make the most of the situation," Elizabeth replied. "As will you."

"Well, if I have to move to Germany you won't be seeing much of your grandchild," Lars said.

"Is that a threat?"

"It is not a bloody threat, it is a promise, you daft woman."

Ruby glared at her husband.

"Don't talk to my mother like that!"

"She started it!"

"Oh, please continue. Show us what you're really like!" said Elizabeth.

"Mum! Don't!"

"But he's being ridiculous!"

"No more ridiculous than you," said Rafael.

"I've an idea," said Demelza. "Why don't we all act like adults and treat each other respectfully."

"Shit! If the banks move, the contract market will collapse, and I might have to go and work abroad," said Crispin.

"You could always go and work in the Channel Islands. Isn't that where your company is registered?" said Elizabeth. "Or is it the Cayman Islands?"

"Blah blah blah…" said Lars.

"Have you thought what would happen to those people who have made their home here?" said Demelza. "Those people who placed their trust in the EU, placed their trust in the UK. What about them?"

Elizabeth sat silently. She breathed in deeply, then out. Then again, in…

"Look, as I said, I don't have all the answers. But I do know we have to ask the right questions and at the moment that is not happening."

"So you'd be happy to see people being sent back, would you?" said Demelza.

"I didn't say that."

"Well, you'd better be careful because this may impact you more than you realise."

"What do you mean?" said Elizabeth.

"Gran…?" asked Ruby.

"Gran, what are you on about?" asked Rory.

Demelza sat silently looking down into her lap.

"Mum, what do you mean?" Elizabeth asked again.

Demelza looked at her daughter, her eyes telling the torment of her secret.

"I have a confession to make," she said.

"What's wrong?" asked Elizabeth.

"Well, it's like this…"

"Yes…"

"Your father and I…"

"Dad? What about him?"

"Well, you see, we never actually got married." She paused without making eye contact. "I'm a spinster."

"What! Don't be ridiculous, of course you're married, January the ninth is your wedding anniversary."

Demelza reddened again and lowered her eyes once more.

"We did mean to, we just never got round to it."

"Please tell me you're joking!"

"So Gran, you're saying Mum's illegitimate?" said Ruby.

"You're illegitimate! Hilarious!" said Rory.

Demelza reddened further, then nodded.

"Please don't use that word," she said. "It's so unseemly."

"I see," said Elizabeth. She shifted in her seat and looked around. "So it appears my whole life till now has been a lie."

"Well, I wouldn't put it quite like that, dear," said Demelza.

"But you and Dad lied to me and to Isobel, our whole lives."

"That is not true."

"Isn't it?" Elizabeth paused and looked at her mother. "Isobel knows, doesn't she?"

Demelza nodded. Elizabeth turned to look at her husband.

"What about you, did you know?"

"I found out last week."

"Oh great!"

"I told him," said Demelza.

"So you're telling me this now because…?"

"Your father's permission to stay in this country ran out last year. He forgot to renew it. If we vote leave there is a good chance he may not be able to stay, what with us splitting up and his trips back to Poland."

"At last, something to make you see sense," said Lars. "To focus your attention."

Elizabeth turned and looked at him.

"You think?" she said.

"Well done, Gran. I'm glad you didn't get married. It's brought Mum to her senses at last," said Rory.

There were nearly two minutes of silence; all eyes were on Elizabeth.

"You're not married? Are you joking?"

"I wish I was, dear."

"But why on earth not?"

"He never asked me… well, that's not strictly true. He did once, in January 1968. We'd drunk a couple of bottles of wine and we were out in the garden wassailing around the apple tree and he asked me."

"So what did you say?"

"I said yes, of course."

"And…"

"And nothing… he never mentioned it again. I think it's because he was so drunk at the time he forgot he'd asked."

"So didn't you remind him?" asked Elizabeth.

"No! Of course not."

Elizabeth paused and looked at her mother. Everyone else sat silently and looked at Elizabeth. Eventually she spoke.

"I see. Well, I'm glad you and Dad are talking again," she said. "But this changes nothing."

"Elizabeth!" said Demelza.

"What?" Rafael looked at his wife.

"Mum, what about Grandad?" asked Ruby.

"Oh, come on!" said Rory.

"If anything, this makes me more determined to vote leave."

A gasp whispered around the room like a breeze through treetops.

"How can you even consider it now?" said Rory.

"I'll tell you how," said Elizabeth. "Because I won't be a hypocrite."

"What! What on earth are you talking about?" asked Rafael.

"I will not vote to remain in the EU just because it has an impact on my family!"

"But he's very worried, dear…" said Demelza.

"So why do you care?" said Elizabeth. "After the way he's treated you…"

"Of course I care," said Demelza. "And so should you. He's your father."

Rafael coughed and then turned to Elizabeth.

"Elizabeth, look at me," he said. "Do you care about me? Do you care about Sydney and Rory and Ruby? Do you care about the life we've had? The life we've got now? The life we're going to have when the kids are grown?"

"Of course I do." Elizabeth was quick to respond.

"Then you need to stop this now. Because if you don't…" He spoke quietly to an attentive audience. "And you do vote to leave, I will divorce you."

A cry made them all turn to look. There, stood in the doorway was Sydney.

FARMER GARLIC

Farmer Garlic had lived in Bedwell House all of her life. The mansion farm had been handed down from generation to generation and with each handover the once resplendent example of Elizabethan architecture descended another step towards rot and decay. Exposed beams kept the original features visible while the toxic water that ran through the deep leaded pipes ensured the 'curse of the Garlic's' myth was kept alive as another descendent died of cancer.

The farmer was more fortunate than most of her descendants. Her body did not show signs of tumour and other than a dizzy spell now and then - most often after a drinking spree - she showed no signs of slowing down even though she was in her fifty-third year. She had a thriving business renting out her land and a large marquee for parties and weddings. She also still worked her farm, employing local people to help with the horses and cows and seasonal workers to help with the vegetables.

Farmer Garlic owned a donkey which had come into her possession as repayment of a bad debt. It was her original intention to sell it but she became attached to the animal as it would follow her around her land twitching its ears, braying loudly and nudging her for food. The animal had no name and so she just referred to it as 'Donkey'. As Donkey got older the once placid animal turned into a spiteful beast but she did not bite the hand of her keeper so she was allowed to stay. However, both her name and demeanour changed after Romeo arrived at Bedwell House. Farmer Garlic won Romeo in a bet while at a livestock show in Scotland. The farmer was drunk at the time and it was a source of bewilderment to her when she awoke on the morning she was meant to return home to find a Wagyu bull taking up space in her horsebox.

The farmer had heard about the quality of Wagyu beef and during her return trip she decided she would get herself a Wagyu cow and start up a herd of her own. When she arrived home, she unloaded the animal and tied it up in a stall in her barn. Within weeks it became apparent that her bull was not like other bulls - his sperm being little more than tadpole jelly – and so she devised a new plan – this time to slaughter the animal and live off the high-quality steak. So she ordered a new freezer to house the beast once it had been killed and cut into Sunday-lunch-size slices.

By a stroke of luck the Wagyu bull was saved by Donkey. The day before Romeo's intended demise and carve-up, Donkey kicked her way out of her stable and headed for the barn. The moment Donkey and Romeo set eyes on each other an act of bestial amour occurred: it was a love which crossed the animal intersection. The spiteful donkey and infertile bull did not acknowledge their differences. The disparity in their looks, size, colour, characteristics and vocal comprehension were set aside and an unseen bond took hold. Farmer Garlic was so touched by the cross-species love affair that she cancelled the slaughter and returned the freezer. Romeo was saved, the spiteful donkey was rechristened Juliette and the two of them were moved to live out their unconventional union in a secure field a couple of miles from the farm.

It was one afternoon while Farmer Garlic was watching the two of them grazing side by side that she realised she was due at a Parish Council meeting. She had spent the morning patrolling the farm in her tractor, supervising the spreading of cow-shit on her land before stopping to visit her two pets on her return to the farm. She looked at her watch.

"Bollocks!" she shouted when she realised she had less than fifteen minutes to get there and her only mode of transport was her tractor.

She arrived at the Millennium Community Hub council offices with two minutes to spare. She parked her tractor so that it only partially blocked the car-park entrance, wiped her hands down her green overalls and went inside.

Froggett Barn was the name of the original Bedwell Ash village hall. Two centuries, three fires, four rebuilds and a major refurbishment project later, and it was rebranded the Millennium Community Hub although it was still known as Froggett Barn to many.

The latest rejuvenation project had taken place in the late 1990s. The building was extended ensuring that – as far as financially feasible – it was in keeping with the village setting. Most villagers were happy with the red brick and tile exterior and the tiny windows but older villagers pointed out that it now resembled the Victorian slaughterhouse which had stood on the edge of the village until the mid-1960s.

Every expense had been spared on the inside as well. There was a grand hall and thirteen offices. Matt grey walls served as a backdrop for the pieces of modern art donated by local artists to bedeck them. In the main meeting room hung the largest oil painting, a mass of colour which at first gander looked just that. Only those with patience and an acute sense of observation noticed the outline of a tree emerge from the swirling lines.

The only item purchased new for the building was a piece of furniture. It was agreed after much discussion and a paper trail worthy of a fox and hounds run to purchase a custom-built table. Like the legend of King Arthur, the expense was justified on the grounds that it was large and round, which meant nobody would have the psychological advantage at council meetings. Delivery of the table was mentioned to a select group of villagers who turned out to watch it being carried into the building by a band of uniformed men. The spectacle was on the front page of the local paper the following week under the heading 'Round Table for Former Stable'. The rest of the furniture - worn chairs and splintered desks - were pushed and carried into the building under cover of darkness during the following evening.

Once in the building, the farmer followed the arrows to the meeting room. Just outside the door three children were sitting in silence on the floor.

"What are you doing here?" she asked.

The three girls wore grubby tracksuits and trainers and had long unbrushed hair.

"We're the ica sisters," said the eldest.

"The ica sisters?"

"Yes, I'm Jessica and I'm twelve." The child looked at the sibling next to her.

"I'm Monica and I'm ten," she said.

Then the smallest sibling piped up.

"And I'm Angelica and I'm seven."

"You haven't answered my question," said the farmer. "What are you doing here?"

"Sorry," said Jessica. "We're waiting for our dad. He's in there." She pointed to the door of the meeting room.

"I see," said the farmer as she opened the door.

Everyone looked up as the farmer entered.

"You know there are three kiddies outside, call themselves the ica sisters."

"They're mine," said Bill Inghurst. "Babysitter let me down."

The farmer ignored the response and was about to take her seat but before she did she paused to stare up at the painting.

"What the bloody 'ell is that all about?" she asked, shaking her head.

"You ask that every time you come here," said Bill Inghurst.

"If you look closely enough," said Caleb, "you will see a tree."

"Bollocks it is. It's a bloody mess, that's what it is." She looked around the table. "By the way, I've blocked some of you in - I had to come in me tractor."

"What is it with you? Couldn't you come in a car like everyone else?" said Roman Winters, the local pub landlord.

"Not everyone," Elizabeth interrupted. "I didn't, I came on my bike."

"Excuse me." Caleb coughed to get the group's attention. "Are we ready to start the meeting?"

Farmer Garlic settled into her seat.

"Now we have a new council member and a new minute taker," Caleb announced. "So please can I ask that we all state our names for the attendance record."

"Shouldn't we wait for Hector?" Elizabeth asked.

"Hector has sent his apologies, he will not be with us today," said Caleb. He looked around the table. "So, my name is Caleb Johnson, I shall be chairing today. As most of you will know my lovely wife Ellie and I run a small computer business and we are proud parents to Benedict, Jethro and baby Daisy."

"Elizabeth Rossi, wife of Rafael, mother of three. I'm a social worker."

"Garlic, among other things they call me Farmer Garlic, no husband, no children, just me and me animals. I own the farm on the edge of the village."

"I'm Paul Hollyoak, owner of Paul's Pies, best pie and cake shop in the village. I have two children, Saul, eleven, and Charlotte who's thirteen."

"Zelda Mark, I own the bookshop with my writer husband Markus and we have three children: Somerset who is thirteen, Harper who is ten and Byron eight."

"I am Jan Kowolski. I come here to work in UK from Poland with my wife Sonja, and my daughter Marina."

"Is it your wife who sings Beethoven every morning down Gainsborough Court?" asked Evelyn.

"That is correct. That is my wife. My daughter Marina sometimes sings also. I myself play the violin."

"So that's you lot," Kirk Scott interrupted. "My Honeysuckle was asking me what that racket was."

"Well, I must say, they both sing beautifully," said Evelyn, casting a look of unimpressed exasperation in Kirk's direction.

"Thank you, you are very kind."

"It's a great pity that not all of us can appreciate such talent." Evelyn smiled at him. "I myself play violin and piano."

There was an awkward silence before Evelyn realised it was her turn.

"I'm Evelyn, Evelyn Smith, I've lived in the village all of my sixty-four years. My daughter and my two grandchildren live here as well."

She looked around the table, smiling at each person as she spoke. The smile disappeared briefly when her eyes met with Kirk's but re-emerged again as soon as they unmet.

"Oh, and I have five cats," she added.

"Roman Winters," the voice of the burly Northerner bellowed out. "I own the village pub and the block of flats opposite the church. Oh, and in case you haven't heard, me wife has buggered off back to Japan and left the kids with me. That's Riku, twelve, and Keiko, she's nine."

"Bloody hell, even I'd heard that," Farmer Garlic spoke loudly.

"Oh, fuck off," said Roman.

"Please, no swearing in council meetings," said Caleb. "Alice, will you please minute that."

"Minuted," said Alice.

"Can't think why anyone would possibly want to leave you," Farmer Garlic added.

"You're barred," said Roman, turning to the farmer.

"Haha! Can't, I'm already barred… your barman barred me last week. Barred me for two weeks he did, all I did was…"

"For the rest of the year…"

"My name is Stefan Schmidt and I am originally from Germany." Stefan smiled around the table as he spoke. "And I am here in England with my lovely wife Alexa and my children Elspeth who is twelve and Helga who is ten. Thank you for letting me join your council."

Next to Stefan sat Bill Inghurst. After a brief pause, as if trying to summon up strength, he spoke.

"I'm Bill Inghurst." His whispered words were near silent as if he didn't want to be heard. "I have three daughters who are waiting outside for me… I hope it's okay."

"That's okay," said Caleb. "But try not to make a habit of it."

"I know," said Roman. "Let's all bring our kids to the next meeting and see how much work we get done."

"I… I'm sorry," said Bill. "The babysitter…"

"Roman, please, I won't ask you again," said Caleb.

"What?" He looked around the table as if appealing for support. "I didn't swear, I merely made a statement."

"Please be respectful of other people… while you're here at least…" Caleb glared at Roman. "And of course please welcome our new minute taker, Alice Grubb."

"Otherwise known as Malice…" said Roman under his breath.

"And I have three adorable girls, Mary, my eldest and Betsy and Jane," Alice piped up, throwing Roman a toxic look. "Everybody says they're the prettiest girls in the village."

"I don't," said Roman.

"Don't what?" asked Caleb.

"I don't say they're the prettiest girls in the village."

"Are you insulting my girls?" asked Alice.

"Not at all, I'm just saying I don't think they're the prettiest girls in the village, so that's not everybody…"

"Kirk, over to you," said Caleb.

"My name is Kirk Scott," he said. "I own the car lot in the village, most of the villagers buy their cars from me."

"How'd you figure that one out?" said Elizabeth.

Kirk looked at her.

"As I was saying, a lot of villagers buy their cars from me. I have a wonderful wife, fitness instructor – very bendy - and a daughter Honeysuckle."

"Right," said Caleb, glaring at Kirk. "Let us begin."

1. Apologies for absence

"As I'm sure you will have noticed by now Hector Oliphant has not been able to attend today," said Caleb. "He's at the regional Scrabble finals."

"Bloody cheek," said Roman. "He should be here."

2. Minutes of previous meeting

There was some discussion, nodding heads, shaking heads.

3. Announcements

Caleb looked around the table.

"I now have an announcement to make. I know Hector would have wanted to make the announcement himself but he was well on the way to London when the news came through."

"What is it?" asked Elizabeth.

"It's about Jill Jones," said Caleb.

"But she's resigned, she resigned two months ago," said Elizabeth.

"True," said Caleb. "Well, the police are at her home arresting her as we speak."

"Blimey," said Elizabeth.

"What's she done?" Asked Kirk.

"It's not murder, is it?" asked Farmer Garlic. "She didn't bump off that old guy she was living with? The way she milked him for every penny was disgusting…"

"No, she's been arrested… for misappropriation of council funds."

"I always knew there was something funny about her," said Roman as his phone pinged a message.

"But she was so nice," said Evelyn.

"I always knew she was a wrong 'un," said Alice Grubb. "A nutcase."

"Well, that doesn't say much," said Elizabeth. "You think anybody who doesn't like you is mentally ill."

"I don't…" Alice reddened. "I was…"

"Enough of this," said Caleb. "The reason she was so nice to us all is because she's a fraudster. And that is what fraudsters do, they're nice to you… to gain your confidence and then steal from you."

"Who would have thought?" said Evelyn Smith. "That kindly woman…"

"Anyway, I'm sure there will be plenty of rumours, we just thought you should all know," said Caleb.

As he finished speaking several more phones pinged, alerting their owners to a message received.

4. Cuts to local bus service

"Why has this been raised again?" asked Elizabeth.

"Because we need to save money," said Roman.

"But people need public transport to get in and out of the village."

"Well, we could think creatively," said Kirk. "You know, maybe have them start later, finish earlier, that sort of thing."

"You can't do that. Lots of people are dependent on the buses."

"People are resilient, they're stoic, they'll cope, they'll find a way round it," said Caleb.

"Huuh! Well, I for one wholeheartedly object. Please make sure you minute that." Elizabeth stared at Alice. "Now, can we move on please?"

"We do have a lot to get through today," said Caleb. "I will, however, suggest we do a survey to see how many people use the buses."

"You do that. You reduce the number of buses and put the fares up and in a couple of years you can get rid of the service altogether because it's so unreliable and expensive people won't use it."

"But most of us do have cars…" said Paul Hollyoak.

"And what about those who don't?" Elizabeth spoke more loudly than she intended. "What happens to them?"

"Okay, calming down and moving on," said Caleb.

5. Speeding through the village

"Scaring my bloody horses," said Farmer Garlic. "Put speed bumps in. That'll stop the buggers."

"We don't allow swearing at our meetings," Caleb reminded her, staring at the scruffy farmer over the top of his glasses.

"We could have one of those speed warning signs, you know, the ones that smile if you're within the speed limit and frown at you if you're not," said Bill Inghurst. With his round face, bald head and popping-out eyes, he looked like the emoji he was attempting to describe.

There was some discussion over which methods to use.

"Barriers," said Kirk Scott.

"Speed bumps," said Evelyn.

"No way," said Paul Hollyoak. "They damage people's cars."

"Only because they speed over them," said Elizabeth.

"Speed bumps it is," said the farmer.

"First I think we need to do research as to costs," said Bill Inghurst. "I can do that if you like."

"Good point," said Kirk Scott. "Let me know if you need a hand."

"We'll discuss this again at the next meeting," said Caleb.

6. Annual village party/fete

"So who would like to take responsibility for organising the annual village party and fete?" asked Caleb.

"Well, I can't this year," said Evelyn. "I do it every year."

"Well, I'm not," said Roman. "I'm far too busy."

"Do we really think it's appropriate this year?" Elizabeth asked, looking around the table. "You know, to have a village fete?"

"I do," said Alice. "My Betsy and Jane have already got their fairy costumes ready."

"But it's not up to you," said Evelyn. "You're just here to take the minutes."

"I'd like it to go ahead," said Caleb. "Everyone looks forward to it."

"It brings the village together," said Paul. "My Saul and his mates love it, and we all enjoy a bit of a knees-up. I'm not organising it though."

"My Jethro really enjoys it too," said Caleb. "My eldest Benedict not so much, it's his age - too cool for school, that one."

"My girls love it," said Bill Inghurst. "They really look forward to it every year."

As if on cue there was a knock on the door and the eldest ica sister entered.

"What's up, love?" Bill turned to his daughter.

"Angelica needs to go to the toilet…"

"Okay, take her and take Monica along with you. You know where it is?"

Jessica nodded.

"Come straight back," he yelled after the child as she left the room, slamming the door behind her.

"You know your kids get called the ica sisters at school," said Alice Grubb.

"I know…"

"It's a form of bullying, you know…"

"I know… but it doesn't bother them… so it doesn't bother me."

"Excuse me, can we get on," said Caleb. "Elizabeth, why do you think we shouldn't have a fete this year?"

"Well, I ask myself if it is right to spend taxpayers' money on a – as you like to call it - a knees-up…"

"But we have it every year." said Farmer Garlic. "Everyone loves it, why stop now?"

"Because of the costs," said Elizabeth.

"I could loan you tables and chairs and the like if it helps at all," said Farmer Garlic. "They're good quality ones I let out for weddings."

"I can vouch for that," said Evelyn. "We hired your marquee and everything for our Eve's wedding. It was a wonderful day, perfect."

"Thanks," said the farmer.

"Okay," said Caleb. "So let's take a vote. All in favour of the annual fete, put your hands up."

Elizabeth was the only one who did not put her hand up.

"Okay, so we want it to go ahead," said Caleb. "Now, who would like to take responsibility for organising it?"

This time nobody raised their hand.

"Your silence has been minuted," said Alice.

Any other business

- Planning application received for two houses to be built on land which is currently the front garden of Plutus Manor.
- Checking the safety of playground equipment.
- Complaints about smoke coming from bonfires on the allotments.
- Request for a kiddies' skate park.
- Complaints about dog poo bins being full.

There was a discussion about each item.

"I can confirm that the emptying of dog poo bins has resumed after a misunderstanding over collection dates," Caleb announced. A collective sigh of relief heralded the end of the meeting.

"Well, that's the last item for today," said Caleb. "Thank you all for com…" Before he could finish his sentence the farmer interrupted.

"So what's going on with this bloody referendum then?"

"What do you mean, what's going on with it?" asked Caleb. "The vote is going to be here, everything's in place."

"Shouldn't we be out there campaigning? Telling people to vote remain," said the farmer.

"You mean get ourselves a battle bus?" said Elizabeth.

"There's already a battle bus, haven't you seen it on the TV?" said Paul. "Leavers have got one too. Apparently if we vote leave, the NHS will receive three hundred and fifty million pounds every week – liars, liars, knickers on fire."

"I've seen the lies, how can they get away with it?" said Roman.

"We need to set one up in the village," said the farmer. "I could probably use me trailer. Stick a billboard on it and tow it around with me tractor. It'll look good."

"I really don't think that will be necessary," said Caleb. "Besides, we – the parish council - should not be telling people how to vote, just providing them with the mechanics to do so."

"Bullshit! Course we should be telling people to vote remain. We're bloody doomed if they don't."

The farmer had heard about the Rossi incident in the restaurant and she turned on Elizabeth.

"You selfish bitch," she hissed. "How bloody could you?"

"I'm a voter and I was exercising freedom of speech…" said Elizabeth.

"I need seasonal workers to pick me vegetables. And who is going to muck out me horses and cows? If we vote to leave the EU I'm in deep shit."

SYDNEY

The shock of hearing the 'divorce' word scared Sydney. Two of her school friends had divorced parents and although they both assured her that being a child from a broken home wasn't actually that bad, it was not something she wanted to happen.

"It's great when they don't get along," said her friend Daniela Esposito. "They feel so guilty with all the arguing you just play one off against the other. My dad always takes me shopping after they've had a row. The louder the row, the more I get to shop."

"I got Dancer when my mum and dad split up," said Charlotte Hollyoak, referring to the pony her parents had bought for her. "They felt so guilty."

Sydney would love to have her own pony and for a short while considered the matter before eventually deciding she would rather live at home with both her parents and have everything just as it had been for the last twelve years. She loved the way they would all sit down for breakfast together. She loved the way her father would hand her her packed lunch and never tell her what was in it. She loved that sometimes at school she would open her lunch-box and just one of her sandwiches would have a mystery bite taken out of it - on those days there was always a chocolate bar replacement. She loved that when she got home from school her dad would have tea ready and they would eat and chat and wait for her mum to come home and then they'd all sit together and she'd tell them both about her day at school before she went off and did her homework.

Sydney knew change was on its way. For one thing Rory was going off to university but she considered that a benefit as he could be a bit bossy.

"Are you okay?" her father asked as he handed over her lunch-box on the Friday before the referendum.

Sydney nodded.

"Are you sure? You're very quiet."

"I'm fine," she said. "Honest."

Sydney was an enterprising child and for days after the family gathering and the revelation that her father was considering divorcing her mother, she spoke a little and thought a lot. This was because she was formulating a plan.

She called her plan 'Action Sunday' because it was her plan and she would go into action on Sunday - the Sunday before the referendum. On the Saturday evening before 'Action Sunday' she set her alarm clock for 6am. It turned out it wasn't necessary because she was awake by 5:45am so, bleary-eyed, she silenced her call to action, jumped out of bed, pulled on her dressing gown, trod into her slippers and made her way downstairs, stepping carefully over Dingle who was asleep on the fourth step up. Nutter was in his bed by the door in the hallway and his tail wagged, making a rhythmic thumping noise when he spotted her. She went over to him and tried to shush him quiet.

"Shhhh... you mustn't make a noise," she said.

Nutter's response was to wag his tail even more.

Sydney got up and went to the kitchen and he followed her. She opened the door to the garden and he leapt out, attempting to scare the one-eared tabby cat which was sitting on a rock next to the lawn. Sydney smiled as she watched him. She then re-focussed and looked around the kitchen. She took off her dressing gown and hung it over the back of a chair. Then she unhooked her teapot-print apron from behind the door and struggled into it, looping the straps around herself and tying them at the front. When her dad or mum were cooking or baking cakes she was often an active participant. She knew how to make tea and use the oven. She had never actually cooked a breakfast on her own, though.

She filled the kettle with water and then put it on. She went to the cupboard and took out two mugs and the Mad Hatter teapot which she had bought for her mother the Christmas before last. Then she got two pans and a bowl from the cupboard. She scrambled the eggs, added a little milk – as she had seen her father do – and then very carefully turned on the electric oven ring, poured the mixture from the bowl into the pan and placed it on the heat. She then went over to the kitchen drawer, selected a wooden spoon and stirred as fast as she could. When the mixture scrambled set she went and popped four slices of granary bread into the toaster. Next she prepared the tray, adding mugs and spoons and knives and forks. Fully loaded, she lifted the tray as carefully as she could and made her way – treading each step with caution – up the stairs to her parents' room.

The tray was heavier than she thought. Like a trapeze artist on a wire she paced one foot in front of the other, trying to keep her body and the tray in unison. When she got to the bedroom she balanced it on her knee and tapped on the door. Then she turned the handle and kicked the door open with her foot which entered the room first.

Sydney saw her mother was awake and breathed a sigh of relief when she jumped out of bed to help.

"Thanks. I nearly dropped it."

"Darling, how lovely," said Elizabeth, placing the tray on the bedside cabinet. "Rafael, look, Sydney's made breakfast for us."

"Morning," said Sydney. "I made it all by myself."

Rafael groaned and rolled over, then looked at his daughter through sleep-filled eyes.

"Morning, darling." He sat up. "Well, I must say that is very kind of you. I think that deserves a tickle."

Sydney rolled her eyes.

"Dad, I'm twelve, not eight."

"So what's the occasion?" asked Elizabeth.

"What d'ya think?" She looked at Elizabeth as she spoke. "You two have got to talk."

"Really?" said Elizabeth. "What about?"

"You are not going to split up."

"Of course we're not," said Elizabeth. "We were just having a row, that's all. It happens."

"Charlotte's mum and dad said that to her loads of times but they did." Sydney looked at each of them in turn. "But she doesn't mind because they bought her a pony to make up for it. I don't want a pony." She paused. "Well, I do want a pony but, well, you know."

She watched as her parents – wide awake now - looked at each other. Then she turned around, walked to the door, took the key from the lock, went out of the room and shut and locked the door.

"I'm going to play with Nutter in the garden," she shouted to them. "Then I'm going to do my piano practice. Phone me when you're sorted and I'll let you out."

ELIZABETH

It was all very simple; on the day of the referendum all Elizabeth had to do was to avoid the polling station. It was what was agreed and it was her intention to do just that. However, two days earlier her sub-conscious mind convinced her conscious mind that it would be a good idea to take the day off work in order to catch up on the housework and so that is what she did. In the late afternoon she decided to take Nutter for a walk and so she did that too. Nutter could hardly believe his luck when she took him into the utility room where he expected her to put on her rubber gloves and dish up an early meat tea, but instead she picked up his lead, snapped it onto his collar and yanked him out through the side door.

Usually when Elizabeth walked Nutter she would take him to the open space around the grounds of the ruined castle, but on this occasion she tugged his collar to turn left and go in the opposite direction. He followed her in an act of submissive obedience. He didn't bark when she hauled him past the tabby cat with one ear, even though it hissed at him and flexed its claws in readiness to take out one of his eyes. Like an unwilling accomplice he trod her path as she made her way in the direction of the Millennium

Community Hub which on this day just happened to be the village polling station.

She sat on the bench, wanting to be part of this historic day but knowing observation was all that was possible. Her thoughts returned to the previous Sunday when Sydney had locked them in the bedroom.

"It's agreed then."

"Agreed," Elizabeth said. *"You don't vote and neither will I."*

"We cancel each other out. Simple."

"No repercussions… you know, about what I said at the party?"

"Not from me… I can't promise for Rory though…"

They made love to the strains of a halted Fur Elise played by Sydney practising her piano piece downstairs, then rested together before Rafael picked up his phone to call his youngest child.

So on referendum day when Elizabeth took Nutter for a walk and found herself outside the polling station, it was as an observer only. She watched as men and women of all ages went in and out, doing their civic duty and exercising their democratic right to vote. Nutter sighed and sat down beside her. Elizabeth knew - as had been agreed and sealed in the family bed on the previous Sunday morning – she could not vote, she must not vote.

She sat on a bench opposite the building, then picked up her bag and pulled out her poetry book. She glanced up as five women in their late teens came out of the building. They had taken part in a historic event and Elizabeth wondered if they realised it. Behind them a lady creased with age walked as fast as her arthritic knees would allow, walking stick in one hand, shopping bag in the other; she tripped and the bag dropped to the ground. One of the women hesitated and then ran over, picked it up and placed it back within the old lady's grasp, scurrying back to the others before they noticed.

> *'If I can stop one heart from breaking,*
> *I shall not live in vain…'*

Nutter barked to alert her that the one-eared tabby cat had followed them and was sitting eyeballing him. It hissed and then spat in his direction. He growled and got up, pulling at his lead to chase it. The cat stood its ground for a split second but then spotted a smaller, more vulnerable prey in the form of a solitary bird with a gammy wing pecking at the dust beneath a buddleia bush. Before Elizabeth realised what was happening the cat stalked and then pounced on the bird, running off with the feathered treat into the oblivion of the hedgerows.

'if I can ease one life the aching,
Or cool one pain...'

As Elizabeth watched, the women reached the gate, they giggled, they chatted, but their eyes were on their phones, not on each other. One swore, another belched and they all laughed. '*How lucky you all are,*' she thought. She spotted the cat again underneath a bush with the bird – dead now - between its teeth. The strong overpowering the weak.

'Or help one fainting robin,
unto his nest again...'

The elderly lady was standing kerbside waiting to cross the road. Today she was an elderly lady but who was she yesterday? A wife? A mother? A poet like Emily Dickinson? A suffragette like Emily Davison?

'I shall not live in vain...'

One minute later and Elizabeth had forgotten the promise she made to Rafael and the intimacy that sealed their pact. She had blanked out her father's predicament and her reassurance to Sydney that things were now okay. She was thinking women's rights. She was thinking Emily Davison. She knew it was her duty to vote as it was the duty of every woman. She stood up and marched towards the polling station. Nutter followed head down as if knowing he was now an active participant in her subterfuge.

Once inside, Elizabeth got her slip of paper and went into a polling booth. There was no hesitation; she marked her cross against the 'Leave' option and posted her slip into the ballot box.

Her thoughts were with the poor and the vulnerable, not with her family, not Rafael or Rory or Sydney. That changed several seconds later when she came face to face with them as she was going out of the door just as they were coming in.

Rory spotted her first.

"Mum, what are you doing here?" He paused before adding. "What the hell have you done?"

She turned to her son but instead caught Rafael's eye. She had betrayed this man, her husband, her confidante, her friend, her lover.

"How could you?" he asked. "We agreed…"

Elizabeth was in the wrong and she knew it. In the past when this had happened (there had been a number of occasions) she'd admitted her wrongdoing, things mopped themselves up and life returned to normal usually within a couple of days. Today was different. She turned on Rafael, her guilt manifesting itself as aggression.

"So why on earth are you here then?"

"I've come to see my… our son cast his first vote."

"We were going to ask you to come but Daddy said it might put you in the way of temptation," said Sydney.

"How could you?" Rafael asked again.

"What on earth is wrong with you?" asked Rory.

"Liar! You lied!" Sydney shouted. "Lying is wrong, you always tell me that."

By now several spectators were showing an interest. It was not at this stage a full-on row but the onlookers could see that the incident had potential and were hanging back watching and waiting.

"What the bloody hell have you done?" Rafael glared at his wife, his face flushed, his fists clenched.

Elizabeth had seen him like this only twice before. The first time was when Ruby had stayed out all night with a friend when they were expecting her back at 11pm, and the second was when the police called to inform them that a fourteen-year-old Rory was in a cell sleeping off half a bottle of vodka when he should have been at school. However, on both occasions Rafael's anger had been born out of love and fear. On this day his anger was born of betrayal.

"I was casting my vote as I have a democratic right... a duty... to do..." Elizabeth did not make eye contact.

The group of onlookers looked at each other and seized the opportunity to become involved en masse.

"She has a right to vote," shouted a woman in her mid-fifties.

"Shame on you," shouted a young woman with three children in tow.

"Sir, you cannot interfere with a person who wants to cast their vote," shouted an elderly gentleman from his mobility scooter.

Elizabeth recognised Mr Melford and his wife. They had run the village post office until it had been forced to close five years earlier.

"Well, Rafael Rossi, I would never have thought," shouted Mrs Melford.

"It... it's not what it looks..." Rafael stuttered.

"Our country is a democracy." An unperturbed Mr Melford boomed the words out.

It was this remark that got the attention of the duty clerk and parish council member Hector Oliphant. He was sixty-one with a single mind and a dress code which had not changed since one weekend in 1976 when he had gone to a music festival and returned home leaving his fashion sense in the Spiegel tent. He placed his pen down, stood up and walked towards Rafael.

"Excuse me, sir," he said. "Am I to understand you are attempting to interfere with this lady's democratic right to vote?"

Rafael reddened and stayed quiet. Rory reddened and didn't.

"Hector, bugger off and mind your own business."

Twenty minutes of apologies and explanations later Hector Oliphant returned to his desk and continued his duties satisfied that it was a domestic affray and not a criminal offence unfolding. Elizabeth turned to her husband and two children.

"Now I would like to be clear about this," she said. "I should not have voted. It was wrong of me and I am sorry. We made a pact, I broke it and I shouldn't have."

"Well, at least you have the decency to apologise," Rafael said.

"But I am not sorry I voted Leave."

"Mum, shut up!" said Rory. "You're making a prat of yourself... again."

"Thank you. A woman died to give me the vote... it was my duty..."

"Daddy, is that true?" asked Sydney.

"Yes, it is true," Rory replied. "But it is also true that a horse was injured and a jockey... an innocent man... committed suicide as a result..."

"Thirty-eight years later," Elizabeth growled at him.

"I'm just giving Sydney the facts," Rory replied. "There are two sides to every story."

"That is exactly why I had to cast my vote," said Elizabeth, "because there are two sides to every story."

"Mum, will you listen to yourself." He turned to his father. "Well, I hope you're going to vote now, to nullify hers."

"Too right I am," he said. "Come on."

She watched as they each went and picked up a ballot paper and made their way to the polling booths.

Sydney turned to her mother.

"Will you be getting a divorce?"

Elizabeth looked down at her daughter.

"No, darling," she said. "Of course we won't."

"So he'll forgive you then?"

Elizabeth took hold of her daughter's hand and squeezed it tight.

They stood and watched as father and son went over and posted their votes into the ballot boxes. Once posted, they shook hands; Elizabeth spotted Rory looking at her, as if to reinforce the message that she was a traitor. The father-son bonding was interrupted by Rafael's phone. She watched as her husband pulled his phone from his jacket pocket, answered it and his face turned to one of concern. He hurried towards them.

"It's Ruby, she's at the hospital."

RUBY

R uby was in the bath when she felt an unusual discomfort. Her first instinct was to get out of the bath – which she did - unaware that the popping sensation down below had been her waters breaking. How could she have known? She had never done this pregnancy thing before. They had explained it to her at her ante-natal classes. *'When your waters break,'* they said, *'you will have a discharge. It may be a little – like an incontinent pee when you sneeze – or it may be a lot – like a burst water pipe that floods the kitchen. When that happens, you go straight to the hospital.'* Well, there was no evidence of any leakage at all because it had drained away down the plughole with the rest of the bath water. Besides, how could they have broken? Her baby was not due for another five weeks.

It was all in her plan and 'What to do when my waters break' would not appear in her daily list (which she extracted from the details of her plan on a daily basis) for at least another three weeks. Her plan for today was:

~~Get up and get Lars off to work~~
~~Reset the alarm and go back to bed until 9am~~
~~Have breakfast tea and muesli~~
Have a bath
Paint
Light lunch of pea and ham hock soup

Read baby book
Go to vote
Phone grandad
Cook dinner and wait for Lars.

Wrapped in her bathrobe, she returned to the living room. She picked up her list and pencil from the dresser, sat down on the oversize tartan sofa and crossed through the 'Have a bath' item. Then she picked up the baby names book from the floor - where she had dropped it the previous evening - and flicked through it, first girls names and then boys, wondering which she would have.

After about five minutes she got distracted by a pain in her inners. It was a definite spasm of some sort. It was short, sharp and nothing to worry about. She sat for five minutes before going back upstairs to her studio to change into painting gear.

The first day Lars brought her to this house and showed her around she knew. She knew that this room at the back of the house would be her art studio. It was full of natural light and the view over the fields both relaxed and inspired her.

Ruby didn't paint fields or landscapes, or portraits either, but she knew this room was perfect for what she did paint. She produced scenes of colours and shapes, abstract motifs, contemporary works. Her friends labelled her a modern artist but she called herself a 'present-day painter'. Quite often the only clue to the domain of her canvas construct was a title - 'Land Fen Aurora' or 'Borealis on Market Day' – a detailed construct of paint and colour put together by an over-active imagination and created by a soul dedicated to the cause of her own invented artistic movement. When asked to describe her work she would attempt to detail her meticulous constructs as a cross between Folk and Geometric Abstract Art. It was more often than not a one-sided conversation as it was reliant on the listener understanding something about either. Ruby was never concerned by people who did not understand her creative path. She sold her work only to those who professed to appreciate art, those who understood creativity, and to those willing to pay hundreds of pounds for a piece of her action.

Over the past few weeks she had conceived an idea for a painting and on this day, the day of the body pop and the spasm, she felt ready to give birth to it in her studio. It was a twenty-seven-piece montage integrated into a single work of art depicting a united EU world. She needed to get the picture that was in her head out of there so she selected a canvas – the largest she had ever worked with – gathered paintbrushes and paints and set herself in readiness to deliver her creative icon to the world.

She started work, washing colour and mark making. Then it happened. It was a contraction, a proper one this time. She knew. She stopped painting and went and sat down. Then she picked up her phone and whispered to herself.

Phone taxi. Phone Lars. Phone taxi. Phone Lars.

She phoned a taxi then she phoned Lars – and left a message.

The taxi arrived within ten minutes by which time she was standing on the doorstep with her half packed bag and her phone glued to her ear, having left three messages for her husband.

"Hospital, as fast as you can please."

The driver, a young man of twenty-four years who had recently returned from living in America, looked at Ruby. Then he got out of his car and stood staring at her, looking her up and down while scratching his head.

"What's wrong?" she asked.

"Hang on, Ma'am…" he said, opening the front passenger door of his vehicle and stretching inside to move the seat forward.

"What's wrong?" Ruby asked again.

He stood up and turned to look at her.

"Nothing, Ma'am," he said with a wink. "Just don't want to have to prise you out with a can opener…"

Ruby attempted a smile, got in the car and just about managed to buckle up.

"I need to get to the hospital…" she said.

"My name is Samuel," he said, "I am your driver today."

"And make it quick!"

Back in his seat now he made it clear he understood the urgency of the situation and put his foot down, skidding off the driveway like a kid on black pavement ice.

"No problem, Ma'am," he said, looking at Ruby in his rear-view mirror. "I'll have you there in a jiffy."

Samuel took his driving duties seriously and considered that he had a responsibility to deliver this young woman to her chosen

SALAMA

destination. However, nowhere in his mini-cab job description was there any mention of delivering a baby on the back seat of his car.

It was three miles down the road just after the roundabout that Samuel and Ruby's vehicle was forced to a halt by a police patrol car. A burly woman, her blonde hair tied tight back, got out of the car and approached their vehicle. She opened her mouth to address what she considered to be a young tearaway but any sound about to come out was drowned out by Ruby who started a contraction. This diverted the police woman's attention from Samuel in the front of the car to the back seat and when she saw Ruby's face contorted in pain and her legs apart, she stepped back, stood erect and cleared her throat.

"Ted! TED!" she shouted.

Ted was finishing off his fish and chips in the passenger seat of his vehicle. He looked over.

"There's a woman about to drop a baby, phone the hospital."

The policewoman had never delivered a baby in the line of duty and had no interest in doing so now.

"Follow us," she said, retreating back to her vehicle. "We'll give you an escort."

She went back to her car, slammed the door shut, set the lights flashing and took off.

"Ma'am, you hold on now," said Samuel. "We'll be there in no time."

Overjoyed at this turn of events, he put his foot down once more and obediently chased the police car, pleased he was not in trouble and ecstatic at the sudden realisation of a childhood dream.

On arrival at the hospital a sobbing Ruby was extracted from the vehicle by a waiting nurse and deposited into a wheelchair.

"Here, please, I will take you," said a voice with a French accent.

Ruby turned to try and see the woman. She was young – about Ruby's age - but she took control of the situation which is what the sobbing Ruby needed.

"My name is Francine. Come on, let's get you to delivery."

"I can't get through to my husband," Ruby sobbed. "I've been trying… I want him here."

"Okay," said Francine. "Is there anybody else I can call for you? Your mother… or a friend?"

106

"My dad, call my dad... please."

Forty minutes later Ruby was in straddle position in the care of a midwife and Francine. Both were staring between her legs, fiddling with technical equipment and occasionally looking above the paraphernalia to nod and wave. Ruby was on her own with the baby experts, hooked up to a computer, its rhythmic monitoring counting down to the moment of creation.

Ruby's scream quietened as her contraction receded and it was at that moment Elizabeth barged through the door. She cried when she saw her mother; it was a cry not defined by pain, but by relief.

"Darling," said Elizabeth. "I've had a devil of a job finding you. I feel as if I've been on a treasure hunt. I followed the signs to the maternity wing 'up two flights' it said, but then the signs disappeared." She paused for breath. "Are you okay?"

"Where's Lars?" Ruby shouted. "I've been calling him."

"Sorry, about the signage," said Francine turning to Elizabeth. "We're in the middle of refurbishment."

"It's happening again," shouted Ruby. Elizabeth got hold of her hand.

The midwife nodded and placed herself in the 'catch' position.

"Where the hell is Lars?" Elizabeth asked nobody in particular.

Eighteen shrill minutes, a snip and several towels later, and Ruby was cuddling her first-born child.

"Thank you, thank you, thank you," she said to everyone in the room. Then she looked at her mother.

"Thanks, Mum," she said. "For being here."

There was a commotion outside; the doors pushed in and Lars appeared followed by Rafael.

"Fucking well let me in. My wife's having a baby. Who the hell are you lot? Rubes, what are you doing here? You're meant to be in private."

"Don't speak to them like that," said Elizabeth.

Francine turned to look at Lars.

"Please could you speak quieter? I'm sure you don't want your daughter to hear you shouting like this."

"Daughter! I've got a daughter!"

"Thank God you're here! Come and say hello to your daughter," said Ruby. "Isn't she beautiful?" Tears streamed down her face as she spoke.

Lars leant forward, kissed his wife on the left cheek then leant over to see his daughter.

"Hello," he said. "Beautiful," he turned to Ruby.

"Why aren't you in private?"

"It… it all happened so quickly…" said Ruby. "I tried to phone you…"

"You took your time getting here," said Elizabeth.

"We couldn't find it," said Rafael. "Can I hold her?"

"Me first," said Lars.

Elizabeth turned on him.

"Where the hell were you?"

"I got stuck in traffic. Then they wouldn't let me in. Questioned me, they did." He turned to his wife.

A pager went off.

"Excuse me." It was the midwife. "I must go. I will be back shortly."

"Where's she off to?" asked Lars.

"Got another delivery, I expect," said Elizabeth.

"They were so good. I was so scared," said Ruby.

"But why did they bring you here…?"

"I panicked… I called a taxi." Ruby turned to her husband. "We got a police escort."

"Well, I'm here now," Lars said, smiling down at his daughter. "She is so beautiful, just like her mummy."

"You're not disappointed?" asked Ruby.

"Disappointed?"

"You wanted a boy, didn't you?" Ruby said. "Go on, admit it. You wanted a son."

"It is not a problem," said Lars. "We will make more. We will have sons."

"She looks just like Ruby when she was born," Rafael said.

Lars looked at his baby and then at his wife.

"Thank you, Rubes," he said. "For giving me a beautiful daughter. I am so sorry I wasn't here."

"I'm sure you had good reason," said Ruby.

Lars nodded.

"Was it very painful?"

"Of course it was painful," said Ruby.

"It's bloody painful," said Elizabeth. "Let me tell you what having a baby is like. Imagine you are building up to a really good orgasm."

"Mum! Yuk! Please stop…" Ruby pleaded.

"But instead of pleasure building up and building up… it's pain. More and more pain, excruciating pain and, then, a baby appears." She paused. "And the pain stops."

"Stop it…" said Ruby. "Just stop."

"Have you thought of a name yet?" asked Rafael glaring at his wife.

Ruby and Lars looked at each other. "We are still discussing it," said Lars.

"Look at her. Look at what we made," said Ruby. "Where were you? Why didn't you call me back? You should have been here."

"I know." Then Lars spoke directly to his daughter. "I am so sorry I missed your entrance."

"So are you going to tell us?" asked Elizabeth. "What was more important than being at the birth of your first child?"

"Yes." He lifted his daughter to face him. "Do you want to know why I couldn't be here to see you being born little one?"

"We'd all love to know," Elizabeth interrupted.

"Daddy had something very important to do."

"What on earth could be more important than the birth of your first child?" asked Elizabeth.

"Making sure that child has a future."

There was a short pause before Elizabeth turned on him.

"You went and voted, didn't you?" she shouted.

"Of course. Why wouldn't I?"

"You went and voted rather than be at the birth of your baby."

"I went and voted for my baby," he said. "For her and for all her brothers and sisters."

"Steady on," said Ruby.

"Well, how bloody selfish," said Elizabeth.

"No he's not." Ruby turned to her husband. "You did the right thing. I'm glad you went."

"Well… sorry… I don't get it," said Elizabeth.

"Huuh! We've already established you don't get it," said Rafael. "Come on, let's leave them to it. We need to talk."

"There's nothing to discuss." Elizabeth barked the words back at him.

Ruby looked at each of them in turn. "What is up with you two? Mum, Dad, what's going on? I thought everything was sorted between you."

"You must be tired…" said Elizabeth. "You've had a long day."

"It was," said Rafael. "Everything was sorted…"

Looks were exchanged and like the sun giving birth to a new day, the mist cleared and clarity dawned.

"You voted…" Lars turned and shouted at Elizabeth. "You went and bloody well voted, didn't you?"

"Come on," said Rafael to his wife. "This is not the time or place to…"

"Mum, you didn't! You promised you weren't going to!" Ruby shouted. "Please tell me you didn't."

ELIZABETH

At 4:36am the following morning, the house phone in the Rossi home rang. It was sitting on the bedside table next to Rafael but it woke Elizabeth first. She nudged her husband awake and he leant over and picked up the receiver. In the past such calls had meant a child was stranded, there had been an accident or somebody had been arrested. Elizabeth watched Rafael as he listened to the voice at the other end of the phone. As she did the events of the previous day came back to her. She was now a grandmother and her thoughts turned to her granddaughter.

"Is the baby okay?" she shouted.

Rafael nodded and tried to move the phone away from her, but she leant over and grabbed it.

"Is the baby okay?" she shouted.

Lars was at the other end of the line and he shouted back.

"No, she is not! My daughter has been born into a country with no future. A country of racists and of bigots!"

"Lars. Calm down, what are you on about?" she asked.

"You should be fucking ashamed of yourself…"

"Pardon?"

"It's you and people like you that…"

"Lars, please… is the baby okay?"

"It's a fucking leave vote."

"It's what?" Elizabeth turned to look at Rafael. "Leave?"

"I hope you're fucking proud of yourself."

Elizabeth handed the phone back to Rafael.

She watched as her husband was informed by Lars of all that was wrong with the referendum result and with the country. She could tell by Rafael's facial expressions that sentences were being punctuated with expletives and that acceptance of the democratic process was not something Lars endorsed now that it was a leave vote. She didn't hear all of the one-sided conversation but she could fill in the gaps.

"We've what!" and "Well, who would have thought…" and "Are you serious? You're not playing some kind of joke?"

Eventually Rafael placed the receiver down.

"Well, you've got your wish. We've voted to leave the EU," he said.

"Blimey, but it wasn't my wish! I wasn't expecting that!" Elizabeth leaned back and then turned to look at her husband.

"And I suppose it's all my fault?"

"Of course it is. You and people like you."

Rafael got up and headed for the en-suite. Fifteen minutes later, ablutions complete, he re-entered the bedroom, put his dressing gown on, went downstairs to the dining room and switched on the television. Elizabeth stayed in bed, too stunned to get out, get up and face the music. It was just after 6:30 am when - still tired - she got up, showered, got dressed and trod gently downstairs to where Rafael was sitting in the back room with a pot of tea, watching the TV. She entered the room silently and went and sat at the table, staring at what was unfolding in front of her.

An hour later Rory arrived home.

"How could you do such a thing?" he greeted his mother as he entered the room.

"It wasn't just me, several other million people also voted leave," she responded with a verbal wriggle.

Insinuations and accusations continued for several minutes.

"Enough now!" Rafael shouted.

The racket woke Sydney who appeared at the dining-room door, rubbing her eyes.

"What's wrong?" she asked. "Why is everyone shouting?"

"It's a leave vote," said Rafael.

"A fucking leave vote," said Rory pacing the room.

112

"Language," said Rafael.

"I'm sorry," Rory said to his father. He turned to his young sibling. "I'm sorry, Sydney. I'm just so angry."

"No probs," said Sydney. "I'm pissed off too, my future is ruined."

"Oh, don't be so ridiculous!" said Elizabeth.

"Don't you dare speak to her like that," said Rafael.

Elizabeth looked at her daughter's face.

"I know… look, I'm sorry…" Elizabeth turned to Sydney. "I promise you I have not ruined your future." Sydney looked at her mother unconvinced, then she turned and ran back up to her room.

By 9am they were sitting in the lounge, each with their drink of choice, watching the television and trying to make sense of it all.

"Well, I must say I'm surprised," said Elizabeth. "I didn't think we'd actually vote to leave."

"You didn't think at all," said Rory. "Along with several million other people."

"Please don't speak to me like that," said Elizabeth. "I cast my vote as I thought fit, as I'm sure you did."

"My vote was for the future," said Rory. "Yours was for the past."

LARS

Lars left the hospital just before 11pm. He kissed his wife and baby goodbye and headed home, picking up a takeaway curry on the way. When he got home he settled in the lounge and switched on the television to watch the referendum results as they came in. He opened a newly bought bottle of scotch and Skyped friends, telling them about his new-born. In return he received congratulations and daddy jokes, but as constituency counts trickled in, the jollity slowed and then stopped altogether as his new daughter took a back seat to the referendum results. He tried to comprehend what was going on. Like a dramatist with a planted seed he foresaw the aftermath of this catastrophic event unfold as one of gloom and doom in his own plotted mental adaptation of 'The Waste Land'.

"Fucking stupid cunts!"

The decline of the UK had been kick-started by the stupidity of the leave voters and it would not be long before the economy would be in freefall.

After the call to his mother-in-law and three black coffees, he decided to go to work.

The early train to London was packed. En route the usually near silent carriage gave air time to shock/horror discussions, as men and women talked about the hell of it all. A few kept quiet.

At work there were initial congratulations and handshakes but then commiserations all round. There was head-shaking, table-thumping and gasps of disbelief.

It wasn't until three days later that he went and picked Ruby and his new daughter up from the private wing of the hospital.

Seven days after their return home, Lars, Ruby and their baby were sitting in their back room expecting their first visitors. Lars and Ruby both jumped when the doorbell pealed C sharp.

"Now please be nice," Ruby warned. "She won't stay long; she just wants to see her granddaughter, that's all."

The doorbell rang again and this time Lars went and opened it. Elizabeth, Rafael and Sydney were standing on the doorstep. Elizabeth held out a sponge cake.

"I've brought this," she said.

Lars nodded at Rafael and smiled as Sydney darted past him and headed for the lounge to see her sister and her niece.

Elizabeth and Rafael followed him to the lounge. It was a bright room with double aspect windows overlooking the landscaped garden. Ruby was sitting on the sofa with her baby. Elizabeth placed the sponge cake onto the table and then went and sat next to her daughter.

"Can I hold her?" Sydney was sitting on the floor, gazing at the baby. "I promise I won't drop her."

"Of course you can," said Ruby. "When she wakes up."

"I bought you a cake," Elizabeth said, smiling at the baby.

"Thanks, Mum," said Ruby.

"It's an Elizabeth sponge."

"You named a sponge cake after yourself?" said Lars.

"No, it's named after Queen Elizabeth. Queen Victoria's got a cake named after her so I thought I'd make one and name it after our queen." She paused. "It's got three layers, look, a layer of cream at the top, then in the middle a layer of jam, then another layer of cream. And look, I did an 'E' on the top. I made it out of raspberries."

"A royalist as well as a…" said Lars.

"Lars, don't," Ruby pleaded.

"That's right, Lars, don't," said Rafael. "We've just come to see our granddaughter, that's all."

Lars got his phone from his pocket, sat down in a high-backed leather Queen Anne style armchair placed next to the window and started to check his messages.

"Yes, thanks for letting us… you know… come over," said Elizabeth, gazing at her granddaughter.

"Is she waking up?" said Sydney. "Can I hold her now?"

"Just give her a moment," said Ruby.

"You're going to be Auntie Sydney," said Rafael.

Sydney laughed.

"That sounds funny!" she said. "What's her name? Has she got one yet?"

"We've decided on Georgina," said Ruby.

"Georgina Latymer, very nice," said Elizabeth.

"Georgina Soros Latymer, meet your grandparents," said Lars without looking up from his phone.

"Georgina... Soros...?" Elizabeth looked at Ruby, puzzled.

"After the greatest financier and philanthropist of our times," said Lars. "And an ardent remainer."

"Excuse me?" Elizabeth spoke louder than she meant to. "What?"

"Elizabeth!" Rafael hissed at her.

"It's a great name," Ruby whispered. "It will give her something to aspire to. It's called nominative determinism. And what's more there is scientific evidence that a child can live up - or down - to its name. My... our daughter needs a name that will help make her successful. It's a tough world out there."

"Oh, behave yourselves!" Elizabeth spoke quietly. "You're giving your daughter the name of the person who almost singlehandedly broke the Bank of England. The man who almost bankrupted this country. Why on earth would you do that?"

"Because they can," Rafael joined in, his voice hushed.

"He is a great man," said Lars. "And what he did was just business. Our baby Georgina Soros will be like him, a great philanthropist."

"How bloody ridiculous..." Elizabeth forgot to whisper this time, alarming baby Georgina Soros who let out a scream.

"Now look what you've done," said Ruby, rocking her baby.

"Your problem is you totally fail to see the bigger picture." Lars glared at Elizabeth.

"Can I hold her?" asked Sydney, crawling over to sit beside Ruby.

Rafael got up, wandered over to his wife and leant over to whisper in her ear.

"We said no politics," he hissed.

Elizabeth turned around to look at him.

"But this is so hypocritical," she said. "Look, sorry, here, let me take her."

Baby Georgina was wiped and wrapped and handed over to Elizabeth. She hummed at her, rocked her and it was not long before the child stopped crying.

"You do realise that if it wasn't for George bloody Soros we would probably still be in the EU." Elizabeth spoke quietly, all the while smiling at her granddaughter.

"Why do you think that? You are talking rubbish again," said Lars.

"Because he's the one who took us out of the ERM." She looked directly up at Lars. Then she turned to Sydney who was sitting on the floor cushion. "She's settled, do you want to hold her now?"

Sydney nodded and Elizabeth went over and placed baby Georgina in Sydney's lap. Then she returned to her seat next to Ruby.

"Remember Black Wednesday?" she asked. "That was largely because of him."

"You don't know that," said Lars. "And besides, even if it is true, he probably did us a favour – look at what happened to the Euro."

"True, but think about it, we've been on the fringes of the EU for years. If we had stayed in the ERM and dealt with the fallout after the crash alongside the rest of Europe do you think that would have made us feel more or less European?"

"But I told you it was just business," Lars said.

"And here we come to the root of the problem!" Elizabeth whispered the words. "Just flaming business!"

"Mum, you're wrong," said Ruby. "George Soros gives loads of money to charity."

"Well, it's a pity the charities who receive his money don't question where it's come from. He represents the unacceptable side of the EU – the one where people get rich at the expense of the poor."

"Oh, I've had enough of this!" said Rafael, turning to his wife.

"And I've had enough of you," Elizabeth shouted. "You're all just following a bloody political agenda like bloody sheep."

"What, even me?" said Sydney.

"And you'll brainwash your bloody child…." Elizabeth stopped, aghast.

As if aware of the curse directed towards her, baby Georgina screamed again.

"I cannot believe you just said that." Ruby glared at her mother.

"I'm sorry…" said Elizabeth. "I didn't mean it…"

"Get out," shouted Lars. "Just go."

RAFAEL

A patchwork mist hung above the town of Bedwell Ash. Lights in houses snapped on to chase away the shadows of the low-slung sky. It was so in the Rossi home. Rafael entered the front room, turned on the table lamp and the shadows of the evening were swallowed by a yellow glow.

Rafael went and sat in one of the armchairs but was up within seconds, pacing around the room. A couple of days previously an impassioned family debate had taken place in the room and there was still evidence of the impromptu event in the form of several books spread across the table awaiting their return to the bookshelf. Largest of the tomes was a vintage Samuel Johnson's dictionary which had been selected from its pride of place on the fourth shelf of the back room bookcase to clarify the exact source and meaning of the word 'austerity'.

1. *Severity: mortified life: strictness*
   Now Marcus Cato, our new consul's spy;
   What is your sour austerity sent t'explore? – Ben Johnson.

2. *Cruelty: harsh discipline*
   Let not austerity breed servile fear;
   No wanton sound offend her virgin ear – Roscommon.

Each time Rafael passed the table he stood for a moment and stared at the books before moving to the window and glancing out, seeking headlights turning into the drive, listening for the sound of tyres on gravel.

Eventually a car did turn onto the drive and he went and sat down again.

A couple of minutes later and there was a tap on the door.

"We're back." It was his son's voice.

The door opened slowly and Rory entered, followed by Elizabeth. Rafael looked up, nodded at Rory and then stood up when he saw Elizabeth.

"You bloody fool!" he shouted.

She was limping slightly; she had a bandage around her head, a plaster on her right cheek and her jacket was torn.

"I'll leave you two to it," said Rory.

"Thanks," Elizabeth called after her son as he left the room. "For picking me up."

Rafael sat back down again.

"So they let you out then..." he said.

"Clearly."

"Actually, I'm surprised you weren't arrested."

Elizabeth ignored the remark, went over to the table, shoved the Samuel Johnson tome aside and placed her handbag down. Then she pulled out a chair and sat down.

"Bloody hell, you were, weren't you?"

"Only a little bit," she said, looking at her husband for the first time.

"Only a little bit! How the hell can you be arrested 'only a little bit!'"

"I mean I wasn't locked up or interrogated or anything."

"So they didn't ask you any questions then?"

"A few..."

"Such as?"

"They asked me what happened." Elizabeth turned her attention to her bag and started rummaging through it.

"I see. So what exactly did happen?"

"I... I... fell asleep..."

"You did what?!"

"...at the wheel..."

"Oh, well done!"

"Calm down... I didn't kill anyone."

"Except nearly yourself."

"It's nothing! I'm okay."

"Will you listen to yourself? Did you have a drink?"

"No! Well, yes, but it was only one glass of wine."

"What is wrong with you?"

"I was tired... I've not been sleeping..."

"Huuh... don't I know it. Conscience keeping you awake, is it?"

The door opened, Sydney entered and ran over and hugged her mother.

"Mum, are you okay? Rory said he picked you up from the hospital?"

Elizabeth looked at her daughter.

"Don't worry, I'm fine."

"He said you crashed the car..."

"I did, but as you can see, I am still in one piece."

Sydney stepped back from her mother.

"Was it your fault?"

"Yes."

Rafael looked at Elizabeth and then at his daughter.

"I think we could all probably do with a cup of tea," he said.

"Okay," said Sydney. She went over to the door but before leaving the room she turned to her mother. "So why did you crash? Did you do something stupid?"

Elizabeth opened her mouth to answer but Rafael spoke before her words came out.

"Yes, she did," he said. "She's been making a habit of it recently."

Elizabeth winced.

"I suppose I did. I didn't mean to... it just happened... I was tired."

Sydney looked directly at her mother.

"Don't you love us anymore?"

"Of course I do, what a silly question."

"I don't think it's a silly question at all," said Rafael, standing up. "In fact I think it's a bloody good question." He turned to Sydney. "Tea..."

Sydney left the room and he turned to his wife and added, "And one that deserves an answer."

Elizabeth talked and Rafael listened. Then Rafael talked and Elizabeth listened. Then the shouting began. Then, lost for words, Elizabeth picked up the displaced Samuel Johnson's dictionary and hurled the vintage collection of the Master's words at Rafael. It narrowly missed him, coming to rest next to the fireplace, knocking over and breaking a vase that had been made for them by Ruby as an anniversary gift ten years earlier.

One and a half hours later and the two of them were standing by the front door with one packed bag and a waiting cab.

"I think you're doing the right thing." said Rafael.

"I know," said Elizabeth. "You need to clear your head... and so do I."

"My head is quite clear," said Rafael. I just want things to go back to how they were... before all of this... nonsense..."

"As I said, clear your head..."

"What about Sydney?"

"She'll be fine. I'll still see her."

"She'll be upset."

"She'll understand. She's a bright kid."

"She's only twelve years old!"

"Oy! I heard that."

Rafael went and peeked around the corner. Sydney was sitting on the third step up in her pyjamas.

"Well, you are only twelve years old..."

"Mum needs space. I get that."

Sydney stood up, went over to Rafael and hugged him.

"Don't I get a hug?" said Elizabeth.

Sydney turned her head away.

"You're tired. Get off to bed," said Rafael.

Sydney turned and headed for the stairs again.

"Goodnight darling..." Elizabeth shouted.

"Night," was the muffled reply.

"She's upset," said Rafael, "and confused."

He watched his wife as she picked up her bag, opened the door and left the house.

"We all are..."

ELIZABETH

E lizabeth opened her eyes. Or did she? A moment, and her dreams, hopes and fears created a whole of the total of their parts and delivered a mental synergy. A second, and the moon and stars aligned to her cerebral solar system. White and grey matter united in light and compiled to operate as a single computational algorithm, analysing and harmonising, checking and balancing, simplifying problems and generating solutions.

Clarity delivered confidence and when sleep returned over an hour later it was a slumber not disturbed by tossing, turning and halted breaths.

The phone startled her awake.

"Hello…"

"When are you coming home…?"

"Sydney, is everything okay?"

Elizabeth rubbed her eyes alert to the day.

"No… nothing's okay. When are you coming home? Dad's so upset."

"I am coming home. I promise. Just give me a few more days."

"He doesn't want a divorce, he told me."

"Well, it's a pity he hasn't told me!" She paused just as her phone alarm alerted her to the start of her day: *The sun has got its hat on...'* "Sorry, sorry." She suppressed the tune. "Look, how about I take you for pizza later? I'll pick you up around 5:30."

She could smell cooking bacon and hear her mother singing 'Somewhere Over the Rainbow.' Wide awake now, she half fell out of the single bed; hunted for her red slippers – a Christmas present from Sydney – retrieved them from under the bed and then unhooked her white cotton dressing gown from behind the door. She wrapped it around herself and was about to head for the door when she turned to look at the picture above her bed. The frame was the same as it had been yesterday, rubbed gilt giving it a worn look, but the quote was different. She smiled to herself as she read *'There's No Place Like Home'.*

"Morning!" Her mother turned and sang at her as she entered the kitchen. "And how are you feeling today?"

Elizabeth went and sat at the table, a move perfectly synchronised with the hand-delivered meat-free cooked breakfast placed in front of her.

"Sleep well?" Demelza asked.

"Really good, thanks," Elizabeth replied, picking up her knife and fork in readiness. "Is there something you'd like to tell me?"

"There's lots I'd like to tell you, dear. Did you have anything particular in mind?"

"The quote above my bed?"

"Oh that. It's wonderful, isn't it?" Demelza smiled as she spoke. "And so true."

"Have I outstayed my welcome?"

"No, of course not, dear - don't be silly. I just thought a gentle reminder might help you focus on what's important..." Demelza was about to return to the cooker but instead stopped to look at her daughter.

"Are you feeling any better?"

"Yes, I am," Elizabeth said while assembling a perfectly apportioned mouthful of one third mushroom, one third egg and one third beans onto her fork. "Sorry about the last few days," she said before devouring her designer forkful and returning it to her plate in readiness for a rebuild.

"Well, you're certainly eating better." Demelza pulled out a chair and sat down. "So what's changed?"

Elizabeth continued chewing, eyes glazed, staring in front of her like a bull contemplating a charge.

"I was talking to Sydney."

"Is she okay?" Demelza asked again. "Look, are you okay?"

"Sydney's fine. I… I was confused…" She looked at her mother and smiled. "You know what I'm like."

"So you're no longer confused then?"

"Nope. After breakfast I need to make a few calls, then I'm going out."

"Well, that's a relief. I hope you're going to call Rafael - you know… your husband."

"Is the water hot? I need a shower."

After breakfast Elizabeth showered, got dressed, picked up her bag and took up residence in the front room, shutting the door and setting out her laptop on the table in front of the window.

At 10:05 am Demelza entered with a cup of tea.

"I'm glad you've come to your senses, dear," she said. "When are you going home?"

Elizabeth shut the lid of her laptop, went over to the printer and grabbed two sheets of freshly printed paper.

"My list of tasks," she said, waving them at her mother. "What time are you going out?"

"Very shortly. Would you like me to get you anything?"

Fifteen minutes later and Elizabeth heard the front door slam. She watched as her mother's head bobbed by the window, then she picked up her mobile phone and clicked onto her contact list.

"Hector Oliphant speaking."

"Hector, it's me, Elizabeth."

"Well, good morning, Elizabeth. What can I do for you?"

"I need you to listen to me."

Elizabeth talked and apart from the occasional '*I see*' and '*why?*' Hector listened. Sixteen minutes later he asked, "Are you sure you want to do this?"

"Yes."

"Have you organised anything like it before?"

"Don't worry, it'll be fine."

"That wasn't my question."

"Similar."

"What?"

"Student marches... sit ins... big big parties... hundreds of people. Hector, do you honestly think I'd let you down?"

"I hope not."

"Besides, I'll have people to help me."

There was silence.

"Hector... are you still there?"

"Okay, we can discuss the detail at the meeting next week. We'll need to see the RAMs as soon as possible."

"I'll get them done and bring them with me."

Elizabeth packed up her laptop and bag, then went out into the hall and stuffed them into her bike panniers. She scribbled a note for her mother: *'Thanks for breakfast, see you later'*. She picked up her clipboard with her two-page list of tasks.

Task 1: Speak to Hector – Tick.

Task 2: Sheep stared, goggle-eyed, as Elizabeth cycled down the track towards Bedwell House. She passed two dead chickens - one with its head torn off – and then swerved to avoid a gutted cockerel lying on the track in front of her. She approached the uncared-for farmhouse and spotted Farmer Garlic sitting on her step in front of the splintered oak door cleaning a shotgun. The farmer looked up as Elizabeth approached. Elizabeth got off her bike and smiled at the wind-sculpted face and sparkling green eyes.

"Happen I can do something for you?" the farmer shouted at her before returning her attention to the shotgun.

"Well, yes, I hope so."

Elizabeth leant her bike against the wall of the house and went over to her.

"As a matter of fact I need to speak to you."

"Best take a seat then," she said, nodding at the space beside her.

Elizabeth sat down on the stone step next to the farmer.

"Well, it's like this..." she said.

Twenty minutes later, using her shotgun as a crutch to help her, the farmer stood herself up.

"Best come inside," she said.

Elizabeth tried to ignore the mud, the dirt and the old-fashioned animal smell as she followed the shotgun-wielding farmer into her home.

The kitchen was large with a scuffed flagstone floor, exposed pipes, a butler sink, a battered range and rat droppings. The table in the centre of the room could seat sixteen people comfortably in a different space but in the context of present time and place the only person who could take their place and feel comfortable doing so was the farmer. The table had once played host at family gatherings and parties but as the farmer had no family and few friends its destiny was a life of solitary splendour allowing only her, the occasional visitor and on this day two chickens – which were in a basket on top of it - to take pleasure in its grandness as a piece of antique wooden furniture.

"Don't mind the chickens, I had a visit from fox last night… bastard killed all bar these two. I'm gonna shoot the bugger." As if to point out to Elizabeth that she had the capability, she held up the shotgun. Elizabeth shuddered at the weaponry and the proximity of the farmer's finger to the shotgun trigger. A bullet and a couple of centimetres and their union could produce a sizeable hole in the ceiling, if not bring it down altogether. Elizabeth gasped with horror when the farmer placed the weapon flat onto the table where it came to rest with the barrel pointing directly at her. She got up.

"I'll tell you what," she said. "Why don't I make the tea while you go find the forms?"

Nearly an hour later, armed with a verbal agreement from the farmer and a collection of forms and phone numbers, Elizabeth was back outside loading up her bike.

"Are you sure that's everything?" she asked.

"That's all you need from me. Best speak to Oliphant for the rest."

She packed the forms into the now full panniers, then picked up her clipboard and took out her pencil.

Task 2: Tick.

Elizabeth got back on her bike and with a wave cycled back up the track. She turned onto the road and headed for the village then turned left at the dog-leg junction.

Task 3: Elizabeth peddled towards the centre of the village and fifteen minutes later arrived at 'The Crafty Fox' pub. She peddled off-road onto the tyre-worn verge, then got off and leant her bike against the brick wall. She pulled her clipboard from the panniers and then stood and scanned the beer garden. She spotted

Kevin, a desolate figure sitting alone on a bench with an empty half pint glass in front of him. She sat on the wall, manoeuvred her legs over it to transfer herself from roadside to beer garden and headed over to him.

"Can I buy you a drink?"

He looked up at her.

"Yes please Mrs Rossi," he said, smiling through half sealed lips.

"Has the dentist been able to help you?"

"Yep, I'm getting falsies."

"Good. I'll get you a drink. Then I would like to ask you a couple of questions, oh and ask a favour."

"Anything I can do, Mrs Rossi. If I can I will."

"Well, you can call me Elizabeth for a start," she said, heading for the bar.

Three quarters of an hour later and Elizabeth left Kevin with a full pint of beer and a smile. She returned roadside to her bike in the same fashion that she had entered the beer garden, but before taking to the road again she remained sitting on the wall, feet dangling.

Task 3: Tick.

She retrieved her mobile phone from her pocket and scrolled through her contact list.

Task 4:

"Hi Judy, how are you?"

"I'm at the doctor's."

"Oh, you're okay, I hope?"

"I think I'm pregnant."

"Blimey…"

"After all these years… who would have thought, eh?"

"You okay with it?"

"Not sure… being a mum… I don't know if I'll be any good at it."

"Don't be ridiculous. Congratulations! You'll be a fantastic mum. The kids at school love you."

"Bit different though isn't it, being a teacher… being a mum… anyway, you okay?"

"Can I pop round tomorrow? I need to ask you something."

"I'm off on holiday tomorrow. What's up?"

"Well, it's like this…"

Elizabeth spoke for nearly ten minutes – until she was interrupted by her friend's laughter.

"You're going to do what? Why would you put yourself through that?"

"It came to me in a dream…"

"Sounds more like a flaming nightmare! It's a bit… no, it's a lot mad."

"I know, I know, but are you in?"

"Course I'm in, you mad cow."

Task 4: Tick.

Elizabeth hesitated before making her next call. She took a deep breath.

Task 5:

"Ava, hi, it's me, Elizabeth. Look, first of all I want to apologise for the other week. I didn't get a chance the other day when you were here…"

"Oh, Lizzy, don't worry yourself. It was only a spillage… on the carpet… and the armchair… don't worry, it's all been cleaned."

"I'll pay any cleaning costs…"

"And you just ruined my party…"

"I know… I'm sorry…"

"I'm joking! It's done with. I knew you'd call – what took you so long?"

"Sorry, I've been busy."

"We must get together again soon… you know, to prove that we get over such things as adults…"

"A wonderful idea."

"How is Rafael? Are you talking yet?"

"Not exactly… I've moved out…"

"I know… I heard… I'm so sorry."

"You heard?"

"Now what can I do for you, dear?"

"You said you heard…"

"Crispin told me… men! You know how they talk. Are you okay?"

"I need to ask you a favour."

"I knew you'd want something... I said to Crispin only the other day, she'll ring when she wants something."

"Sorry..."

"It doesn't matter dear. Look, I know you're going through a tough time at the mo... what with your condition..."

"My condition? What condition?"

"This whole Brexit thing... I prefer to think of it as a condition... you know, one that can be cured..."

"Well, funnily enough that's why I've called you..."

Twenty-five minutes later, with a flourish Elizabeth took out her pencil and delivered another tick to her list.

Task 5: Tick.

She looked at her final task for the day and an involuntary shudder whispered down her spine.

Task 6: Forty minutes later and Elizabeth was cycling up the drive of Plutus Manor. She took a deep breath when she saw PeeTurD's distinctive yellow Jaguar parked in front of the house. He was at home. A minute later and she was standing, clipboard in hand, on the doorstep.

She was about to press the 'Rule Britannia' bell when PeeTurD opened the door.

"What are you doing here?" His brown eyes - always angry - bore into her.

"I'd like to speak to you."

"What about?" he asked, stepping out onto the doorstep and pulling the door tight behind him as if he had something to hide.

Their conversation lasted twelve and a half minutes. During the thirteenth minute Elizabeth turned and legged it. Hands shaking, she ran back down the tarmac drive alongside her bike without looking back. She heard him shout though.

"Set foot on my land again and I'll fucking have you."

Once back at the roadside she stopped. She took several deep breaths before getting back onto her bike and peddling the path back to her mother's house.

She was still a little unsteady when she got there. Hoping to sneak in she took her bike around the back and let herself in through the garden gate. She got off, leant it against the shed, managed to unhook her bags and headed for the house. As she walked up the garden, she could see her mother by the kitchen window. Demelza looked up and smiled; Elizabeth nodded back then let herself in through the back door.

"Had a good day, dear?" her mother called to her.

Elizabeth placed the panniers next to the coat stand in the hallway and picked out the clipboard and pencil.

"Mostly," she called back.

Then she placed three question marks where a tick should have been.

Task 6: ???

She tucked the clipboard back behind the panniers and headed for the kitchen. As she entered, her mother was unloading the dishwasher.

"It's Shepherds pie for tea," her mother said, turning round to smile a greeting. "Are you okay?"

Elizabeth paused.

"I'm fine. I'm going out, taking Sydney for pizza. Sorry, I should have mentioned it this morning. I forgot."

"It'll keep," Demelza said. "You know Rafael called earlier... he asked how you are."

"Next time he calls you and asks how I am, tell him to call me and ask me himself."

On the following Thursday Elizabeth was in her mother's front room catching up on paperwork. At 3:45pm she closed the lid of her laptop and then signed, crossed, dotted and full-stopped the remaining papers on her desk before placing them in a file and locking them in her briefcase.

Her last night's sleep had not been as rejuvenating as the previous few nights but she yawned away negative thoughts and decided to walk to The Millennium Community Hub for the council meeting.

She arrived at the meeting room at 5:05pm. It was empty apart from Hector Oliphant who was walking around the table straightening pencils. He looked up as she entered.

"Good. I am glad you're early," he said.

"Is everything still okay?"

"That is what I need to ask you," he said without making eye contact. "Thanks for the RAMs you sent through."

"Were they okay?"

"Looked fine to me, you've obviously done a thorough risk assessment." Hector paused, then turned to look at her. "Are you absolutely sure you want to take this on?"

"Of course."

"Excellent news. I'm sure most people are going to be delighted," he said.

"Most people?"

"You know what some people are like... don't like change..."

Roman entered the room, then Alice Grubb. There were nods and polite greetings as Bill, Caleb, Paul, Evelyn and Kirk followed. By 5:28pm everyone but Farmer Garlic was present and seated. Hector took his place at what was accepted as the 'head' of the round table, straightened the blank A4 sheet of paper in front of him and, at 5:30pm exactly, cleared his throat.

"Well, good evening everyone, and thank you all for coming!" He looked around. "Now I suggest we make a start."

"Farmer Garlic's not here yet," said Bill.

"I suggest we start without Farmer Garlic." Hector spoke loudly, staring at Elizabeth. "She knows the start time. So... apologies for absence."

"What the bloody hell's that all about?" Farmer Garlic stood in the doorway staring at the painting.

In unison they turned to the door and saw her. Dressed in green overalls, straight from a day on the land, the farmer made her entrance.

"You say that every time you come here," said Hector.

"And you say that every time I ask the question yet you still don't answer me. It's just a bloody mess, isn't it?"

"No, it's not," said Hector. "Some people see artistic genius in those lines."

"It's a wonderful work of art," said Paul Hollyoak. "You just don't know how to read it."

"You pretentious twat," Farmer Garlic replied.

"Do you know I wait for the day when you just accept the fact that it is an image way beyond your mental comprehension and just ignore it," said Hector.

"Oh, fuck off, Oliphant," said the farmer.

Hector turned to her.

"No swearing at council meetings." He paused and nodded to Alice. "Please minute that."

"'Fuck off Oliphant' has been minuted," said Alice.

"Shall we all calm down now and start the meeting?" Elizabeth stood as she spoke. She smiled and nodded at the farmer as she settled herself in between Alice and Caleb, each of whom was attempting to shift sideways away from the whiffiness of the farmyard.

"Thank you all for coming." Hector nodded to Elizabeth and she sat down. "Let us begin again. Apologies for absence... I am pleased to say that for once we are all here."

They went through the items on the agenda, discussing, agreeing, ticking off, discussing, disagreeing and ticking off.

"And now," said Hector. "To the matter of the annual fete."

"Is there going to be one?" asked Evelyn.

"Yes, there is," Hector intervened. "As you all know the same people run the show every year." He paused and looked around the table. "Well, not this year."

"What's happening?" asked Roman Winters.

"I'm pleased to be able to tell you that we have a new volunteer who has offered to run the whole event this year."

A smile lit around the table like a circular Mexican wave.

"Really," said Caleb. "Who?"

"Great," said Kirk Scott. "Who is it?"

Hector looked to Elizabeth.

"Elizabeth," he said.

All eyes turned on Elizabeth. She saw surprise, shock and was that disbelief?

"Well I never," said Evelyn.

"What a surprise. Are you sure you're up to it?" asked Kirk Scott.

"Cheeky!" said Elizabeth, and then added with a wink, "But I'll let it go for now." She stood up. "It's true; I shall be making all of the arrangements this year."

"Excellent," said Evelyn. "My services are available if you need me."

"Oh, I'm so pleased," said Alice. "My Betsy and Jane have their fairy outfits all ready for it. They would have been so disappointed if it hadn't been going ahead."

"Fairy outfits? I thought the theme this year was going to be Unicorns and Dragons?" said Paul Hollyoak.

"Fairies can ride unicorns…" said Alice.

"Sorry, sorry," Elizabeth interrupted. "I've made some changes…"

"Changes? What changes?" asked Paul.

Elizabeth looked around at the shocked faces staring back at her.

"I've changed the theme."

"But you can't do that," said Alice. "It was agreed on and announced last year, in the garden outside, you remember, at the end of the fete."

"As it always is, every year," said Evelyn.

"You really must follow procedure, Elizabeth," said Bill Inghurst, "if you're going to organise it."

There was silence; all eyes were on Elizabeth.

"I am going to organise it," said Elizabeth. "And so I get to decide."

"But that is against protocol…" said Paul Hollyoak.

"Oh, sod protocol!" Elizabeth replied, her voice louder than she intended.

"Elizabeth!" said Hector. "Language please!"

"'Oh, sod protocol' has been minuted," said Alice.

"I'm organising it so I'm bloody well…" She turned to Alice. "Make sure you minute that."

"'I'm organising it so I'm bloody well' has been minuted," said Alice.

"It's going to be my theme or no theme… no event…" Elizabeth looked around the table. Smiles had long since flat-lined.

"So may I on behalf of all of us ask what your theme is?" asked Evelyn in a hushed voice.

"The EU," said Elizabeth. "In light of everything that has happened this year I think we should have an EU-themed village event."

"I can work with that," Roman was the first to speak.

"So can I," Paul Hollyoak added. "I think it's a good idea."

"I think that sounds rather jolly," said Bill Inghurst. "And it is a good idea… you know… in light of what's happened."

"Can my girls be fairies?" asked Alice.

"Fairies, unicorns, dragons… we can have the flipping lot," said Elizabeth. "But the main theme will be the EU." She paused. "Now do you want me to organise this event or not?"

"Yes, I for one think it's a brilliant idea," said Hector. "I wholeheartedly want it to go ahead."

"And so do I," said Caleb.

"Thank you, Caleb," said Elizabeth, smiling at him. "There is another thing…" Not daring to look around the table this time, she picked up her pencil and pretended to write on the A4 sheet of white paper in front of her.

"What other thing?" asked Kirk.

"I, well, I thought we'd have a change this year."

"Another change?" asked Evelyn.

"I've booked a different venue."

"You've done what?" said Paul, clearly unsettled by the reveal. "But it's here. It's always here, in the gardens and the hall."

"It's always here," echoed Alice.

"Nearly twenty years it's been here," said Evelyn. "Why change?"

Elizabeth placed her pencil down and looked up.

"I thought we could have it somewhere different this year." She paused. "And Farmer Garlic has kindly offered us one of her fields…"

"A field? What if it rains?" said Alice.

"And she's let us have her marquee and tables and chairs, everything… you know, that she hires out for weddings and the like."

Amazed faces turned to the farmer but she didn't spot them - she was too busy checking her mobile phone.

"Won't that be rather expensive?" asked Caleb.

"She has kindly offered the field and marquee and everything for free, and she'll get her people to take them to the site and erect them and put everything together."

"That is very nice of you," said Paul Hollyoak, turning to the farmer.

"What's come over you?" asked Alice.

There was a short silence which made the farmer look up from her phone and realise for the first time that she was the centre of attention.

"I've gotta go," she said. "Vet's on way - me bull can't shit proper." She got up and looked at Elizabeth. "Let me know if you need anything else."

"Donkey rides would be nice," Elizabeth shouted after her. "You know, for the children."

"You can have Juliette," the farmer shouted back as she headed for the door. "Do her good to do some work. You'll have to watch her, mind – she'll bite your arse soon as look at you."

Back in the room the group turned and looked at each other, then all faces turned to Elizabeth.

"Well, I'll be buggered," said Alice.

"Language," said Elizabeth. "Make sure you minute that."

"How'd you persuade her to let us use her land for free," said Caleb.

"Yes, and the marquee?" said Roman Winters. "She's never been community-minded."

"She joined the council, didn't she?" said Elizabeth.

"I don't wish to sound mean," said Evelyn, "but I always thought that was just her being nosey and safeguarding her own interests."

"Good point," said Elizabeth. "I think you're probably right. But I told her that it would be a very nice thing to do."

"And…?" said Alice. "We all know that wouldn't persuade her."

"I think the EU theme helped persuade her. She's very worried about not having enough workers once we leave…"

"She's got a point," said Hector.

"I also mentioned it would, of course, increase her standing in the village. She particularly liked that."

"Such a wonderful idea," said Evelyn. "An event to support the EU - well done, Elizabeth."

"But hold on a minute," said Paul. "Didn't you vote leave in the referendum?"

PART 2

BEFORE THE STORM

I'll tell you how the sun rose,
A ribbon at a time
The steeples swam in amethyst
The news like squirrels ran
The hills untied their bonnets,
The bobolinks begun.
Then I said softly to myself...
'That must have been the sun!'

Somewhere a cockerel sounded sun-up. The animal locked in a windowless shed, a shard of light filtering through a crack in the rotting planks of its wooden prison was all it needed as evidence to start his day.

As the cockerel crowed, a few miles down the road Elizabeth opened her eyes to the sound of her alarm. She picked up her phone and held it directly in front of her to gaze at the time in case it was telling her lies. But, like the cockerel, it wasn't. *'The sun has got his hat on and is coming out to pla...'* was silenced in its prime.

An hour later she was in her VW bumping along the time-worn farm trail heading towards the festival site. As she gazed across the morning fields she selected optimism as her emotion of choice - the judgemental backchat of the Parish Council or the sceptical comments of her disillusioned family were not going to dampen her spirits. She slowed down to allow a snuffling hedgehog cross her path. It paused momentarily and turned to look at her as if to offer a polite 'much obliged' for not squashing it. *'I'll show them I'm not a bad person,'* she whispered in a voice unheard.

She rounded a bend and gasped at the undulating landscape and the flora and fauna that called it home. A mist which floated like an over-exposure of dry ice on a set of a mystical stage show was dissolving in front of her as the air warmed. The ever-changing light source painted a picture drawn by nature, coloured in by the weather. A badger meandered alongside the track. She smiled at a fox, whose scented walk and low-slung crawl suggested malicious pursuit. She watched as a curious hare surveyed her from the side of the trail before taking to the fields in a slalom speed show disappearing into a far-flung hedgerow in a matter of seconds. It was a joy ride, in its most literal sense - an enjoyable ride - before the words 'joy' and 'ride' were united and used by nut-jobs who live in a back-side world of social misunderstanding to explain away the havoc they wreak.

She continued past an ancient orchard and in the field opposite she spotted Romeo. He stood grazing close to the gate, Juliette at his side. He raised his head to watch her pass, then pounded a cloven Wagyu hoof into the ground as if in readiness to charge. Elizabeth smiled to herself; she knew this bull was no bully. She was more frightened of Juliette; with her high-pitched vocal range and devious aggressive nature, the donkey was far more intimidating than Romeo could ever be.

A bridge, a copse then she turned left through a gateway and into the field which was granted village use for the day. The marquee had been delivered and erected two days earlier in readiness for the 'Bedwell Ash EU Family Fun Day'. It was a quality structure, however, on this chaste morning in the context of the indigenous countryside it looked like an un-lanced boil simmering on the landscape, its sides wheezing in the breeze as if breathing in and out to the rhythm of its own life.

Elizabeth drove up the hill to the marquee and parked by the entrance to unpack the boxes and bags stacked up in the boot and on the back seat of her car. She piled her stuff up by the door of the marquee and then, clutching her handbag, got back into her car and drove it back down the hill to the designated parking area which on this day happened to be a field enclosed on all four sides by a prickly red berried hedge hiding several strings of barbed wire. The entrance to the field – a wooden five-bar gate - was secured back and a 'Car Park' sign hung over a post which hid the public warning message 'BEWARE DANGEROUS BEASTS!' The field was the home paddock of Romeo and Juliette. No evidence of their homestead remained; a haze hovered over the grass adding a sense of theatrical romance to the scene by painting the bullshit and donkey poo out of the picture.

She parked her car at the furthermost point of the field hoping it would act as a starting point for people to line their vehicles up against when they began to arrive. Then she walked back across the field out of the gate and up the hill towards the marquee. Her shoes darkened as the dew soaked them, dampening her feet and leaving imprints as evidence of human interference - redrawing a scene whose celibacy was now forfeit until the break of the tomorrow sunrise. She reached for her phone to check the weather forecast: sunny, with rain due later. She looked skyward to review the evidence. The sun had its hat on but in the distance it was the dark clouds coming out to play.

She returned her attention to the task in hand and looked around. Her plan was for the events to take place outside until the late afternoon and she smiled when she saw that – as per her instructions – an outdoor stage had been erected for the Bedwell Ash talent contest. In addition, there were stalls in place for the village crafters, bottlers and bakers to sell their wares and a fenced-off area for kiddie donkey rides.

She headed to the marquee, went inside and looked around. The structure had two rooms: a main room with a sizeable stage, dance floor and allocated buffet area, and a smaller room at the back which was to be used as a crèche. In the main room mat flooring had been laid but the stacked tables, chairs and boxes filled with decorations provided evidence of the work that still needed to be done. Elizabeth went over to tables and managed to lift one off the stack; then, using a combination of dragging and pushing, she claimed it as her own by manoeuvring it next to the stage. She went back outside and carried in the boxes and bags and planted them onto it.

Next she went to inspect the crèche and - as ordered by Farmer Garlic - in the corner there was a roped-off area for Juliette to take sanctuary should the heavens open.

Stefan Schmidt arrived at exactly 8:00am with daughters Elspeth and Helga.

"Morning! Good to see you, you're early," said Elizabeth.

Twelve-year-old Elspeth turned on her father.

"You see! I said we'd be too early!"

Helga turned to Elizabeth and giggled.

"She didn't want to come. Daddy forced her."

"Yeah, like I'm his flaming slave."

"Elspeth!" Stefan looked at her.

"When I said you're early, I didn't actually mean early," said Elizabeth. "What I meant to say was well done; you're the first here and bang on time."

Stefan turned to his daughters.

"Now you go and sit over there until Elizabeth gives you something to do." He turned to Elizabeth. "I wanted to get here early," he replied. "There's so much to do. I need to look at the outside stage and put up two more stalls."

At just after 8:15am Elizabeth went outside to watch more of the volunteers arrive. A chauffeur-driven Bentley belonging to Markus Mark pulled into the field and stopped. The uniformed driver got out and opened each of the doors to release, first, the three Mark children, and then Noah and Ellis Smith, the two grandsons of Evelyn Smith. Once all of the children were out of the car they raced up the hill towards her, arms flailing, rucksacks bouncing, the breeze catching their laughter.

"Steady, you lot!" Elizabeth shouted to them. "It's going to be a long day."

Several of the older volunteers arrived in their own cars smiling a greeting, while most of the younger ones were deposited by one of the two designated parent power pick-up vehicles circling the village plucking bleary-eyed children from their homes while being waved off by parents grateful for the gift of a child-free morning.

Other youngsters made their own way. Moses was helping out and he decided to jog the route passing the ica sisters who had donned their track suits and hard hats in an effort to pedal power their way there. The on-road bit went okay but when they reached the off-road part they soon realised their kiddie bikes and cycling expertise were no match for the worn trail. Monica stopped as she thought she had a flat tyre and at the exact same time Angelica fell off her bike and grazed her knee. Jessica attempted to rescue the situation and made a decision for the three of them to abandon their wheels and walk the rest of the way. So they leaned their cycles against an apple tree near the entrance to the ancient orchard and under the watchful eye of an increasingly unsettled Romeo and Juliette, they headed through the copse and over the bridge towards the festival site.

By 9am Elizabeth counted twenty-eight volunteers. She ushered them into the marquee and took up her place on the stage.

"Morning! Can I have everybody's attention please?" she shouted.

The laughing and chatting quietened. A couple of young lads laying on the matted floor catching up on sleep were kicked awake by one of three laughing teenage girls.

"Good morning and welcome," Elizabeth shouted. "Thank you all for coming today."

"Good morning," was the shouted reply, some tagging 'Elizabeth' onto the end, while a few of the younger ones tagged 'Mrs Rossi'.

She went over to her table and pointed to one of the boxes.

"In here…" she said. With the deftness of a magician pulling a rabbit from a top hat, she pulled a light blue tee shirt from the brown cardboard box and held it up. First she displayed the front which showed a picture of the Bedwell Ash village sign, then the back which had the EU flag printed on it.

"Please will you each take a tee shirt and put it on."

Several of the girls giggled.

"Get us a small…" shouted Honeysuckle Scott who had been dropped off by her father in his battered four-wheel drive.

"Are there any ones for little children?"

Elizabeth turned; it was Monica Inghurst.

"Yes there are," said Elizabeth, looking at Monica and her two sisters. All three were small for their age, pale and undernourished; their track suits hiding their bony frames. Each had their hair pulled tightly back into a straggly pony tail. She spotted blood on Angelica's grubby pink track-suit leg. "What on earth has happened to you?"

"She fell off her bike," said Jessica. "Have you got a plaster?"

"Of course. Come with me and I'll fix you up." Elizabeth held out her hand but Angelica shied away. "Follow me." She walked slowly to the crèche and the three sisters followed her.

The four of them emerged ten minutes later.

"There," said Elizabeth turning to Angelica. "If your knee starts to hurt again you must sit down."

"Thank you, Mrs Rossi, I will."

"Thank you," said Jessica. "Mrs Rossi..."

Noise levels had increased again in the marquee and Elizabeth didn't hear her. She shouted in an attempt to silence the chatter and laughter.

"Silence please, we've a lot to do."

"Mrs Rossi..." Jessica said again, louder this time.

"Yes?"

"Are you going to go back and live in your house again?"

Elizabeth stopped and turned her full attention to the wide-eyed child.

"What a question." She paused. "Why do you ask?"

"Sydney's ever so upset. She was crying at school the other day."

"Was she?"

"Yes. She really was."

Stunned, Elizabeth turned to Jessica once more.

"Well..." She paused before adding, "I'm... I'm going home very soon."

"That's what our mum said when she left - she said she'd be back but that was two years ago and we've not seen her."

"Well, I'm not your mu..." Elizabeth stopped herself from completing her sentence. Instead she smiled as Monica, hand in hand with Angelica, joined them.

"My dad says you're a busybody..." Monica piped up.

"Does he indeed?"

"No he doesn't," said Jessica. "He doesn't use the word busybody... exactly."

"Thank you, so what word does he use?"

"Meddler... he says you meddle in other people's business..."

"I see," said Elizabeth.

"And he says you should sort out your own life before you nosey in others," Angelica added.

"Really? Thank you for letting me know." Embarrassed, she turned her attention back to the crowd. "Okay, now that you all have your tee shirts," but nobody was listening.

She coughed but it was not heard above the chit-chat, laughter and ringing phones. She coughed again, louder this time. Then she shouted.

"Quiet!"

And it did the trick.

"Now that you all have your tee shirts I would like to put you into teams."

"Teams? We're in teams?" Honeysuckle shouted. "Bagsy I be a team leader..."

"No. I have already decided on the team leaders," said Elizabeth. "Now, each team leader has a list of who is with them and a list of tasks. Can I ask that when I have called your name you go and find your team? Our team leaders are Barry Jones, you're going to help Stefan finish off setting up the outer stage and stalls."

Barry smiled and nodded. He was the eldest son of Jill Jones but he could not have been less like her. He was well liked in the village although since his mother's arrest things had been difficult for him.

"I've got the younger kids with me; I'd like them to stay with me if that is okay? They can be a bit of a handful."

"Of course," said Elizabeth.

"Pearl! Buster! Spike! You're with me. I want you in my sight at all times, you hear me!"

Three sheepish-looking children with unkempt hair and designer trainers appeared from under the stacked tables and stood up in a military line.

"You are to do as you are told. If you misbehave I'll tell Mum and it'll be early to bed and no pocket money next week. You hear me?"

The three children nodded in unison.

Elizabeth turned her attention to the rest of the volunteers.

"Charlotte Hollyoak, you're a team leader and I'd like you to do the inside tables and decorations and the like. Francesca Esposito, you're on food with Daniela, Mary Grubb and Jessica, Monica and Angelica. Moses, thanks for coming and sorting out the techy stuff."

Elizabeth had bumped into Moses one day while walking Nutter around the ruined castle.

"How are you?"

"Great! I've just been offered my dream job, working backstage as a sound engineer."

"Congratulations! Well done."

"How are things?"

"You know I'm arranging an EU-themed family fun day..."

"Rory told me. Great idea! If I can help at all just ask."

"Well, we do need a sound and lighting technician..."

"Put me down..."

"And actually, there is something else. Can I ask a favour?"

"Go ahead... anything..."

Elizabeth had known Moses since he was four years old. He was a friend of Rory's but he had also come to her attention officially when his father was put in prison for burglary and his mother turned to drugs and alcohol. Despite his poor upbringing Moses had grown into a decent lad who had been a good friend to Rory.

"Jan Kowolski..." No sooner had Elizabeth shouted his name than his head popped up.

"I am here."

"Jan, you're on signage, and anything else," she said, handing him his task list. "And that includes car-park duties. If you have any queries at all let me know. She turned to address everyone once more. Now will all of you please find your team leader and get on with what you have to do. Any questions, I'm over here."

She returned to her table, sat down, pulled her 'EU Fun Day' file out of her bag, selected a sheet of paper and started to read it.

"Right you lot, follow me," shouted Jan, having found his team of workers. Leading the way out of the marquee he shouted. "Let's start with the signage."

"Oh goody," said Monica. "We're on food."

"Can I ask that you just get on with your tasks and not chatter, I'm trying to concentrate," Elizabeth tried to make her voice heard. "No mobile phones – turn them off please – oh and you lot on food - no eating it."

"Bloody cheek," shouted fifteen-year-old Mary Grubb who had been deposited at the site by the second pick-up vehicle along with her younger sisters Betsy and Jane. Their mother had waved them off with a smile and a sigh of relief then promptly returned to bed for energetic snuggles with her new boyfriend. "Who the fuck does she think she is? It's not as if she's paying us or anything." She picked up a chunk of cheese from the table, unwrapped it and bit into it.

"I said don't eat the food," Elizabeth shouted over. "It's for the buffet later." She noticed but chose to ignore the whispers and sideways glances cast towards her from some of her helpers as they settled into their tasks; instead she returned her attention to her file and carried on reading.

"Oy…"

She looked up. Honeysuckle was standing in front of her.

"Honeysuckle, have you nothing to do?"

"No."

"Aren't you helping set out tables with Charlotte?"

"I don't like moving stupid tables."

"She's frightened she'll break a fingernail!" Charlotte shouted with a giggle.

"Let's save the giggling for when we've finished." Elizabeth turned to Honeysuckle.

"You're here to help, so go and help."

"You can't talk to me like that," said Honeysuckle. "Bossy cow."

"Thank you," said Elizabeth. "Go and find something to do or go home."

Honeysuckle turned and went back to where the group were sorting out decorations. Charlotte picked up a box of table centrepieces and handed them to her.

"One on each table," she said.

At that moment Honeysuckle's phone rang.

"No phone calls," Elizabeth shouted. "Turn your phone off."

"I've had enough of this," Honeysuckle shouted, phone in one hand and box in the other. She dropped the box, leaving the decorations to spill over onto the mat.

"Same here." Mary Grubb looked up from buttering slices of bread. "This is really boring."

"What? So you didn't think there'd be any work involved?" asked Elizabeth.

"Course... I just thought it would be more fun," said Mary.

"I see," said Elizabeth. She bent down, opened her bag, which was under the table and took out her poetry book. The top right corner had turned in and she bent it back the other way in an effort to straighten it out before opening it at a random page. "Now, both of you, get on and do some work."

> I lost a world the other day,
> Has anybody found?
> You'll know it by the row of...

"Excuse me, Elizabeth."

Elizabeth looked up; it was Kirk Scott.

"Kirk, what are you doing here – come to volunteer?"

"Honeysuckle forgot her purse; I've just nipped back with it." He paused. "What's going on?"

"We're setting up for the fun day."

"Don't be bloody sarcastic. Why are you being so rude to my girl?"

"Was I?"

"You were. And not just her, some of the others are complaining too. A couple of lads over there are leaving."

Elizabeth could see two boys aged about sixteen - rucksacks in hand - heading for the exit. A girl was fiddling with her bag in readiness for hers.

"They're volunteers, I can't stop them leaving." As she spoke she spotted a man at the entrance dressed in overalls, clipboard and pen in hand. "Just means more work for the rest of us. There's plenty to do if you want to stay and help?"

She got up and walked towards the entrance, dodging Kirk, boxes and rucksacks.

"Two portable toilets," the man shouted as she approached. "Where d'ya want them?"

"Just over there," she said, stepping outside the marquee and pointing to an area to the left.

She stood and watched the man as he pressed buttons and hoisted, then lowered the cubicles into position. Then she returned to the marquee, almost bumping into Kirk who had taken up his own viewpoint just inside the doorway.

"Just the two, is it?" He said.

"That's right." She avoided eye contact as she manoeuvred passed him.

Once inside she went to her table and sat down again, breathing a sigh of relief that he had not followed her back in. She rummaged through her bag to find her flask, then poured a drink and surveyed the work taking place while taking sips of green tea.

During the next hour she read her poems, glancing up occasionally to monitor progress. She watched as tables and chairs were set out and made functional, decorations were put up and bread was buttered.

"Is there any tomato or cucumber or anything for the sandwiches?" Francesca shouted to Elizabeth.

"No."

"Isn't just cheese or ham a bit plain?"

"Probably," Elizabeth replied returning to her book.

"You know there are only three water jugs..."

"I know."

Elizabeth stopped reading, placed her book face down on the table, got up and headed for the crèche. Inside the doors there were red, blue and yellow plastic mini chairs and tables, and boxes of toys and books and crayons. Along one wall stood a clothing rail packed tight with children's costumes hanging like flattened bodies, each one waiting to be brought to life by a living, breathing child.

She spotted Mary sitting on the floor leaning against one of the kiddie tables talking on her phone.

"Mary, will you get off your phone, you're here to work." She looked at the torn jeans and tie-dyed tee shirt. "And where's your festival tee shirt? Go get one."

"Get lost."

"Okay." Elizabeth smiled to herself, headed back to the main room and was about to sit down again when she heard a rasping noise from outside so she changed direction and headed for the entrance.

Once outside she could see the source of the racket. Chugging slowly up the hill was a tractor with the recognisable shape of Farmer Garlic perched at the helm. It was moving at a steady pace, not looking as if it was going to stop anytime soon. Elizabeth went and stood in line with the vehicle and waved at the farmer. The tractor ground to a halt not a shadow's distance in front of her. On this occasion the farm vehicle was towing a trailer, which was pulling a reluctant Juliette who was tied to the back of it. The donkey's reluctance was reinforced by her constant braying as she bellowed for her mate. The animal was wearing a pad saddle, a bridle and an expression of '*must I?*'

Elizabeth turned. In the distance she could just see Romeo in his temporary paddock four fields away. He was charging around, pausing every few minutes to paw the ground, snort and shake his head.

Farmer Garlic climbed off her recently acquired possession, waddled towards Juliette, unhooked her and pulled the reluctant donkey towards where Elizabeth was standing.

"Here she is," she said. "Watch her mind, she's being right monkey."

Puffing heavily, Farmer Garlic handed the reins and a nosebag full of chaff to Elizabeth, obviously pleased to relinquish control of the beast and its baggage. "Behave yourself, you little git." She waggled a finger in the donkey's face, scolding it as one might an errant child.

"Thanks," said Elizabeth, accepting the donkey in one hand and the nosebag in the other. "She's a wee bit vocal, isn't she?"

"If her hollering gets on your nerves stick the nosebag on her, that'll shut her up."

As if to reinforce this statement Juliette stretched her neck, shook her head then opened her mouth and bellowed out a bray.

Elizabeth used the opportunity to loop the nosebag around her ears.

"Thanks again." She turned to the farmer. "The kids will love her. Will Romeo be okay on his own?"

"Don't worry about him, he'll settle down."

Elizabeth watched as the farmer walked over to the marquee and peeked in.

"You sure you got enough chairs and tables in there? I've plenty more in the barn if you need 'em."

"No thanks," said Elizabeth. "What's there is just fine."

The Farmer shrugged, and as she turned she saw the toilets.

"Blimey, they look rum. Why don't you use mine? I've got great portables, much better quality than them."

"Thanks for the offer but no thanks, they'll do."

Farmer Garlic lifted her flat cap and scratched her head.

"Just let me know if you need anything else. And remember; watch your arse with that one." She pointed at Juliette.

"Will she be alright with the children?"

"She'll be fine with kids... and men, loves 'em she does. Can't get enough of 'em. It's women she got a problem with."

She waddled back to her tractor, shaking her head and mumbling under her breath. Elizabeth watched her mount her machine as a knight would its' charger and as she did so, two figures darted out of the marquee and headed towards the slowly reversing vehicle.

"Oy! Garlic!" Mary shouted out. "Give us a lift back."

Elizabeth watched as Mary and a lad of about sixteen climbed onto the trailer. Once they were on board the farmer continued her reversing manoeuvre, a little forwards, a little backwards, near jack-knifing the two separate parts of her transport while Mary and her friend clutched the sides of the trailer laughing like a pair of kids on a bull ride. Eventually the farmer managed to reunite tractor and trailer into a cohesive roadworthy position and they were transported back down the hill towards the track and civilisation.

"See you later. I'll be back when the fun starts!" Mary shouted and waved two fingers at Elizabeth.

Farmer Garlic was a thoughtless driver on a public road but in her own tractor, driving on land she owned, she was a one-woman force with the ultimate advantage. Elizabeth watched her drive back up the track, with her two passengers clinging to the side of the trailer like limpets, swaying backwards and forwards and laughing as they disappeared into the copse.

A nudge in the back reminded Elizabeth that she now had a donkey to take care of. She turned to attend to the animal just as an earth-worn set of molars were about to close around her buttocks. She led the beast to the newly hammered post outside the marquee and tied her up. Several of the younger volunteers stopped what they were doing and approached to pat the animal.

"No patting the donkey," Elizabeth shouted. "Until you've finished your tasks." She returned to the marquee and as she entered she felt all eyes upon her. There were mumblings, she heard her name, but whispered, not requesting her attention.

'I thought it would be more fun' and *'who the fuck does she think she is?'*

"Elizabeth."

Elizabeth looked up. It was thirteen-year-old Somerset Mark with his younger sister Harper and brother Byron on one side along with Betsy Grubb - the middle child of Alice – and eleven-year-old Saul Hollyoak on the other.

"Well now, we appear to have a delegation, what can I do for you?"

"You're lucky we're still here," Somerset said. "Everyone's saying you're being really mean."

"Yeah, you've been treating us like shit! My sister's gone home." Betsy Grubb added.

"I'm aware of that," said Elizabeth.

"We're here to help but you're not being very nice to us," said Somerset.

"I know."

"You do?" Somerset looked at Elizabeth, surprised.

"Yes." Elizabeth nodded.

"Our daddy says you should always treat other people respectfully," said Harper. "He says you should treat people as you would like to be treated yourself."

"I'm going to tell me mum," said Betsy Grubb. "That you've been horrid to us."

Elizabeth looked at the five youngsters.

"Please just bear with me... trust me." She winked at them.

"You're up to something," said Somerset. "Aren't you?" He looked at Elizabeth and then turned. "Okay, come on you lot, let's go and finish up."

Elizabeth turned and spotted Honeysuckle on the phone.

"I won't ask you again! Will you put your phone away," she shouted. "And get on with your tasks."

"Hang." Honeysuckle spoke to the caller before turning on Elizabeth. "Are you me mother?"

"Fortunately not."

"It was a rhetorical question."

"Clearly."

The girl returned to her call.

"I'm done here, I'll be with you in half hour," she said, heading for the exit. "Will you come and pick us up? Else I've got to walk back up that bollocking track."

Before she walked out Honeysuckle returned her attention to Elizabeth.

"What did your last fucking slave die of?"

"She got beaten to death for being lazy," Elizabeth shouted back without a second for thought.

She returned to her table, sat back down, took a deep breath, then picked up her book once more and flipped it open at a random page.

'I'm nobody! Who are you?
Are you nobody, too?'

"Have you gone mental?"

Elizabeth looked up. It was Caleb.

"If you're here to volunteer you're a bit late," said Elizabeth. "Most of the work's been done."

"What is going on? These kids have given up their time to come and help set everything up and you're talking to them as if they are your skivvies!"

"I think they could do with a hand outside…," she said.

"Charming."

"Dad!"

Benedict, Caleb's eldest son, came over.

"Hi son, how's it going?"

"It's okay. But I've got something to say."

"What's up, son?"

"Not to you, to her," he said, pointing to Elizabeth.

"Okay," said Elizabeth. "I'm listening."

"I... I've been elected as a sort of spokesperson."

"Have you indeed?"

"Yes," he said. "I've been asked to ask you if there are going to be enough tables?"

"I see," said Elizabeth.

"And chairs," he added.

"It's a good question," said Elizabeth. "But please don't concern yourself, it'll be fine."

"You know, he's got a point," said Caleb, looking around for the first time. "Is that all there is? Hasn't Garlic got any more?"

"I've got the number I asked for." Elizabeth snapped her book shut and returned it to her bag. "Now please excuse me, people will be arriving soon." She stood up and headed for the exit.

Once outside the breeze cooled her face. She closed her eyes and inhaled deeply before opening them again to face up to the day that had come to her in a dream.

In the distance she saw Jan giving a group of older helpers a semaphore lesson on how to point and position cars into the car park. The high viz volunteers had little time to digest their newly acquired skills as vehicles belonging to early-bird arrivals bumped their way along the track towards them.

Juliette's brays returned Elizabeth to the present. Somebody had removed the donkey's nosebag and she was bellowing for her mate. In the distance Romeo did try to respond to his distraught friend but his efforts were captured by the breeze and wafted in the opposite direction.

She spotted a van with 'Paul's Pies' written on the side of it; it turned into the car park followed by a yellow Jaguar and she breathed a sigh of relief. PeeTurD had arrived.

Some families had brought picnics and lugged their food and belongings, ready to claim an afternoon piece of the farmer's land just as large as their groundsheets would permit.

"Have a wonderful day!" was the chant, as each volunteer thrust a programme and an EU flag into the hand of every arrival en route up the hill.

At 2:35pm, Elizabeth stood on the outside stage and stared out across the crowd. She saw a community coming together, meet ups, greetings, people sitting on the grass, some standing chatting, village people connecting with village life. She picked up the microphone, the sound system screeched and then quietened. There were nods, shaking heads and eventually a thumbs-up from Moses. She was about to announce a welcome when she spotted Rafael in the distance standing by the entrance to the car park. Lars and Ruby – the latter carrying baby Georgina close to her chest in a baby sling – joined him and they headed up the hill towards her.

'Stop being silly, don't feel intimidated by your own family.' She turned to the audience smiling a greeting.

"Good afternoon and thank you all for coming to our EU themed family fun day." The crowd responded with a cheer, a few included a flag wave.

"We've got lots to entertain you this afternoon. We've got a show, then the children of Bedwell Ash are putting on a play for us, we have a debate on the EU, and of course we have a buffet and disco in the marquee later."

The crowd cheered, clapped and flag-waved some more.

"So to start we have a talent show. We asked for entries and you all responded. Bedwell Ash has got talent! But first, to officially open our day we need to crown our carnival queen."

"Carnival Queen?" shouted Alice Grubb. "What! No one mentioned a carnival queen."

"I didn't think we were having one this year," shouted Jill Jones, who, in spite of her bleached blonde hair and red lipstick, looked older than her thirty-eight years. "My Pearl wanted to be queen. It's not fair!"

"What the bloody hell are you doing here?" Roman turned on her. "You should be in prison."

"I got bail," Jill shouted back. "And let me remind you I'm innocent until proven guilty."

"That won't be difficult," shouted Kirk. Several people cheered.

"Oh get lost." Jill Jones showed not a hint of embarrassment at the remarks lobbied in her direction. "Can someone explain to me why my Pearl didn't get the chance to be the Queen?"

"Or my Betsy," shouted Alice, glaring at Jill. "She'd be the best queen."

"The reason the post of carnival queen wasn't advertised is because…"Elizabeth smiled at both of the women. " I decided we should do something a little bit different this year." She breathed a sigh of relief as she saw PeeTurD approaching. "In these enlightened times I decided that we wouldn't actually have a carnival *queen*."

"But you just said…" Jill interrupted.

"What I meant," said Elizabeth, turning to face her, "was that this year we are not going to have an actual carnival queen. In the interest of equality we are going to have our very own king of the carnival instead."

Cheers and some laughter bubbled through the crowd.

"About time too!" shouted Hector Oliphant from his place at the side of the stage. "Equality for all. Well done, Elizabeth, who is it?"

Elizabeth turned to Hector and winked.

"I also decided to break with tradition and instead of having a good, honest and decent person…"

"Elizabeth, what have you done?" Hector Oliphant hissed at her.

"We have a baddie for you… you know… like in a pantomime. Please welcome our king for the day, Bedwell Ash's very own King Herod, PeeTu… sorry… Peter Dawson."

For a few seconds there was silent shock and aghast faces. From his place at the side of the stage PeeTurD approached, and as he did so the crowd started to jeer.

"Oy," PeeTurD hissed as he approached Elizabeth. "King Herod? I've not killed a kid."

"Well, that's a matter of opinion!" Elizabeth spoke under her breath, not looking at him as the words spilled out.

"What do you mean?!"

"Remember, it's just for one day, come on. Be a villain, it'll be a laugh. Let everyone see you're a good sport underneath all of that… that…" She leant forward to whisper something to him.

PeeTurD paused then turned to the crowd and hissed at them. "Losers," he shouted.

The jeers continued, as did the booing, and then hisses were combined into the welcome.

Elizabeth picked up a heavily embroidered cloak folded neatly on the chair beside her.

"Now, come here and turn around and behave yourself," she said, placing the cloak carefully around his shoulders. "Now kneel down."

As PeeTurD got down on one knee Jessica stepped onto the stage carrying a handmade cardboard gold crown. She walked towards him in a rhythmic beat; then, stopping in front of him, she curtseyed and placed the crown onto his head.

"Huuh," said PeeTurD. "You know when I was a kid and me mum used to take me to pantomime my favourite character was always the villain."

"So now you're living your dream," said Elizabeth. "Please go sit on your throne and enjoy the day. There's food later."

Amidst the boos and jeers from the crowd PeeTurD, dressed in his cloak and gold paper crown, went and sat on his battered gold sprayed chair-cum-throne which had been placed at the side of the stage.

"And now to show that this really is a family affair, to open our 'Bedwell Ash Has Got Talent' show, please welcome our very own Kevin 'the kilt' Dawson."

A cheer went up. Elizabeth left the stage, the cheer cooled to silence.

"Please welcome Kevin to the stage," Elizabeth shouted from the sidelines.

Another cheer was raised, but the stage still remained bare and silent. A few seconds and slow clapping started, a few seconds after that chanting: '*why are we waiting, why are we waiting*'. It started low, good-humoured; there were smiles as the families had their fun.

Elizabeth went over and peeked behind the screen. Kevin was there, bagpipes positioned in readiness to play their part, unlike himself who – although looking immaculate in full Highland dress – was standing stock still with a glazed look. Moses appeared to be doing his best to communicate with him but it was obvious to Elizabeth that he wasn't getting through.

"Kevin," she hissed. He turned to look at her and she saw an expression of panic. "Please... just play."

The words acted as a spur and he acknowledged then bonded with his instrument and within seconds 'Ode to Joy' was piping out. The sound was drowned out by the clapping and singing at first but as Kevin ramped up the volume the audience hushed their chanting. Their singing stopped, their clapping slowed until all audience interaction ceased.

Kevin, clean-shaven, eyes tense shut, landed on the stage with a jolt and a missed note as a result of a gentle push from Moses. He recovered his composure and played as if in a trance.

Many of the villagers had heard Kevin play, most often during one of his alcohol-induced High Street parades, but here in front of them he stood as if born to this moment in time. They listened, they looked, mesmerised by his party.

Even Juliette stopped chewing her nosebag to watch and listen, and from his distant field Romeo stood still and faced the sound that shimmered over the fields towards him.

Like Bagger Vance and his golf clubs, Kevin was at one with his bagpipes; people were paying attention to his playing. He tuned into their picnics with a melodic feast and they loved it. Their silence spoke their respect while his Royal Stewart tartan kilt, blowing flag-like in the breeze, added to the intrigue.

As 'Ode to Joy' faded there was a few seconds of silence before the cheers started. Kevin blushed and bowed his head. Elizabeth returned to the stage got hold of his hand and held it up.

"I now declare our fete open!" she shouted. "Thank you, Kevin that was beautiful." She addressed the audience. "Just to make you all aware, Kevin is now available for weddings and parties or you can see him in town at weekends by the arcade."

Out of the corner of her eye she could see Crispin and Ava climbing the hill from the car park. She watched as they spotted Rafael and the others and headed towards them; then she looked again as she spotted the overweight figure of Bob Windass lugging a cool box following them and almost getting run over by Mr Esposito in his pizza van.

'What's Bob doing here?' she asked herself before returning her attention to a now tearful Kevin.

"Thank you, thank you so much, Mrs Rossi," he said.

"Elizabeth, please call me Elizabeth."

"Elizabeth, thank you… for everything." He shuffled off the stage with the half-winded bagpipes tucked under his arm.

"And now please welcome to the stage Helga Schmidt."

Young Helga stepped up onto the stage and turned to face the audience. She had her blonde hair tight in plaits tied up on top of her little head and she wore a red tunic with a frilly ruff around her neck. As she stood there not moving and making no sound, she looked like a noble child painted as a miniature adult in a portrait composed before the Enlightenment. The moment did not last. She opened her mouth and bellowed out to the crowd.

"What do you call Postman Pat now he's retired?" and after several seconds of silence from the crowd, "PAT!"

Several other jokes followed; most were well established Christmas cracker funnies. But the audience joined in the fun and laughed loudly at every one.

She left the stage to cheers and Elizabeth introduced the next act.

"And now please welcome to the stage two brothers, Buster and Spike Jones, who are apparently going to show us their acrobatic skills and throw each other around the stage a bit."

Buster and Spike did routine somersaulting and flipping in near perfect unison. Their mother Jill looked on proudly until their act came to an abrupt halt when Buster sidestepped into Spike's way mid-cartwheel.

"You wanking idiot!" Spike stood up and shouted as older brother Barry headed for the stage.

"I told you two little buggers to behave!" he shouted at them before ushering them off.

"Thank you, Buster and Spike," Elizabeth shouted. "Maybe a little more practice is needed. And now please welcome Sonja and Marina Kowolski."

The mother and daughter sang 'There's a Place for Us' in perfect pitch, silencing the crowd and bringing tears to the eyes of some. Elizabeth looked out to the captivated audience and spotted Kirsty and Miriam sitting on a blanket.

"Hector take over will you please," she approached him offering the microphone. She went over to where they were sitting.

"Hello, Mrs Rossi," said Miriam.

Elizabeth was relieved to see the child was smiling.

"Miriam, Kirsty, how are you both?"

Kirsty looked at her.

"Better," she said, "much better."

"We're going to see a flat tomorrow." said Miriam. "In Motley Barton."

"I'm so pleased," Elizabeth said.

"I'm not sure how Miriam's going to get to school if we get it. Have to change schools, I suppose," said Kirsty.

The singing stopped and Elizabeth clapped to join in the applause.

"Mum, it's a roof over our heads," said Miriam. "Don't worry, I'll get to school…"

Laughter from the crowd drew Elizabeth's attention back to the talent show. A young man with a bushy moustache wearing a yellow morph suit was on stage setting up a table. When the table was stable he climbed onto it and lay on his back, arse out towards the crowd with his legs in the air.

"Will you excuse me? I'd better go and see what's going on." Elizabeth smiled at them.

The young man sat up and shouted to the audience.

"Good afternoon, ladies and gentlemen. My name is Christoph Roberto Urquhart Nickolai Trump and I am a traditional flatulist. Please bear with me while I warm up."

He lay back down again and with legs positioned to face the crowd let out a resounding fart.

Hector Oliphant jumped onto the stage and stood in front of the table, facing the audience arms outstretched, at the same moment as Elizabeth reached the stage.

"Get him off," Hector hissed to her.

"I think they've already spotted him," she said.

"And heard him!" said Hector as Christoph let out another gust of tuning-up farts.

Elizabeth went over to the young flatulist.

"Christoph, I'm sorry, I don't think Bedwell Ash is quite ready for your act," she said.

"But it's traditional, my act is traditional," Christoph pleaded. "It's a Victorian art form."

"If that's the case my ex hubby's a flaming artist!" shouted Jill from her place in front of the stage. "Especially on Sunday morning when he's had curry on Saturday night!"

"Let him fart!" shouted Alice Grubb who was sitting next to her. "Let him fart, it's freedom of expression!"

Several people in the audience laughed. Elizabeth turned to Christoph.

"I'm sorry," she said. "You can't go on."

Christoph turned and glared at her, tear-like spittle seeping from each corner of his mouth. She opened her mouth to say something but before any words came out, Christoph, in a single flexible upswing, leapt off his table, manipulating his body out of ordinary human form - as a child would a rubber toy – and landed back onto the stage in an accomplished gymnastic motion. He stood still, perfectly composed for a couple of seconds as if awaiting a perfect ten from the judges, then addressed his audience.

"Ladies and gentlemen." He gave a short bow. "In spite of accepting my entry into this talent contest I have been asked not to perform for you today." He turned and glared first at Elizabeth and then at Hector Oliphant. "In my view this is clear discrimination."

Some of the audience cheered, but most did not. Unperturbed, Christoph continued.

"I have prepared myself especially for today. It takes a lot of time and it costs me money." He turned to address Hector. "I'll have you know my act was very popular in Victorian times." Another cheer. "My act requires skill and I think, sir, that you are being extremely small-minded."

"Let him stay." A chant went up from a small number of people in the crowd. "Let him stay."

Elizabeth could see the disappointment on the lad's face. She went over to him and put a comforting hand on his shoulder.

"Look," she said. "I'm sorry your times been wasted, why don't you hang around. There's lot's going on later this afternoon. I'm sure you'll enjoy it."

Christoph looked at her and then, with a pout droopier than his well-oiled moustache, he turned, went back to his table and started to fold it up. When compacted, he carried it and his carrier bag with clothes concealing a near full bottle of vodka and headed for the crowd.

Hector Oliphant turned and followed him, ushering him along with arms outstretched while simultaneously keeping a safe distance in case the young man should exercise his self-professed right to freedom of expression through his backside. Only when the lad was well on his way to the back of the crowd did Hector return to speak to Elizabeth.

"Have you completely lost it?" he hissed at her.

"I didn't know he was a farter," said Elizabeth. "He said on his form he was a bubble act. I thought he was going to blow bubbles."

The acts continued. There was a Rumanian dance troupe. Jan Kowolski played 'Somewhere Over the Rainbow' on his cherished violin. A drummer beat out his improvised composition which was almost frantic enough to ward off evil spirits.

They kept on coming.

"And next up we have twelve-year-old Elspeth Schmidt, who is going to yodel God Save the Queen for us." Elizabeth stood back to welcome Elspeth to the stage.

The child belted out the national anthem as it had never been belted out before, yodelling her way through the first and second verses to enthusiastic cheers from her family and most of the audience.

"Really, Elizabeth, do you think this is appropriate?"

Elizabeth turned around; it was Paul Hollyoak.

"What's up?"

"The national anthem, I thought this was a day to celebrate the EU?"

"Oh, don't be so bloody ridiculous." She spoke the words as Elspeth let rip her final yodel. "Why don't you take your finger out of your back side and grow up."

"Pardon?"

Microphone in hand Elizabeth headed to the front of the stage.

"Thank you Elspeth."

Elspeth curtsied then stood and beamed at her audience.

"And now please welcome to the stage nine-year-old Jethro Johnson who is going to do a street dance for us."

Elizabeth and Elspeth just managed to escape the stage as Jethro bounded onto it. The audience watched open mouthed as Jethro twirled and flipped around to cheers from appreciative onlookers. When the music stopped so did he and the audience let rip their applause. Elizabeth - satisfied there was no danger - got back onto the stage.

"Thank you, Jethro, that was very entertaining... and very energetic."

Jethro beamed his pleasure.

"And now another unique act, please welcome Jane Grubb to the stage. Hector, I hope this act is okay with you, it involves bodily gases so get lost for a few minutes if you're offended. Jane is going to burp the alphabet for us. Is that right, Jane?"

Eight-year-old Jane climbed onto the stage the minute she heard her name. She was dressed in jeans with a blue woollen top and matching blue bow clipped into her shoulder-length brown hair.

"Yes, Mrs Rossi, I can do it. I'm really good at it." Jane stood there for a moment and then turned to Elizabeth. "When you've left the stage, I'll start."

As soon as Elizabeth was off the stage, Jane turned to the crowd, smiled, then put herself into what looked like a semi-hypnotic trance.

"Come on, Jane, you can do it," Alice Grubb shouted from the front row.

"A B C D E..." The child belched every letter. "M N O P..." She didn't miss a single one. "X Y Z."

The final act was a Steam Punk Morris dance troupe led by Demelza who, with bells jangling and black headwear bobbing in rhythmic unison, completed the show with attitude. Elizabeth watched as her mother and the rest of the team danced, tapped and grimaced in a variety of aggressive poses. The cheering went on for several minutes after they steam-punked their way off stage. Elizabeth waited until they had hushed.

"Thank you all," she said. "Great acts, great show. Thank you." She watched the nods and smiles. "The next item in the programme is a discussion about the EU."

Some smiles disappeared and there were a few groans but they were out-voiced by cheers.

"Oy, Elizabeth, before that I've got a question," a voice shouted.

Elizabeth turned to address the question asker. It was Mr Melford on his mobility scooter.

"Why the hell are we sitting in the middle of a field in the middle of friggin nowhere?" he shouted. "It's been a right bugger getting here."

"Yes, why aren't we at the town hall as usual?" shouted a woman with five children of various ages and hair colour sitting around her. "We had to bloody well walk here."

"It's not very easy to get here," another voice shouted.

"Oh, come on," Elizabeth shouted back, looking around the crowd. "I thought we could have a change - where's your sense of fun?"

"But why here? In the middle of chuffing nowhere?" Mr Melford shouted again.

"It's as good a place as any," Elizabeth replied.

"I for one," Evelyn Smith offered, "think it is quite selfish of you. I thought that at the council meeting but didn't say anything. I wish I had."

Elizabeth turned to her.

"What's the problem?"

"It's so difficult to get here. I know several people who haven't been able to come."

"Oh dear," said Elizabeth, before turning back to the crowd. "What a shame." Out of the corner of her eye she could see Rafael watching her. "You know I was going to arrange for a minibus to pick up people who didn't have transport but then I decided to cut it to save money and let people make their own way."

"Utter madness," said Mr Melford shaking his head.

"What are we debating?" asked Caleb, changing the subject. "About the EU, I mean, where do we start?"

"Who the hell wants to talk about the EU?" shouted PeeTurD. "You said this was gonna be fun."

"Shut up, PeeTurD," a voice shouted from the back. "King of the fair, bloody hell!"

"Why you here anyway?" Roman Winters addressed PeeTurD. "You don't even support the EU." Elizabeth glared at Roman.

"I asked him to come," she said. Then she turned and smiled at PeeTurD. "And he kindly accepted my invitation. If we're going to discuss the EU we need all views – even those we don't necessarily want to hear."

PeeTurD smiled through expensive dental wear.

"Didn't even have to pay for me ticket." He paused. "Not like you deadbeats." He looked at the families sitting on the grass. "Losers."

Elizabeth looked skyward in despair and for the first time noted the clouds circling directly above.

"Right, let's get on," she said. "So would anybody like to start? Maybe we could begin by asking why people think we voted to leave the EU?"

She looked around, but people were talking to each other, not paying attention to her. She opened her mouth to say something but PeeTurD got in first.

"Because of all the migrants," he shouted without warning.

"Racist!" shouted a voice from the crowd.

"Stop! Let's discuss that point, shall we?" said Elizabeth.

But the weather had other ideas; as if competing for the attention of the crowd, it made a statement of its own. The clouds - which until now had intimidated the event from the sidelines – invaded Bedwell Ash EU Family Fun Day like a bunch of unruly louts jeering the losing side at a football match. A lightning flash threatened rain, a grumble of thunder confirmed its arrival. Belongings were grabbed, children and the elderly were organised. Everyone made a dash for the marquee.

"Get the throne!" Elizabeth shouted to Jan Kowolski. "Don't let it get wet!"

THE STORM

The marquee was the port in their storm and they entered en masse, at speed, united in their quest for shelter. Once undercover, their common goal evaporated and those with the most pliable knees and sharpest elbows claimed tables and chairs as their own.

"Where we meant to sit?" a voice shouted.

Jan Kowolski was heading towards the stage carrying PeeTurD's throne.

"Get out me bloody way." PeeTurD pushed Jan, nudging him into the path of Somerset Mark. "I'm fucking soaked."

"Ow! Watch it!" shouted Somerset. "You nearly pushed me over!"

"Sorry… sorry…" said Jan then he placed the throne down and turned on PeeTurD.

"You must be more careful!" he said. "And please, do not use your bad words. Children are here."

"Thank fuck you've brought me chair in," said PeeTurD. "Somewhere to sit!"

"Come on, you king for the day, join in the fun properly now." Elizabeth winced as PeeTurD looked at her with eyes imaging contempt.

Jan Kowalski placed the throne at the back of the stage, approached PeeTurD and in a hushed voice said, "and no bad words, please."

"I'm not fucking well being told what to do by the likes of you." PeeTurD's voice was not as hushed.

Elizabeth walked up to him and switched off the microphone. He stood a head above her.

"We had an agreement." She smiled as she spoke. "Please, sit here, you'll get a great view of the play."

"Fuck that!" PeeTurD's crown was sitting lop-sided on his head, and he started to unbutton the cloak at his neck.

"If you go there will be consequences."

The words caught his attention and he stopped. "You fucking bitch…"

A minute later he was sitting on his throne casting menacing looks to the crowd.

Elizabeth returned her attention to the now settling audience. Some gathered into groups and vocalised their opinions in hush-hush circles while others just shouted their viewpoints to anybody prepared to listen.

"Why so few tables?"

"Where are all the bloody chairs?"

"Where we meant to sit?"

Microphone still in hand, Elizabeth headed for the stage.

"We need more tables. And are there any more chairs?" Caleb shouted to her.

"Sorry, no," she shouted back.

"Excuse me, Elizabeth, but we can't find a table… and there are no chairs either." Mrs Melford pointed at her husband. "He's alright, he's got his scooter, but what am I supposed to do?"

Elizabeth turned to Mrs Melford.

"There's plenty of floor space…"

"But we bought tickets. Why should we sit on the bleeding floor?"

"Elizabeth, I need to speak to you about the volunteers." Elizabeth turned around, it was Kirk.

"What's up with them?"

"They're annoyed at the way you treated them. They want an explanation. Not just Honeysuckle, all of them. You know she didn't want to come back this afternoon. I had to drag her."

"Really?"

"They gave up their time to come and help you."

"Look, Kirk, as you can see I'm busy just now. I'll speak to you about this later."

As she turned she saw Paul Hollyoak making a gesture, running his hand across his throat. He stopped as soon as he saw her, reddening and lowering his eyes.

"Are you okay, Paul?" asked Elizabeth.

Paul reddened some more.

"If you must know I was merely gesturing to a friend of mine over there," he nodded in the general direction of the crowd, "that this event has been really badly organised."

Elizabeth looked at him and smiled.

"You know, Paul, for once you could be right."

"Elizabeth, what's going on?"

She recognised the voice. She took a deep breath, turned around and smiled at Hector.

"You know we've run out of tables and chairs?" he said. "Where is everyone meant to sit?"

Elizabeth shrugged her shoulders and opened her mouth to reply but before the words came out she spotted Judy over his shoulder.

"Judy, can you organise the kids now?" She yelled over.

"Will do."

"Looking good," Elizabeth added, nodding at her baby bump.

"And I'm feeling great," said Judy. "This pregnancy lark suits me, I've decided."

"I said what's going on?" Hector asked again.

"Not now, Hector I'm busy. But don't worry, all will be revealed."

PeeTurD was sitting on his throne at the back of the stage surveying the scene. Elizabeth climbed up and stood at the front facing the audience, microphone in hand.

"Children and parents who are helping with the play, please follow Judy to the crèche," she shouted, pointing for those who had not yet discovered their bearings. "Your costumes are in there, please get yourselves changed."

She watched as children formed an orderly queue in front of her and Judy stream-lined them to the crèche.

"Mum! What's going on?" From nowhere Sydney appeared.

"Hello, darling, how did you do in your piano exam?"

"What the fuck's going on?"

"I beg your pardon? How dare you speak…"

"Hypocrite!"

"Excuse me?"

"You've been treating everyone like shit!"

"Now that's enough." Rafael appeared.

"Dad, tell her. I've had loads of horrible texts."

"Texts? What texts?" asked Elizabeth, jumping off the stage and launching herself forward as if to grab the phone from her daughter's hand.

Sydney sidestepped out of reach to ensure parental access to her phone could not be realised. She held it up and started to read.

"'What the fucks wrong with your old lady?', 'Your mothers doing my head in', 'Your mum's a bitch', 'Have a word with your ma', 'Your mum's such a cu…'"

"Enough!" Elizabeth shouted.

"Okay, okay, we get the gist," said Rafael.

"Dad, tell her. She's embarrassing me."

"I'll speak to her. You go and sit down, look, Crispin and Ava are over there." Rafael pointed towards the group who had given up their table and were now sitting on mats near the entrance. "Go."

Sydney looked at her mother and then her father. With her face set in a look that did not invite further communication, she headed off.

"No, go to the crèche… the play! You need to get changed," Elizabeth shouted after her.

The words did not persuade Sydney to change direction; she continued to head towards where Ava and Crispin were sitting.

"Please!" Elizabeth shouted after her. She turned to Rafael. "Is that Bob with Crispin? What's he doing here?"

"He's over at the moment, wanted to come apparently… you know, to support the EU. It's not a problem, is it?" He paused and looked at his wife. "That is what we're doing here, isn't it?"

Elizabeth turned away from her husband.

"Yes," she said in a voice unheard.

"I said, that is what we're doing here?" Rafael asked louder this time. "Showing support for the EU."

Elizabeth turned and their eyes met.

"Of course it is." She smiled at her husband. "Did I tell you Ava's written a play for us?"

"She mentioned it."

"Please will you go and ask Sydney to get changed? She'll listen to you."

Children were still heading towards the crèche, chattering excitedly. Elizabeth watched as Rafael battled through the crowd and interrupted Sydney as she spoke to Ava, then sighed with relief when – after a brief threesome discussion – her daughter turned and headed to the crèche. As she passed they made eye contact for a moment. Elizabeth was about to smile, but instead her heart near stopped when she saw the hurt in her daughter's eyes.

A lightning flash jolted her to the present and she returned her attention to the spectacle still unfolding in front of her. It was a scene where the slow were literally left standing.

A roll of thunder hammered overhead and as it did so Angelica appeared at the crèche doors dressed in a pink trouser suit. She made a dash for the exit doors.

"Angelica, come back here!" Monica with a half painted white face was the next to appear.

"Juliette," Angelica shouted back at her as she shimmied through the throng. "She's getting wet!"

"Juliette!" Elizabeth shouted at no one in particular. "Will somebody please go and get that bloody donkey in?"

A lightning flash, the passing of a couple of minutes and a sopping wet Saul Hollyoak re-entered the marquee dragging a drenched donkey.

"She's soaking wet," he said.

"And so are you," his father Paul added. He turned to Elizabeth. "Really, Elizabeth, look at him. He could catch cold now! This really is not good enough, you know."

Elizabeth turned to Saul.

"Stick her in the pen in the corner of the crèche," she said.

"What about my son? He's soaked!"

"It's just a bit of rain."

"No, Elizabeth, it's not a bit of rain, it's a lot of bloody rain," Paul shouted. "Have you seen it out there? Loads of the stuff. In fact it's the opposite of the tables and frigging chairs, there's not loads of those."

"Oh dear," said Elizabeth. "Don't you think we have enough?"

"You know well enough there's not," Hector shouted, closing in.

"This wouldn't have happened if we'd have stuck to the original venue," said Paul.

"You're right," Elizabeth replied. "It wouldn't have happened. In fact nothing would have happened. There wouldn't have been a fete this year because nobody wanted to take responsibility for organising it."

Mrs Melford approached.

"Are you talking about tables and chairs, dear?" she said. "Are you going to get some more?"

Elizabeth turned to the elderly lady.

"No. We were hoping some people wouldn't mind sitting on the floor."

"We! We? Don't even attempt to suggest the Parish council had anything to do with this... this..." Hector jumped in.

"Calm down, Hector, all I meant was..."

"My dear girl, if I sit down on the buggery floor I won't be able to get up again."

"Don't worry," Roman shouted from behind her. "We'll borrow Garlic's crane to hoist you up." He laughed at his own humour before going to sit at his table.

Elizabeth returned to the stage and attempted to switch the microphone on but it was dead. She turned to face the audience.

"Excuse me, everyone" she shouted. "I'm sorry to see some of you haven't managed to get your own table... or been able to find a chair to sit on. Please can I ask you to share?"

"Couldn't organise a piss up in a brewery!" a voice from the crowd shouted.

"Elizabeth, I need to speak to you." Hector grabbed her arm.

"Steady on, Hector," said Elizabeth, looking at his hand. He let go.

"Sorry," he said, red-faced.

"What is it?"

"Elizabeth, I know you've not organised an event like this before but it's clear to me you underestimated the number of people coming."

"I knew how many were coming."

"People need places to sit. They need to easily be able to get to and from the event."

"Why?" said Elizabeth.

"What do you mean why?"

"Why? We're a stoic group, we're resilient, we cope, we get on with things." She looked directly at Caleb as she spoke, and then turned to Hector.

"Yes, we are all of those things, but I thought you did a risk assessment and put everything in place based on the number of people coming." Hector's words were quiet - but spoken with urgency.

"I did most of that," said Elizabeth.

"Most?"

"I did the risk assessment, and I calculated how many people were coming."

"So what went wrong?"

"I decided to ignore my risk assessment and just let the people come."

"You did what?!"

"I ignored it."

"Ignored it?"

Elizabeth nodded.

"Not all of it, just some of it. I made cuts."

"Cuts? Why would you do such a thing? When you said you'd organise the event I thought you'd do it properly... responsibly..."

"I'll have you know I have organised it properly." She paused and looked directly at him for the first time. "Responsibly? Maybe not so much, now shove off and let me get on."

"You can't talk to me like that."

"You can't talk to him like that," said Caleb, closing in.

"I can speak for myself, thank you." Hector turned on him.

"While you're all here, what about the volunteers?" asked Kirk Scott, approaching.

"What about them?" said Hector.

"They were treated appallingly this morning," said Kirk. "My Honeysuckle was near tears."

Elizabeth attempted to stifle a laugh.

"Something funny?" asked Kirk.

"Look," said Elizabeth, regaining composure. "I've already told you I'll discuss this with you later. But as for your Honeysuckle being in tears, I don't think so."

"What do you mean? What are you saying?"

"I'm saying that your daughter is more likely to be the cause of people's tears," she said.

"Bloody cheek!" said Kirk.

Still holding the broken microphone Elizabeth turned to the audience once more and bellowed the words out.

"Now anybody who hasn't got a chair but needs one please put up your hand."

"What're you talking about? We all bought a ticket, we should all have a flaming chair," somebody shouted back.

"Of course they should," Hector hissed towards her.

She ignored him and turned again to the crowd.

"Please bear with me," she shouted again. "Okay, first of all let's just make sure that those who can't sit on the floor do have somewhere to sit. Cheer up, everyone, there's food and a disco later."

She got down off the stage. Hector followed her and together with several of the volunteers they went around table by table in an effort to make sure that everybody who needed a chair had one.

Ten minutes later Moses nodded to Elizabeth. Technology was up and running again.

"Please can I have your attention," she switched the mike on and addressed everyone. "Earlier I was asked to explain why I would think it acceptable to host an event like this and not adequately cater for everybody."

"Yeah, what's bloody going on?" shouted Alice Grubb.

"What about health and safety regulations?" shouted Paul Hollyoak.

"Good point." Elizabeth nodded to him. "So are we agreed that if you invite people to an event you have got to ensure you have enough places for them to sit, decent transport links to and from the event, enough facilities for them…?"

As if invited to join the conversation a grumble of thunder completed the rest of her sentence.

"Will you please explain the point you are trying to make," Paul Hollyoak shouted at her.

"Well, as this is an EU event I thought I'd follow the example of our government and invite a lot of people to our gathering while at the same time cutting the budget… let's call it an austerity package."

"Austerity! What are you on about?!" Paul shouted.

"I decided to cut costs, it was easy."

"Have you gone mad?" shouted Alice Grubb

"I don't think so," Elizabeth replied.

"If you've got a marquee with two hundred chairs and three hundred people…" said Paul.

"Some people are going to have to either stand or sit on the floor." Elizabeth finished his sentence for him.

"But you can't expect people to sit on the floor, they've bought tickets!" Paul shouted back.

"…and as we are experiencing in front of us, most of those who have a chair to sit on aren't actually that worried about those who haven't."

"Is it time to go home yet?" PeeTurD shouted from his throne at the back of the stage.

"Okay, okay, you've made your point," said Hector. "Albeit in a somewhat irresponsible way."

"Why, thank you."

"Now will you explain to us all why you treated the volunteers so badly?" Kirk Scott shouted out.

There were several shouts and nods of agreement from the crowd.

"You were bloody rude to them," Alice Grubb shouted.

"Elizabeth, please, I really do think we all deserve an explanation." Hector hissed from the side of the stage.

Elizabeth turned to him.

"Hector, please, come up here and join me."

Hector waited a moment and then with some hesitation stepped onto the stage and turned to face the crowd.

"Well, Elizabeth," he spoke in a normal voice but he had the attention of the crowd. "Will you please share your actions with us? Please tell us why you have organised this event in such a haphazard fashion? We would all of us like to know why and try to understand your thinking. Thank you for your co-operation."

A cheer went up and this time it was Elizabeth who reddened.

"Right everyone!" She shouted. "Firstly, I have been asked to explain myself and my actions this morning regarding our wonderful team of volunteers. Please all of you, even those of you who walked off this morning, come and stand at the front here, with me."

At first there was no movement. Then, led by Barry, a gradual trickle of young people, including Honeysuckle, Francesca and Charlotte, got up and - curving around tables and treading over bodies - made their way to the stage.

"Please, stand in a line along here," she said, pointing to the front of the stage. Energised, she turned and addressed her audience once more.

"This morning this group of young people came to work for me."

"Volunteer!" Kirk Scott shouted from mid-audience.

"Work? Volunteer? Is there a difference?"

Honeysuckle turned from her place in the middle of the line-up and shouted, "Minimum wage!"

A laugh shimmered through the crowd. Elizabeth breathed a sigh of relief.

"Thank you, Honeysuckle. Very true," she said.

"Excuse me, Mrs Rossi…"

Elizabeth looked along the line; a hand was up.

"It wasn't the work. It was you, you were so rude to us," said Jessica, the eldest ica sister.

"I know."

"You know?" Jessica looked surprised.

Elizabeth nodded at her.

"First of all, I would like to thank you all for doing a wonderful job." She paused and then spoke again, louder this time. "And I would like to apologise to you all."

Along the line of volunteers all heads turned in unison to look at her.

"I knew you were up to something," Jan hissed from the sidelines. "You are not a nasty person."

"You should have treated the volunteers respectfully, Elizabeth," shouted Bill Inghurst.

"I agree," she replied. "Not because they are volunteers, but because they are people... people at work. Whether they are getting paid or not is irrelevant. I just wanted to make a point..."

"Another point." Hector spoke quietly, still standing at her side. "How many more points do you intend to make?"

Elizabeth ignored him.

"Everyone at work, and I mean everyone - volunteering or not – should be treated respectfully. This morning our volunteers had the option to walk away." She turned to the line-up again. "Which many of you did, doubtless feeling disgruntled and possibly angry. Well first of all I'd like to thank those of you who did leave for coming back."

"You've got a bloody cheek!" Kirk Scott shouted at her.

"I know." Elizabeth paused; all eyes were on her. "Upon reflection maybe it wasn't my best idea but every day people are going to work and being treated badly, zero hour contracts, no sick or holiday pay and employment rights being eroded. It's all wrong. It's as if we are returning to Victorian times."

At that moment Christoph Roberto Urquhart Nickolai Trump, who had drunk half a bottle of his vodka and taken his place at the back of the marquee, broke wind loudly. There was a stunned silence followed by giggles.

"And now, will you clear the stage, please. There's just one more point I want to make before we start our play."

She nodded to Stefan and Barry who were standing on the other side off the stage. It was not just a nod, it was an instruction, and together they went over to a large wooden easel by Elizabeth's table, picked it up and carried it onto the stage, placing it at the front facing the crowd. Hector looked concerned but sidled around to get nearer to it in order to have a vantage viewpoint.

On the easel there was a picture covered by a royal blue sheet. Elizabeth walked over and stood by it, then she turned and - all the time looking at the audience as they peered back at her - she tugged the sheet from the easel. It revealed a large print.

"Now," she said. "Tell me what you see."

"It's a picture," someone shouted. "A country scene."

"A landscape," shouted another voice.

"It's a horse and cart stuck in a river," shouted another.

"Why, it's The Hay Wain, of course," shouted Hector Oliphant. "By Constable."

"Thank you," said Elizabeth. "A landscape, a country scene, a horse and cart stuck in a river, The Hay Wain by Constable."

She turned her back on the crowd, lifted the print and placed it on the floor, leaning against the easel. Its removal revealed another picture: this time a painting. She turned to her audience again.

"Now tell me what you see."

"No idea," somebody shouted.

"A load of blue squiggly lines," another voice shouted.

"A work of modern art," shouted Paul Hollyoak. "And it looks like a pretty good one."

"A load of splodgy paint," Bob Windass yelled from his place near the entrance. "Absolute rubbish!"

"No... no..." Hector's voice was calm. He approached the painting slowly, as if stalking prey, and then closed in on it. The crowd watched as he weaved one way and then another, the painting mesmerising him like a hypnotised snake dancing to the flute of its captive master.

"This... is..." he spoke quietly at first, his voice becoming louder the nearer he got, "...a work of art."

"And not a very good one," Bob shouted.

"You are wrong, this is... ...beautiful" said Hector. "A fine work... it is superb... it is a masterpiece."

"Okay, okay," said Elizabeth. "Hector, please, enough."

"But look, it is artistic perfection... who is the artist?" He gave a satisfied sigh.

Elizabeth shimmied into the gap between Hector Oliphant's face and the painting in an effort to return him to the present.

"Please, enough..."

"What a load of rubbish," shouted Kirk Scott. "How can you call that art?"

Hector turned to glare at Kirk, the two united only in their contempt for each other's viewpoint.

"My Honeysuckle could paint better," said Kirk. "Hell! I could paint better!"

"No, no, it is a brilliant work of art, the work of someone who understands paint... who understands detail... colour, light and shade... composition..."

"Thank you, Hector," said Elizabeth. "Ruby will be very pleased to hear that."

"Ruby...?"

"My daughter, she painted it." Elizabeth pointed to Ruby who was sitting on the floor near the entrance breastfeeding Georgina.

"Really?" he said, looking over and then quieter, "Really?"

Ruby reddened and gave her mother a look of darkness at being forced into the breast-feeding limelight.

Elizabeth returned her attention to the easel. With both hands she lifted Ruby's painting and placed it on the floor in front of The Hay Wain. Its removal revealed a third picture.

"Now what do you see?" she asked.

"A town," a voice shouted.

"With what may be a cathedral... and a river?"

"And a bridge."

"Yes, anything else?" she asked.

"People, there are some people."

"Okay, what about the people," asked Elizabeth.

"They're going about their business... they look quite wealthy."

"Why do you say that?"

"Most of them are quite plump and they look well dressed."

"Good point. What about the other people?"

"Where?"

"What other people?"

"I see... it looks like there are some on the bridge."

"Yes, lots on the bridge."

"Who would like to come and examine them more closely? Kirk, how about you?"

Kirk Scott accepted the challenge. He got up and stepped around the bodies on the floor to get to the stage. He glared at Elizabeth. She ignored it but held out her hand as he passed her which made him stop.

"Here," she said, handing him a magnifying glass. "This might help."

Kirk snatched the magnifying glass and approached the painting peering through it as a nosey child might peer through an out-of-bounds peephole.

The audience made no sound apart from a couple of coughs. The only other noise came from PeeTurD who sounded like an obscene phone call as he snored gently on his throne.

Kirk stepped forward. He closed in, then retreated, breathed on the lens, rubbed it clear using the end of his tee shirt, then holding the magnifying glass in front of him like Sherlock searching for a comedy clue stepped forward to examine the people on the bridge once more.

"There're no people there, on the bridge," he said. "There are just little blobs of coloured paint."

"Thank you," said Elizabeth. "Please, go back to your seat." She held her hand out for the magnifying glass as he passed. "This painting is the 'View of Dresden with the Frauenkirche at Left' by Bellotto."

"I knew that," Hector shouted to her.

"So what's your point now?" shouted Alice Grubb.

"I'm glad you asked that," Elizabeth replied. "My point is simply this. When remainers say 'leavers need to see the bigger picture' then let's face it, Brexit is not this one." She pulled out the Constable print and held it up for everyone to see before placing it flat on the floor. "It is more like this one," she said, pointing at Ruby's painting. "However," She paused and looked around before turning to the Bellotto print still on the easel. "This is the picture our government is painting, and those insignificant little blobs of paint at the back represent the poor and the vulnerable in our society." She paused to look around the audience, trying to judge who understood, who was with her. "And for the record, those who represent us and profess to understand 'the bigger picture' also need to understand the detail."

"But why?" asked Evelyn.

"Because without that understanding all they have is a concept from a text-book. They have no comprehension of the social consequences of their actions."

Someone somewhere started to clap. A couple of people joined in but within seconds it had fizzled out.

"There are too many people, the poor, the vulnerable, who are just little blobs of paint in a picture painted by our government and we must speak for those people because many of them cannot make their own voices heard."

"I agree!" a voice shouted.

"Governments everywhere need to be reminded that our world is not just a business enterprise." Elizabeth paused before turning to the crowd again. "And now I would like to hand you over to the children of Bedwell Ash who are going to put on a play for you." A cheer went up. "But before we start I would like to thank my dear friend Ava for her help in writing this play." She nodded towards Ava who was sitting on the floor at the back between Crispin and Ruby. Ava stood up and took a bow amidst some clapping. "And Judy." She pointed to the entrance of the crèche where she was standing; from behind her small faces were attempting to peek out into theatre-land.

"Oh, it was nothing." Judy reddened and smiled.

Jan and Moses carried the easel and pictures off stage and then returned each carrying a square table. They placed them next to each other in the centre of the stage, and positioned benches on either side. They then put six chairs in a line at the back of the stage, just in front of PeeTurD. The scene was set.

"And now let our play begin." Elizabeth nodded a thank you.

A moment later, the lights dimmed and Sydney walked onto the stage dressed in a blue suit and colour co-ordinated top hat. She made her way to the front and stood facing the audience. Six children followed her on, each one dressed in purple. There were hushes and shushes amongst the audience as the children went to the back of the stage and sat on the chairs in front of PeeTurD.

The lights went down further, and a spotlight shone onto Sydney. She opened her mouth to speak but before the words came out a figure swathed in a black cloak swooped onto the stage. The audience laughed as it circled the area flapping its arms like wings before coming to rest just behind PeeTurD's throne where it stood statue still and wrapped itself cocoon-like in its cloak.

"Oy! What are you up to behind there?" PeeTurD shouted.

"Sssshhhh," Jan hissed from the side of the stage.

"Shut up, PeeTurD," Barry shouted from mid-audience.

PeeTurD stretched around the back of his throne to look and when satisfied that the chrysalis-type figure was doing no harm returned to his position, sitting back, placing one arm on the armrest and closing his eyes once more.

Sydney addressed the audience.

"Welcome to our play 'The Brexit Trilogy'. I would like it if you can to imagine for a moment that..." She turned to the children in the chairs. "...that this is our government. Ladies and gentlemen, will you please introduce yourselves."

First in line was Oliver Goodchild. He stood up and headed for the front of the stage. Once there he stopped and stood looking out to the crowd. He was about to open his mouth but first sniffed and then wiped his nose on the sleeve of his jacket. At the same time - concerned he might have forgotten his line - Judy prompted him in a whisper from the side of the stage.

"My name is..."

This bumped Oliver back to the present. He returned his snotty hand to his side and stood up straight.

"My name is Blarney Scumbag," he shouted out, "of the Hertfordshire Scumbags and I am a very nice person." He headed back to his chair amidst claps from the audience.

As he sat down ten-year-old Buster Jones got up, headed for the front of the stage and without hesitation announced his role.

"My name is Giddyup Stirrup and I am here to represent myself. Just so's we're clear." He walked solemnly back to his chair but before sitting down turned and yelled, "Giddyup all!"

When the laughter stopped whispered voices could be heard but no movement took place on the stage. Only when complete quiet inhabited the marquee once more did ten-year-old Betsy Grubb stand up, her purple ballerina skirts flopping, her lilac tights shimmering, and her white ballet shoes disguising her flat feet. She jete'd, frappe'd and pirouetted around to a melody in her head, waving her fairy wand like a maestro of a massive orchestra conducting an audience in silent watchfulness before coming to a finish position at the front of the stage with a curtsey and a buck-toothed grin. Alice Grubb clapped enthusiastically, others followed in a more restrained manner - more of a polite refrain than applause for a formidable talent.

"Well done, Betsy," shouted Alice. "That was brilliant."

Elizabeth was standing at the side of the stage watching when a whispered voice from behind made her jump.

"We need to talk."

It was Rafael.

Her heart fluttered but her manner conveyed indifference.

"I'm a bit busy…" She nodded at the children on the stage. Betsy Grubb was addressing her audience.

"Good afternoon. My name is Bellyflop Rudder. "I go where my wind takes me." She curtseyed again and then danced back to her chair amidst gushing noises and claps from her mother.

The next to stand up was Saul Hollyoak, the eleven-year-old son of Paul. He wore several gold chains around his neck and carried a briefcase with the word 'Money' painted on the side of it. He arrived at the front of the stage with a nod to the audience.

"Good afternoon, ladies and gentlemen," he said.

There were some giggles and a few claps. He fiddled with one of the chains while waiting for the return of silence. When it arrived, Rafael whispered to his wife again.

"It's not a bad idea," he said. "All of this – sort of."

"Sort of?" Elizabeth said without looking at him, directing her attention to the stage where Saul was now bellowing out his lines.

"My name is Stonking Rich, my friends call me Stonky."

There was a burst of laughter and more giggles. Stonky bowed and then went and sat down, and Ellis, Evelyn Smith's eight-year-old grandson, got up from his chair. He wore a purple onesie and a smile. He toddled to the front of the stage.

"I can see where you're coming from," said Rafael. "The play, it's a good idea…"

"I know," said Elizabeth. "And if you pay attention you might learn something."

Rafael looked at his wife, not able to disguise the hurt at her rebuke.

Meanwhile, onstage Ellis was whispering his words as if he were imparting a secret.

"Hello," he said. "My name is Diddums Hardheart. I have had the same nanny for over forty years." To the sound of some laughter and echoes of 'what did he say?' Ellis was about to turn around when Judy intervened again. She put one foot onto the stage, leant over and whispered as loudly as she dared.

"Pssst... Ellis... say it one more time, would you? Louder please."

Ellis looked at her, then returned his attention to the audience and stared at them until complete silence reigned once more.

"My name is Diddums Hardheart," he shouted. "I have had the same nanny for over forty years." This time his voice was so loud that the audience responded with laughter and a cheer. He beamed before heading back to his chair.

The last child up was Jessica. Perfectly colour co-ordinated, with powdered face and purple eye shadow, she wore a blouse tied at the waist and a lengthy tight skirt. Her normally long straggly hair was backcombed into a beehive with a few wisps of straw sticking out, looking like broken chopsticks stuck into the hair of a Geisha gone wrong.

"My name is Bimbo Haystacks," she said. "When I look out of my boudoir window I own all the land that I see." She paused and headed back to her chair but before sitting down she spoke to the audience again. "Even if I'm looking through my long-sighted binoculars. Haw haw!"

Elizabeth turned to her husband and half smiled. He opened his mouth to say something but she got in first.

"Shhh! It's Sydney in a sec..."

"And who the hell are you," Blarney Scumbag shouted to their daughter.

Sydney turned to look at him, then she returned her attention to the audience.

"I, my friends, am your Collective Conscience."

"You're our what?" shouted Bellyflop Rudder.

"I am your Collective Conscience. I see what you do, I hear what you say. I know what you think."

"Haw haw!" said Giddyup Stirrup. "What are you doing here?"

"I am the one who keeps each of you awake at night."

Elizabeth looked at her husband, his gaze had barely left her. She nodded a smile and she felt herself redden once more when he smiled back.

"Well," said Diddums Hardheart, "I would like to point out that I sleep very well at night."

"So do I," said Stonking Rich.

The other children in the chairs nodded agreement.

The lights on the stage snapped to darkness. Then, after a few seconds, through the skill of Moses' fingers on buttons, the lighting mimicked a dawn - of sorts. A group of children led by pink-suited Angelica walked onto the stage and sat around the tables. Once they had settled, a tinkling tambourine sounded and Monica, the middle ica sister, stepped onto the stage dressed in a white sheet with a hole for her head, grey wig and painted white face.

"Wooooh…" she said. Then she hissed and motioned a flight to the front of the stage. The audience giggled. She stopped and stared out at the sea of attentive faces. They waited. They waited some more. Eventually the words came out.

"I am… the Ghost of Brexit Past." Her first words were hesitant.

"In the olden days - back in the 1970s."

After the laughter she gathered pace.

"There were strikes and three-day weeks. The UK was known as the sick man of Europe." She turned and pointed at the children dressed in purple sitting on the chairs at the back. "Then in 1975 you, the government, gave us a referendum to see whether we should stay in the Common Market."

"I remember all that!" Mr Melford shouted from the audience. "Like it was yesterday!"

A laugh and a half-hearted cheer rippled through the crowd.

Rafael nudged his wife.

"Nice touch," he said, "telling how we got here."

"Ava wrote the play," Elizabeth said. "She didn't want to at first."

"I know."

"You know?"

Rafael returned his attention to the stage. Stonking Rich stood up with such gusto that his chair fell backwards onto the half asleep PeeTurD. He jumped awake and glared at the child.

"What the fu…!"

"Language!" shouted Jan from his position at the other side of the stage.

Stonking Rich leant over to pick up his chair, then stood up and faced PeeTurD – not as Stonking Rich but unscripted, as Saul Hollyoak.

"You are very rude, you know, going to sleep while we're putting on our play."

"I'm the king, I can do what I like," PeeTurD said with a smug grin.

"I suppose," said Saul. He took a deep breath, turned his back on him and returned to the audience in character.

"We will ask the question," he shouted. "'Do you think the United Kingdom should stay in the European Community Common Market?'"

Pearl Jones and Riku Winters dressed in bright coloured clothes from the acid scene that was the Seventies, appeared and walked across the stage chatting.

"Ooooh, I'm so so excited," said Pearl.

"So am I," said Riku. "I can't wait to vote."

Elizabeth had expressed her concerns to Judy about giving young Riku such a major part in the play. Sydney had told her that since his mother had returned to Japan the lad kept bursting into tears in class. But Judy had assured Elizabeth that Riku was a very capable boy and that a large role in the play was just what he needed to bring him out of himself.

"What box you gonna tick?"

"Doohh, the 'stay in' box of course…"

The children laughed and walked off the other side of the stage.

Bimbo Haystacks stood up and headed to the front of the stage, patting the back of her beehive.

"May I have your attention please," she shouted. "We the government would like to announce that the United Kingdom has voted to become a proper member of the Common Market."

All the children on the stage cheered, the audience cheered, flags were waved and the spotlight returned to the Ghost of Brexit Past.

"And we became a proper member of the EU and lots of people were very happy as the UK thrived."

There was another appreciative cheer.

"Then in 1986 things changed."

From his chair at the back Stonking Rich stood up.

"We will have a big bang," he shouted and sat back down again.

From behind the screen the crash of two cymbals made the audience jump.

Bimbo Haystacks stood up.

"We will deregulate the financial markets," she said.

"And so you… the govern…" The Ghost's line went unfinished.

"Have you seen the bogs out there?" Everybody turned to look. It was Roman Winters standing by the exit door. "They're bloody disgusting."

"I've seen them, they're a real health hazard," Paul shouted. "Bloody disgrace if you ask me."

"What's up with them?" asked Rafael, looking at his wife. She ignored him and went onto the stage to face the audience, nearly knocking over the Ghost of Brexit Past.

"Sorry for the interruption," she shouted. "Look, is this really necessary now?"

"But they're a health friggin' hazard," Paul shouted. "I didn't use 'em, I went in the bushes earlier."

Several people jeered again.

Elizabeth stood her ground, unsure if they were jeering at the interruption to the play or the state of the toilets.

Hector appeared to be in no doubt.

"Right, that's enough!" He got up and approached the stage, then turned to face everybody. "I'm sorry but this event must stop now. I'm going to have to close it down."

"But why?" Elizabeth shouted to him. "The children are in the middle of their play. Most people are enjoying themselves." She turned to the audience. "Aren't you?"

There were a few cheers – mainly from parents.

Hector turned on Elizabeth.

"You've really messed this up, Elizabeth. You've been extremely childish, not to say irresponsible."

"Okay, okay," said Elizabeth. "Maybe a little childish…"

"Get lost, Hector - let the kids get on with it," Jill Jones shouted.

For once Elizabeth agreed with her. She turned and faced Hector.

"I don't mean to be rude but you don't actually have the power to close us…"

Her sentence went unfinished as a roll of thunder interrupted proceedings.

Hector bristled.

"I'll have you know I am part of the Health and Safety executive," he said in his official voice. "A fact I know you are well aware of."

"Health and Safety only deal with accidents," said Elizabeth. "So if there's an accident, you'll be the first to know. Now go away and let us enjoy the play."

The audience cheered. Hector opened his mouth to speak but Elizabeth got in first.

"Besides," she said, as another clap of thunder interrupted the discussion, "hear that? I suggest you do a quick mental risk assessment and think about how hazardous it would be to throw everyone out into that storm right now."

Hector looked at the audience.

"Sit down, Oliphant," Jill shouted. "Give your ego a rest."

"Let the kiddies get on with their play," Alice shouted. "Look at my Betsy; she looks like a little angel."

"Bugger off, Hector," John Goodchild shouted from mid-crowd. "You always try and spoil things."

Hector turned to look at the audience. The blank looks of some and aggressive chants of others made him re-evaluate the risk to his own personal safety.

"Okay, okay," he said. "Maybe I'm being a bit hasty."

"Thank you," said Elizabeth. She turned to the stage once more and nodded to the Ghost of Brexit Past.

"Sorry about the interruption children. Please continue."

The children re-positioned themselves and waited for the focus of attention to return.

"After Big Bang," the Ghost of Brexit Past repeated the words and the cymbals clanged once more, "financial services were deregulated and this made lots of people lots of money and that made lots of people very happy."

A cheer went up in the audience and as they quietened Bellyflop Rudder stood up to take centre stage.

"Now that investment banks are not using their own money, do you think they are taking more risks?"

"Yes we are!" said Stonking Rich. "Why on earth wouldn't we?"

"Shouldn't we monitor them or something?" Bellyflop Rudder positioned a finger to her lip to ask her question.

"I know!" said Diddums Hardheart. "We'll create the Financial Services Authority; they will monitor each bank to make sure they are doing things properly."

"But who will pay for it?" asked Giddyup Stirrup.

"Why, the Financial Services Industry of course," said Stonking Rich.

Off-piste, Elizabeth turned to Rafael.

"So go on, tell me what she said then."

"What who said?"

"Ava! You said she said she didn't want to do the play."

"I said she wasn't keen that was all." At that moment the lights on the stage shone into his face and he put his hand up to shield his eyes. The Past Ghost was addressing the audience.

"And lots of people made lots of money and lots of people were happy," she bellowed out.

Elizabeth was not happy. She looked at her husband.

"So, tell me why wasn't she keen?"

"I think she felt you would want her to write something... you know..."

"No, I don't know. Wha...?"

The lights on the stage dimmed once more.

"...hang on, Sydney's up."

"Oy you lot!" Sydney was addressing the children in the chairs. Rafael and Elizabeth both fell silent to watch their youngest child.

"When deregulation happened, things changed. Large companies took over smaller companies. Young people went to the cities for work and didn't return, so councils cut down the bus routes and put up fares, cutting many of the smaller villages off. Did any of you think this was a problem? No!"

There was a short pause in the theatrics, a silence reflected by the audience.

"You know, what we need is plenty of cheap labour." Stonking Rich stood up and shouted the words so loudly that many in the audience giggled.

"You can't say that!" said Bellyflop Rudder. "We need to put a positive spin on it."

"Okay," said Stonking Rich. "How about, what we need are lots of hard-working talented people."

"Much better."

The spotlight returned to Sydney.

"So in 2004 you lot said we won't bother to limit the flow of people into the country as most other EU countries did so lots of people came from Europe."

A group of seven children walked onto the stage, they went over to the tables but there was only enough space for three of them to sit down so four of them had to sit on the floor.

Bellyflop Rudder stood up.

"We must make it easier for businesses to hire and fire people."

Blarney Scumbag shouted from his chair.

"We must curb people's employment rights. Make them think twice about going to a tribunal if they feel hard done by."

Elizabeth turned to Rafael once more.

"Talking about feeling hard done by, are you sleeping with her? Again…"

"What! Who?"

"Well, 'Raffy darling'… you're always so bloody close."

"Ava? No! Have you gone completely mad? We're friends, that's all…"

"With benefits?"

"Where is this coming fro…?"

A drum roll interrupted the pair of them and the Ghost of Brexit Past appeared at the front of the stage once more.

"Then in 2008 there was another big bang. Only this time it made lots of people poorer and that made lots of people unhappy."

Blarney Scumbag stood up.

"Oh dear, it's not our fault. It's because of what's been happening in America."

As he sat down Bellyflop Rudder stood up.

"Oh dear, silly us. It's not really our fault, we have been monitoring each individual bank. We should have been monitoring the banking system as a whole."

Stonking Rich stood up.

"There's only one thing for it."

Together all the children on chairs shouted out:

"Budget cuts! Austerity!"

Rafael laughed. Not at the play, his amusement was directed to his wife.

"You thinking I'm having an affair with Ava is like me thinking you're having an affair with Crispin…"

Elizabeth reddened. Rafael spotted the change of colour.

"You look embarrassed… you're not, are you?!"

Elizabeth turned her back on him to watch the children on the stage.

"My God, you are!"

"Don't be ridiculous!" she said without turning around.

"You just blushed. That means something."

"Shhhhh." This time Elizabeth did turn round to look at her husband. She pointed to the stage. "The play."

Stonking Rich and Blarney Scumbug were walking over to where the children were sitting at the tables. They got hold of a bench end and tipped it up so that the children slid off. Then Jan strode onto the stage, picked up the bench and carried it away. There was a scramble to sit on the remaining bench and those who managed it were crushed up close to each other. The rest of the children sat on the floor.

Rafael watched the performance without taking any notice.

"I want to know what's going on." He hissed at his wife louder than he intended.

"How much have you had to drink?" Elizabeth's voice matched her husband's decibel for decibel. "Have you been smoking?"

"Maybe," said Rafael.

"Dope?"

"I might ha…"

"I say this is a marvellous play you've put on." It was Crispin. "Here, I bought you a glass of wine each. Thought you might need it."

Rafael glared at Crispin, standing there with a glass of red wine in each hand. The lights went down on the stage casting shadows across the three of them.

"We were just talking about you." Rafael turned to Crispin. "I hear you and Elizabeth have..."

Crispin turned to look first at Rafael and then at Elizabeth. His smile evaporated.

"Have what? Elizabeth and I have what?"

"Been sleeping together," said Rafael, nodding first to him and then to Elizabeth.

Rafael was not prepared for the look of shock on Crispin's face, or the laughter that followed. There were shushes from the audience. Someone even shouted 'Shut up!'

"Sorry!" Crispin shouted out. Then he spoke quietly. "Me sleep with Elizabeth? That's bloody hilarious!"

Rafael reddened. He returned his attention to the stage once more, children were squashed together sitting on benches and on the floor. Pearl and Riku, this time dressed as elderly people, got up from their place on the floor. To help the audience buy into their charade of old age Pearl had been given a walking stick and Riku an ear trumpet which they each used with gusto.

"I'm so excited," said Pearl, leaning over her stick.

"Sorry, what was that? I didn't hear you," said Riku, waving his ear trumpet.

"I said I'm ever so excited," Pearl shouted again.

"So am I," Riku shouted back. "I can't wait to vote."

"What box you gonna tick?"

"Doooh, the leave box, of course..." said Riku as they headed off the stage.

The other children got up off the floor to follow them. There was a delay of a few seconds during which a grunt and then a snore could be heard.

"Blast!" hissed Elizabeth almost to herself. "It's PeeTurD! He's properly crashed out!"

Pearl and Riku returned and stood centre stage together. Riku was just about to open his mouth when there was another louder grunt and another snore, but not just one. The noise continued, in, out, in, out, rasping like a pneumatic drill on a kerbstone.

Riku stood facing the audience and burst into tears.

"I... I can't..." He turned and pointed at PeeTurD, who had slid down the side of his throne and was laying with his head on the armrest. "He's making too much noise."

On her own initiative Pearl stepped out of her character, went over to PeeTurD and stood in front of him.

"Somebody shut him up," shouted Roman, "before I do."

Elizabeth got onto the stage and was heading towards Pearl but it was too late. The child kicked PeeTurD in the shin and he jumped awake.

"What! Where the fuck am I?" he shouted.

"Hey! No bad words in front of the children," shouted Jan.

Several audience members booed.

"You're the bad king in our play," said Pearl, staring directly at him. "And you're ruining it cos you're snoring. And you've made him cry." She turned and pointed at Riku, who had stopped sobbing and was rubbing his eyes.

"Is it time to go home yet?" PeeTurD asked with a yawn.

"Not long now!" Elizabeth spoke briskly.

She put her hands on Pearl's shoulders, turned her around and guided her gently back towards Riku, then she knelt down to speak to him.

"Are you okay?" she asked. "Do you want to continue?"

Riku set his mouth firm and nodded his head.

"Good boy," she said, smiling at him. Then she turned and left the stage.

"Hurrah!" Riku shouted the words loudly to a huge cheer from the audience. When they quietened he shouted out once more. "It's leave!"

"How could they?" said a voice from the group of children sitting around the table.

The lights went down until a single spotlight shone on a spare space on the stage. Sydney stepped into its glare and turned to the children representing the government sitting on their chairs.

"I as your Collective Conscience would point out that every ten years in this country you send us a census questionnaire asking us for loads of information about ourselves. You apparently do this to enable you to target resources properly, but since the year 2000 our country has seen large increases to our population and..."

"You should give us facts and figures, love, not just make vague statements," Paul Hollyoak shouted out.

Sydney stopped and looked off-stage to her mother. Elizabeth saw a fleeting look of panic.

"Oh shut up Paul," shouted Rafael.

Elizabeth looked at her husband. He acknowledged the look by way of a wink and then turned into the crowd heading towards Paul who was sitting at a table mid-way in. Without another thought Elizabeth got up and joined her daughter on the stage.

"Do you mind if I take over for just a second?" she whispered.

"Go ahead," Sydney said, stepping back.

Elizabeth stood and stared at the audience, paying particular attention to Rafael who was standing over Paul talking to him.

"Actually, I do have some statistics for anyone who's interested." She continued without waiting for a response. "For your information, the estimated population in 2000 was fifty-nine million and now in 2016 our population is estimated at sixty-five and a half million people. Since 2010 the number of police officers has fallen by twenty-one thousand." She paused to jeers from several people in the audience. "Now only a complete fool would suggest that that won't increase crime levels. And did you know the UK spends slightly less than the EU average on public and private healthcare? I could go on about housing and our infrastructure but I for one would prefer for the children to get on with their play."

"So would we," shouted Alice Grubb.

Elizabeth turned to Sydney.

"Well, Collective Conscience, are you okay to continue?"

Sydney nodded.

"Thanks, Mum," she whispered.

Elizabeth retreated and Sydney took her part once more.

"Instead of growing our infrastructure and building longer tables to cope with the increase in our population, our government did the opposite. They started to dismantle our infrastructure to save money. They devised cruel cuts which impacted the most vulnerable in our society and called it austerity!"

The lights went down, leaving the stage in darkness.

"And now it's time for a break," Elizabeth shouted out.

Hector Oliphant came and stood beside her.

"Please tell me you ordered enough food for the buffet," he whispered.

"Depends how much people want to eat."

Hector put his hand up to his head as if in deep thought before looking at her again.

"More cuts?" he said.

Elizabeth nodded.

"Please help yourself to food," she shouted.

"At last," said Alice. "I'm starving."

"So am I," said Evelyn.

"You should have brought a picnic," said Roman Winters. "We did, I'm a bit peckish now though," he added before heading to the buffet with a couple of his own plates.

"I hope there haven't been any cuts made to the food budget," Kirk Scott shouted from his place in the queue.

Elizabeth didn't respond. Kirk addressed her again.

"It was meant as a joke. Please tell me you think it's funny…"

"Not so much funny," said Elizabeth, "as accurate…"

"Is that all there is? Measly old crisps and a few sandwiches?" shouted Bill Inghurst.

Elizabeth nodded.

"Due to cuts in the budget" she said. "However, I do prefer the word austerity, it seems more in context… you know, language more in keeping with the EU theme."

She listened to complaints of 'All the cheese sandwiches have gone' and 'Any more crisps?', and she watched as it was those with pointy elbows who came away with their plates full.

"So you wanted to make a point."

Elizabeth jumped; Hector was beside her again.

"Do you honestly think this was the way to do it?"

"I just wanted people to understand how irresponsible it is to host an event – any event – without putting in place the correct..."

She spotted Rafael approaching.

"All sorted, Paul's apologised," he said with a smile. "For the interruption, I mean." He looked at his wife and then turned to his daughter.

"This is why I fell in love with your mother," he said.

"Why?" said Sydney. "It's only a play."

"Because your mother is nutty," said Rafael. "A right proper nut case."

Elizabeth felt herself redden once more. She looked at Sydney, imploring a reaction. A few seconds later a smile appeared.

"Crispin seemed very relieved just now," said Rafael almost to himself.

"When?"

"When I accused him of sleeping with you... "

"Mum! No! You haven't! Not with Uncle Crispin..."

"Don't be ridiculous, of course I haven't. Your father wasn't thinking straight." Elizabeth turned to Rafael. "Will you be more careful what you say in front of her."

"I am here, you know."

"Sorry..." said Elizabeth as she stood on tiptoe, attempting to look over the heads of the people queuing for food.

"I know something's going on," said Rafael.

"You know what your problem is?" said Elizabeth having placed both feet back flat on terra firma. "You're a bloody fool sometimes. You don't see what's staring you in the face."

"So, Mum, are you coming home now?"

"Of course, come here - give me a hug."

It was a long-lost bear hug until Sydney realised where she was and stepped back to regain her composure. Rafael turned to Elizabeth.

"Come on; tell me what I'm missing."

"Now is not the time or place to discuss this." Elizabeth looked at her husband. "Besides, it's not my secret to tell."

"Secret? What secret?"

"I'm just going to go and say hi to Ruby. Will Lars be okay, do you think?"

"Best wait till he goes out for a smoke; he's not quite there yet."

Elizabeth looked over to Ruby, caught her eye and waved. Ruby returned her smile.

"They'll be a riot soon unless you find more food from somewhere," said Rafael.

Elizabeth turned to Judy who was sitting at the side of the stage, a group of younger children around her examining her swollen belly. Their eyes met, Elizabeth gave a polite nod and Judy stood up.

"Come on children, it's time for Part Two," she said.

"And now we have Part Two of our play," Elizabeth shouted from the sidelines.

Several shushes, a single 'shut up you lot' and the chats and whispers hushed to silence.

The lights went up on the stage revealing a scene of calm. At the back, Bellyflop Rudder, Blarney Scumbag and the others were sitting on their chairs asleep. Another group of children sat crushed around the table, also asleep, while the rest of the children lay dozing on the floor. The sound of a tambourine whispered over the crowd and as it did so a figure dressed in a long overcoat strode onto the stage carrying a plate of cakes in each hand. The figure walked along the front of the stage smiling and nodding to the audience, teasingly offering out the plates. Then he walked up to the children at the back sitting on the chairs.

"Wakey wakey! Time to get up!" It was the voice of the ever-confident Byron Mark.

The children on the chairs jumped awake and their eyes widened as they spotted the figure in front of them, arms outstretched, offering cakes on plates.

"Morning! Fancy a Fondant Fancy?" Byron shoved the plates into their faces. "Or there's éclairs, Swiss roll, Eccles cake, Tottenham cheesecake, Death by Chocolate?"

Bellyflop Rudder stretched out and was about to take a cream horn.

"I'll have one," shouted Stonking Rich, making a grab for a whole plate. The cake holder laughed and pulled back both plates, making the audience cheer. "Who are you?"

"Who am I? Why, I am the Ghost of Brexit Present of course and we need to talk."

"Blimey," shouted Diddums Hardheart. "Can I have cake? I want one."

The children sitting crushed around the table started to wake, rubbing their eyes and yawning. The Ghost of Brexit Present turned and smiled, then walked over to them.

"Want some?" The Ghost placed the two plates with just a couple of cakes left onto the table. The children made a grab for them and they were gone.

On the floor Riku, Olivia Goodchild – the younger and better behaved sister of Oliver - and the other children stretched awake.

"I dreamt of cakes," Riku said. "It was yummy; there was cream... and chocolate..."

"That wasn't a dream, silly," said Olivia. "He brought us some." She pointed to the Ghost of Brexit Present. "But they ate them all."

Hector sidled up to Elizabeth. She felt his presence but deliberately didn't make eye contact.

"You do realise your actions will reflect badly on all of us on the council," he hissed at her.

"Just blame it all on me, I really don't mind."

Meanwhile back on stage Riku leant over and tugged the end of the Ghost's coat. The Ghost looked down at him.

"Please can I have a cake?"

The Ghost shook his head and nodded towards the table.

"Too late, all gone," he said.

The lights shone onto the empty plates then blacked out. They stayed that way for a few seconds and then came up again, this time shining on the children sitting on the floor.

At the side of the stage Hector was hissing at Elizabeth.

"You know you've broken all manner of regulations."

This time she turned and looked at him.

"So what?"

"So what? Is that all you've got to say - so what?"

"Shhhh! Watch the play." Elizabeth pointed towards the children.

The Ghost of Brexit Present was striding around the stage.

"Okay," he said stepping over the children on the floor. "You sir, why did you vote to leave the EU?" He pointed at Riku.

"Because I thought the government needed to be punished for how they've treated people."

"I see," said the Ghost, turning to the children on the chairs.

"The trouble with people like you," Diddums Hardheart shouted out, "is you just don't see the bigger picture."

"And you do see the bigger picture, but we're just blobs of paint to you," Riku shouted back.

"Old people like you shouldn't be allowed to vote," Blarney Scumbag shouted out. "You'll be dead soon."

"But I fought for our democracy in the last war AND voted to join the EU in 1975," said Riku.

"What about you, sir, what do you think?" The Ghost turned to a boy sitting on the floor twizzling his long hair. He looked up, his face dirtied with face paint. It was Caleb Johnson's son Jethro.

"I had a job but I kept being late cos the bus was late, so they sacked me. Plenty of people looking for work who can get here on time – that's what they said to me. So I lost my job, I couldn't afford to pay the rent so I lost my home…"

"Loser," shouted out Blarney Scumbag.

"I'm just an ordinary bloke who doesn't have a fancy degree or anything like that. I just want to work, be treated respectfully and provide for my family," he said. "I can't do that anymore… so I guess you're right, I am a…"

At that moment a commotion by the entrance claimed the audience's attention.

Standing just inside the doorway was a group of sopping wet young people. The unseen – those stuck outside - were pushing and shoving them from behind, trying to get in. The Ghost of Brexit Present looked at them and then at Elizabeth.

"What shall I do?" he mouthed to her.

Elizabeth walked onto the stage, stood in the middle and addressed the children.

"Hold on a sec." She spoke quietly. "Just sit down and I'll go and see what's going on." She left the stage and, zigzagging across the room to avoid tables and bodies, made her way to the entrance. On the way she passed Mr Esposito; she smiled at him and gave a short nod, then continued her journey. By the time she got there,

there were more than twenty sopping wet young people crowded inside the doors.

"What's going on?" asked Elizabeth. "Who are you?"

"We heard there was something going on," said a youth with torn jeans and an anorak.

A young lady next to him, barely dressed and supping from a bottle of cider, butted in.

"Yeah, we thought we'd come along."

"Excuse me, this is a private event," said Hector, approaching.

"What, it's not a rave?" asked a young lady with long black hair, ripped jeans and a top cut to her naval.

"No, it's not," said Hector.

"It's private," said Bill Inghurst. "And you must have a ticket."

"I've got money," said the long-haired youth at the front, putting his can of beer down onto the floor and attempting to interrogate the pockets of his overly tight jeans. After dipping his hand into each front and back pocket he opened his palm out flat. There was a ten-pence piece and three two-penny pieces.

"Oh, er, not much though…"

"I'm afraid all of the tickets have been sold," said Hector.

"Oh man," sighed the young woman. "But we've walked all this fucking way."

"We just wanna party…" said the lady with the torn trousers.

"…and get out of the rain," added a more smartly dressed bearded lad who was standing beside her.

"Now look," said Hector. "You cannot come in here, we're completely full. I'm sorry. Please go away."

"But you can't send them back out there, it's pouring," said Ava, approaching the group. "They'll all catch their deaths. Look at them; they've barely got any clothes on."

As if aware of the intrusion, Juliette let out several loud brays from her settlement in the crèche.

"Was that a donkey?" asked a red-haired girl in an orange jumpsuit.

"Definitely yes. It's a donkey honk… room for a donkey, but no room for us," said the chap with the beard.

A lightning strike and there was more pushing and shoving as the few remaining outside attempted to cram into the marquee.

"Hold on a minute," Elizabeth shouted into the microphone. Everyone jumped and turned to look at her.

"These poor people have trekked all this way and want to come in out of the rain."

"But they haven't got tickets," said Roman Winters. "So they can't."

"We can't turn them away," said Evelyn. "Not in this."

"I agree," said Caleb. "It would be a very mean thing to do."

"Couldn't agree more," said Elizabeth. She looked over at Rafael. He looked back at her but there was no smile.

"I think we should vote on it," she said. "Come on in, everyone, and get out of the rain while we have a vote."

There was some shuffling and pushing and soon the entire group were standing just inside the entrance.

"I'm starving," said an obviously pregnant young lady. Elizabeth heard, walked over to her and got hold of her hand, pulling her near. Then she turned to address everyone.

"Now, who here thinks we should turn this group of soggy young people back out into the rain? All in favour of allowing them in please put up your hands." She counted fifteen hands. "All those who think they should be chucked back out into the rain put up your hands."

Most people abstained from the vote but there were certainly more than fifteen hands up; she didn't bother to count them. Instead she turned to the new arrivals.

"I'm sorry, you are going to have to leave," she said.

Another crack of thunder made everybody jump.

"Maybe they could stay a few minutes," said Hector.

"Until the rain stops," Caleb added.

"Wait a minute," said Elizabeth. She turned to her audience again. "Can I ask why we can't let them in?"

"They've not got tickets," shouted Roman Winters.

"Not enough tables and chairs," shouted Paul Hollyoak. "Not enough for us, let alone them."

"And obviously there's not enough food," shouted Alice Grubb.

"So we're not going to let these people in, even though they are stranded, because we don't have enough tables or chairs or food." She paused and looked around. "So, supposing we did have enough tables and chairs and food, would we let them in then?"

"Of course," said Paul Hollyoak.

"Course we bloody would," Roman shouted.

People looked at each other. Elizabeth noticed a flicker of comprehension amongst some. There were whispers through the crowd and then silence.

"Look," said Elizabeth, "it's too late to do anything about the tables and chairs but I can do something about food. Mr Esposito has kindly offered to get his son's to drive over in their Land Rover with pizzas for us. So who here thinks we should turn this group of soggy young people back out into the rain now? All those in favour of allowing them in please put up your hands."

As hands went up, the result was clear: an overwhelming vote to allow them in. There were shouts of approval as they were invited to disperse and mingle with the crowd. A loud bray from Juliette in the crèche suggested her buy-in.

A couple of minutes later and the young people were integrated, sitting in spare spaces on the ground. Many were offered coats to help them dry off. Elizabeth and Rafael's eyes met; he smiled at her and she smiled back before heading for the stage.

"For all our newcomers, the children of Bedwell Ash are putting on an EU-themed play for us, then later we have a band and a disco."

"A disco? Is that like a rave?" asked the lady in the orange jumpsuit.

"A bit, I suppose, but without the trespassing and drugs," Ava shouted across.

"We'll go from your bit." Elizabeth nodded to the Ghost of Brexit Present.

The children repositioned themselves, and the audience turned their attention to the stage once more.

The Ghost of Brexit Present went over to the children on the floor.

"Room for a little one?"

"And so you all voted to leave the EU." He placed a pretend microphone in front of Olivia Goodchild. "Can I ask why?"

"Because my pensions been delayed twice now, and I'm really struggling."

"That's nothing to do with the EU," shouted Bellyflop Rudder.

"She's right, you know," said the Ghost of Brexit Present.

"I know," said Olivia. "But I can't vote for more of the same, can I? We need things to change."

"Aren't you being a wee bit harsh?" said the Ghost.

Olivia shook her head. Then Riku put his hand up and the Ghost went over and handed him the microphone.

"It's simple." The boy was well spoken, but the words were quiet, the audience hushed to silence.

"When you invite people to a party you make sure you have enough food and tables and chairs for them."

"You build longer tables," Pearl shouted over from her place on the floor. "Not make the tables you've got shorter."

"Hear hear," a voice shouted from the audience.

Sitting leaning against one of the tables, dressed in jeans and an oversized top, was Charlotte Hollyoak. The Ghost went over and stood next to her.

"And you, Madam, why did you vote to leave. What were your reasons?" he asked.

"I voted leave because I am concerned about the difference in our cultures," she said.

"Now that sounds a bit racist," said the Ghost.

"Listen, young man, I said I'm concerned about the difference in our cultures, not the difference in our races."

"Aren't they the same thing?"

"There are people who would like us to think they are but they most definitely are not."

"I see." He turned to nine-year-old Keiko Winters. "And, Madam, why did you vote to leave?"

"Because I'm a racist," she said. "I don't like people from different countries coming over here."

"Best move on," said the Ghost. He turned to the children sitting on their chairs at the back. "And now I would ask you all…" He took a deep breath and pointed at the children sitting on the floor. "To walk in their shoes." He pointed to Keiko. "Except hers. Don't walk in hers. Shoo!" he said, making a dismissive gesture towards her.

Keiko got up and snarled at the Ghost.

"Go for it!" shouted PeeTurD.

"You seriously need to shut up and stop interrupting these children." Roman Winters stood up and shouted.

"And who's going to make me?" PeeTurD shouted back from his splintered throne.

"I will if you don't shut up." Roman yelled back.

Several audience members cheered.

"And me!" Kirk Scott shouted when the cheering had died down.

Elizabeth stepped onto the stage and went up to PeeTurD.

"Now the play is nearly over, please sit down and do not interrupt the children again." She turned to the Ghost of Brexit Present and smiled. "Go from 'And now I would ask you all...'"

The Ghost of Brexit Present turned to the children on the chairs.

"And now I would ask you all..." He turned around and pointed to the children sitting on the floor. "To walk in their shoes."

"Do we have to?" asked Diddums Hardheart.

The Ghost nodded. The children on the chairs bent forward to slip off their shoes, got up and padded towards the children on the floor.

Giddyup Stirrup made a face.

"But look, their shoes are all worn," he shouted.

"Put them on," said the Ghost of Brexit Present.

"Do we really have to wear them?" asked Diddums Hardheart. "They're all tatty."

The Ghost nodded.

The children put on the shoes and walked around the stage, acting out their discomfort through their facial expressions. Then they returned to their chairs and sat on the floor in front of them.

The lights went down and it went dark. In the darkness a voice spoke; it was Bimbo Haystacks.

"Did we do this?"

"No, they did it to themselves!" shouted Stonking Rich.

"Silence!" shouted the Ghost of Brexit Present. "Yes, you did do this, and there will be worse to come."

From darkness came light, there was movement in the shadows. Onto the stage walked Miriam, her skinny frame padded out to make her look fat. She carried a stick in one hand and held a lead in the other. The end of the lead was tethered to a small boy, her little brother Leo dressed in rags. Miriam pushed herself onto one of the benches causing two children at the other end to fall to the floor. Then she used her stick to forcefully guide her little brother to lie down on the floor beside her.

"Who are they?" asked Diddums Hardheart.

"That one," said the Ghost, pointing to Miriam, "is Greed." Then he pointed to Leo. "And that one is Integrity."

The lights went down again leaving only the Ghost in the spotlight. Riku got up from the floor and crept over to the Ghost. The Ghost stooped down and Riku whispered in his ear while pointing to the black cocoon-like figure still lurking in the shadows behind PeeTurD. The Ghost stood up straight again and looked down at Riku.

"You ask me who that is?" he said. "Why, that is Bilderberg."

Riku beckoned the Ghost down and whispered into his ear again. When he had finished whispering, the Ghost stood up once more.

"You ask why he is here?" he said. "I'm sorry lad, I can't tell you, you'll have to Google that one." Then he turned his attention to the children sitting on the floor in front of their chairs.

"You must all learn from your mistakes," he said. "Greed must make way for Integrity. It is Integrity who should have a seat at your table."

What should have happened next - had the original script been observed - was a short contemplative silence followed by appreciative applause followed by a visit from the Ghost of Brexit Yet-to-Come. It had worked perfectly in rehearsal, but this was no rehearsal and instead of a visit from the Future Ghost the attention of everyone on stage and all those in the audience was diverted to the entrance once again where an intoxicated Ghost from Demelza's past appeared in the form of Freddy - pushing people aside and stepping drunkenly over sitting bodies as he attempted to make his way to the stage.

"Demelza! Demelza!"

It was a melancholy cry.

Elizabeth turned to look at what was going on.

"Dad!" Then she spotted her sister. "Isobel?"

Isobel was attempting to follow in her father's footsteps, but he was no Good King Wenceslas and she was no Page, and instead of marking his footsteps, between them, father and daughter trod boldly on hands, tripped over feet and trampled on bags and bits and bobs en route to a showdown already taking place in Freddy's head.

"Dad! Come back," Isobel shouted. But it was not to be; her father was unhearing, unseeing of either of his daughters. He only had eyes for Demelza but try as he might he couldn't spot her anywhere.

"Demelza!"

Elizabeth turned her attention to Isobel.

"Isobel!" she shouted. "What are you doing here?"

"Dooh, trying to catch him." She pointed in Freddy's direction.

Elizabeth headed for her father - who was heading for the stage - attempting to cut him off.

"Dad!" she shouted.

"Demelza!"

Freddy swerved to avoid Elizabeth but she could see Rafael was closing in on him from behind. He sped up and reached the stage.

"What's going on?" Elizabeth shouted to Isobel.

Freddy reached the stage and stepped over the children without treading on even one. Centre stage he turned, faced the audience and, teetering slightly, put his hand inside his jacket.

"Demelza!"

"He's getting a g…!" a voice shouted from the audience just as Freddy pulled out a small box from an inside pocket.

He got down on one knee, held the box high and turned and addressed the audience.

"Demelza, wherever you are… will you marry me?" He held out his hand with the boxed ring, offering it to the audience, scanning for his would-be bride. "I know you're here somewhere."

There were oooohs and ahhhs and cries of 'how romantic'.

Demelza was sitting up the back with the Morris Dancers, still in her steam punk garb and adorned with hair feathers. She turned and bellowed at her would-be suitor.

"You silly old sod, you're drunk again, aren't you?"

"Mum!" Elizabeth shouted to her. "Please…"

"Trust you to interrupt the kiddies!"

"Say yes," the audience started to shout. "Yes! Yes! Yes!"

"Not on your flaming nellie!" Demelza turned to the audience and shouted back at them. "I'm glad we never married! I'm proud to be a bloody spinster!"

"Thanks for that, Mother," said Elizabeth under her breath.

"Dad!" Isobel shouted. "When I suggested you propose to Mum…" She stopped when she spotted Elizabeth's face.

"You did what?!"

"All I said was, if you want to marry Mum then you should ask her." She hesitated. "I didn't mean today… not here… not now…"

Elizabeth attempted to close in on her father. Meanwhile he had dropped to both knees and looked like a wounded bear sitting on all fours to steady himself. She approached him, stooped down and whispered,

"Dad, do you really think this is going to make Mum realise how madly in love she is with you?"

From his place on the ground he looked up at her.

"Pro… probably not."

"How much have you had to drink?" She felt her anger return as she spoke. Then she felt a presence beside her. It was her mother.

"You daft old goat," said Demelza. "You're only asking because you're scared of being kicked out of the country after Brexit!"

"That's not true! I love you!" Freddy shouted to her.

Elizabeth looked closely at her mother.

"Mum, have you been drinking?"

"Just a few drops of dessert sherry, dear…"

Freddy attempted to stand up but it was obvious he wasn't going to make it without help. Between them Isobel and Elizabeth pulled him up. Once back on his feet again, he leant on Isobel's shoulder and she struggled to help him walk off the stage. As he left he turned to Demelza.

"Marry me, please... that other woman, it was a mistake... I love you... only you." He spoke slowly so as not to slur his words. "Forever ..."

"Yes! Yes! Yes!" shouted the audience.

"No! No! No!" shouted PeeTurD. "No more migrants...!"

"Shut up, PeeTurD!" Elizabeth shouted at him as she watched her father and sister leave the stage. Then she turned to face the audience once more. She had their attention, a sea of faces all engrossed in her family business.

"Please let me apologise for the little domestic incident which you have all just witnessed," she said. "It was totally unexpected." Before anybody could reply she turned to the children.

"Come on, children, let's finish the last bit."

Like a tampered chess game, the children once again re-assembled in readiness for their next move. As they slotted themselves back into position the audience hushed once more. For several seconds there was a noiseless dusk and then, like aurora borealis, the marquee lit up with swirls of light capturing the full attention of the adults and mesmerising the children. As if to reward their stillness a single child's voice broke the silence. It was the voice of thirteen-year-old Somerset Mark.

"April is the cruellest month...

Several audience members stirred recognising the first line of The Waste Land. As the boy spoke, the light and shadow slowed and then stilled. The stillness encompassed the marquee as if a magical wand had been waved hypnotising his audience into quiet. It lasted until the mention of the word 'summer.' Suddenly a spotlight flashed on like a flare in mid-ocean. It searched the stage before settling on the row of purple dressed children now sitting back in their chairs, momentarily highlighting each child before passing on. Once it reached the end of the row it shone briefly on PeeTurD who was trying to doze.

"What the...!" He grizzled awake.

The spotlight moved to its next target: a sign reading 'Polling Station'. It held the position for several seconds before snapping the stage into darkness once more.

A few seconds of silence and Moses turned a knob and reset a switch to return the stage to a misted visibility. He struggled with the limited technology at his fingertips but eventually presented to the audience a semi convincing sunrise. Darkness turned to light as the spotlight increased its luminosity but a broken bulb and a haphazard switch finger ensured that, as dawn broke onto the stage, the marquee encapsulated a majesty of morning more akin to a disaster area than a poetic sunup.

As visibility became sharper it revealed a scene of children, some sitting, and some lying on the floor. Nature stepped in with an obliging thunder clap, providing a sense of haunting reality.

A single figure swathed in a dark coat and wearing a top hat walked slowly onto the stage, a spotlight picking up and following the movement.

"Aw shit!"

"Ow! That was my foot!"

The lights on the stage brightened. The figure dressed in black turned to the audience and grinned.

"Sorry," said Somerset Mark to his audience. "That wasn't meant to happen." Then he turned to the child sitting on the floor. "Sorry, sis."

"You did that on purpose!"

"Harper! Somerset! Behave!" The voice of Markus Mark boomed out from where he was sitting on the floor mid crowd. The two children froze and turned to look at their father. After a few seconds he bellowed again. "Continue!"

Somerset immediately returned to the scripted shadowy character. He walked to a sign; 'Polling Station' and bowed his head.

"What's he doing? What's going on?" Blarney Scumbag shouted out.

"I think it's the Ghost of Brexit Future," said Bellyflop Rudder. She turned to the figure. "Excuse me, young man."

The figure turned to her with features unseen.

"Am I right in saying that you are going to show us things that are going to happen to us?"

There was a movement, a possible nod of its shrouded head.

"I say, he's a rather sinister character," said Giddyup Stirrup. "Didn't bother to bring cakes or anything."

"Where's security? Get them in here now," shouted Stonking Rich.

"Why doesn't it speak to us?" shouted Blarney Scumbag.

The figure beckoned to the children at the tables and they got up and started to follow him; then the children on the floor got up and – led by Riku - they followed him to the 'Polling Station' sign. Standing in front of the sign Riku started so sing.

"London Bridge is falling down,
Falling down, falling down,
London Bridge is falling down..."

"Are you going to vote?" Pearl interrupted him.

"No," said Riku. "Are you?"

"Of course not," she replied. "There's no point."

"What's going on?" said Bellyflop Rudder.

"Nobody wants to vote," said Riku.

The lights went down on the stage and after a couple of seconds there were cheers and clapping from the audience.

Sydney returned to the stage as the clapping stopped.

Without warning PeeTurD let out a loud yawn.

"I've had enough of this," he said, standing up, stretching and accidently whacking Somerset Mark on the head.

"Watch it, you big bully," the child shouted out.

"Karma." Harper giggled as she spoke.

"Quiet!" Markus Mark stood up and shouted. "Sit and be quiet! Behave yourselves!"

Somerset and Harper froze then sat down. PeeTurD obeyed the order too, sitting back down as a disobedient dog might when confronted with a whip-carrying master.

"Blimey," Rafael whispered over to his wife. "He sat down."

"That's because he's a cowardly bully. It's what they do when they're confronted," Elizabeth whispered back. "Now watch this bit…"

On the stage Sydney looked at her mother. An encouraging nod and she turned to address the audience.

"Now, we have a favour to ask. We need you to…"

"Help! Shut the doors! Shut the doors!" A voice shouted, distracting the attention of the audience once more. Mr Esposito's two first-born sons entered the marquee at speed, both heavily laden with pizza boxes. The voice belonged to son number one, twenty-two-year-old Enrico.

"We're being chased by an enormous fucking cow," shouted son number two, twenty-one-year-old Franco.

The soggy pair pulled up sharp once inside, causing the pizza boxes to fall forward.

"Shut the door! Shut the door!" shouted Enrico.

"Yaaaay, pizza!" shouted Roman.

"It was waiting for us when we parked the Landover. Biggest cow I've ever seen!"

Elizabeth manoeuvred herself through the crowd, shimmying around tables and stepping over bodies as she headed for the entrance. Once there she pulled open one of the tightly shut doors and there, merging into the darkness - sopping wet and slobbering - stood Romeo. As soon as he saw Elizabeth, he bellowed, then gave a soulful stare and a stepped-forward nudge, as if to suggest a meeting of like-minded souls.

"Oh, it's only Romeo," said Elizabeth, trying to regain her footing after the shove from Romeo's nose. "He wouldn't hurt a fly."

She stepped aside and there was a scuffle to get away from the entrance as Romeo took the opportunity to lumber in. Once inside he stood and looked around the room, searching for his missing donkey mate.

It may have been Romeo's bovine bouquet that alerted Juliette, or it may have been the screams from the crowd because as soon as she sensed her buddy was in the vicinity she upped her vocal volume and began to eee and aaaw, repeating the sound as a vocalist might a chorus in a melodic refrain recorded onto a buckled vinyl track.

From his seat near the entrance Bob's heart pounded excitement.

"Don't worry! I'll get him!" he shouted. He downed his fifth near full glass of red wine and picked up his jacket which was lying next to him. "I'll sort him out, get him under control."

"Here, let me help," said Crispin, offering a hand and a smile.

After several tugs Bob was upright on unsteady feet, peering at Romeo through thickened glasses.

"Try and get him to…" said Crispin.

"Husband, sit down," said Ava. "You've been drinking, you might hurt yourself."

Crispin returned to his space beside his wife and sat down.

"You be careful now," he reached for his camera. "I'll video it - this'll go viral for sure."

Bob held his jacket up and gazed at the bull as if attempting to psych the creature out. He took his bottle-end glasses off and gave them a wipe on his shirt before replacing them.

"Holy shit," he whispered to himself as he confronted the huge form. "He's a big bastard."

Romeo turned to Bob and as the two of them made eye contact, the animal lowered his head and walked towards him in an act of submission. The moment was lost in animal to human translation as Bob interpreted Romeo's meekness as an act of bovine aggression.

"Fucking hell!" he shouted as Romeo closed in. "He's coming at me!" He fell backwards, narrowly missing Ruby and Ava.

"Watch out!" shouted Ruby, glaring at him.

Once on the ground he struggled to get himself back onto his feet so that he could further distance himself from the animal. But the only thing that moved was Bob's bowels. He shat himself.

"You alright?" Crispin asked.

"Did you see it?" he said, his voice muffled, his underpants dense. "It went for me."

"Don't be ridiculous." Elizabeth stepped forward. "It's only Romeo. He's gentle as anything. He's got his, you know, his thingies, but they don't work… he's not a proper bull." She turned to Crispin. "He's looking for Juliette you see. Quick, go open the crèche door. He'll hear her and wander through."

Crispin obediently went and opened the door to the crèche, then ushered the few children in there out. Standing tied in the corner was Juliette, still vocalising her unhappiness at the current arrangement.

"Stand back," Elizabeth shouted.

Slowly and deliberately Romeo pawed the ground with his cloven Wagyu hoof. As if on cue, Juliette brayed; Romeo responded and started to lumber forward heading towards the dance floor.

"Just get out the way," Elizabeth shouted. "I'm sure he'll be fine when he sees Juliette." She looked around. "Farmer Garlic's here somewhere, she'll sort them out."

Each step Romeo took removed audience members from in front of him and it was not long before there was a human-free pathway across the dance floor en route to the crèche.

Elizabeth turned to Enrico and Franco who had taken refuge within the crowd. "Could you grab the pizzas and set them on the table, please?"

"I've found her!" It was Rafael; he pointed to the corner.

Elizabeth followed the point to the furthest corner of the marquee where Farmer Garlic was sitting propped up against a table leg singing to herself.

"Once upon a time there was a little white bull…"

Instead of her green overalls she wore embroidered jeans and a white cotton coat. It was what she called her 'country best' outfit. But with a near-drunk bottle of scotch hanging out of her patch pocket she looked like a drunken medic ready to give out advice on the current situation but completely failing to understand the urgency re the uninvited presence of her bull. Rafael went over and helped her up. She leant on his shoulder and they approached Romeo, who was by now standing in the centre of the dance floor. When Farmer Garlic spotted her pet she smiled, reached out, stepped forward and then fell onto him, grabbing him around the neck and hanging on tightly like a human garland. She attempted to stand up straight once more, whispered in his bull ear, turned around and then, like an uncertain tight-rope walker, did her level best to put one foot in front of the other as she headed to the crèche.

"Romeo! Romeo! Follow boy! Follow!" she shouted.

But Romeo stood his ground. She turned to look at him.

"Romeo! Follow!" she shouted again when she realised he hadn't moved. "Here boy!"

Romeo's only response was to raise his tail and let out a fart loud enough to contest the overhead thunder.

The breaking wind noise awoke young Christoph Roberto Urquhart Nickolai Trump who, after having completed his bottle of vodka, had fallen into a doze under one of the tables next to the dance floor. He jumped awake to the melodic pattern of flatulence and crawled out.

"Why, that was… beautiful," he said, attempting to stand upright. "So beautiful*...*" Once upright he staggered over to Romeo, headed for his rear end, and then leant against him and stared at his tail.

"That was beautiful, beautiful… more, please… again… I must remember this for my act."

Romeo obliged immediately by orchestrating a melody in gas. He turned his head, raised his tail and let rip a fume cappella. But this time as the refrain slowed his tail stayed raised and he opened his bovine bowels and pumped out a pile of bullshit large enough to grow a bed of roses.

Taken by surprise Christoph's initial instinct was to remain bullshit free so he stepped in retreat but it was too late.

"Aaaaargh!" The yell was more one of shock than horror. He tripped, slid backwards and landed amidst the steaming vapours. Rather than fight the moment he decided to go with the flow and unite with the bull and his bodily excretion cum last meal, so he lay back on the ground, manoeuvring arms and legs in unison, performing bullshit angels on the dance floor.

"I love my job!" he shouted.

Farmer Garlic turned and looked, first at the bull, then at Christoph and then at the crap resembling spinach stew spreading around the dance floor. Instantly she was semi-sober and her face lit up like a torch in a sewer.

"Good boy! Well done!" She turned to the crowd. "That's the first decent shit he's done in weeks!" she said as she patted her pet once more.

"Come on boy," she said, heading for the crèche once more. "Romeo! Follow!" This time Romeo followed her like a chick would its mother. When Juliette caught sight of them, the three enjoyed an un-staged, unadulterated, linguistic unification ritual expressed through Farmer Garlic's joyous coos, Romeo's moos and Juliette's braying. So content were they to be reunited they failed to notice the crèche doors close and were not aware they were theoretically barred from escaping should they wish to do so.

Elizabeth breathed a sigh of relief and smiled at Hector who was standing in front of the doors like a silent protector ensuring the captive trio stayed just that. She turned to Enrico and Franco.

"Would you like to stay?" she asked. "Join us?"

"No thank you," said Enrico.

"Best not," said Franco. "We're short-staffed in the restaurant."

"Can we come with you?" a voice shouted from the crowd.

"And me," another shouted.

"Sure," said Franco. "We can take five people."

"I'm done here," shouted PeeTurD, standing up and taking off his crown. "I've had enough of this." He unhooked his cloak.

"You're not done just yet," said Elizabeth. "I thought you could help me close the play. Not long now."

PeeTurD glared at her and sat down again.

"Now then," Elizabeth shouted, calling everyone to attention. "Let's clear up this mess as much as we can and let the children finish their play."

Paul Hollyoak and several other parents set about cleaning up the dance floor. A mop appeared, and a bucket.

"What do we do with him?" asked Kirk Scott, pointing at Christoph.

Elizabeth bent down to look at him.

"He seems happy enough," she said. "He's sound asleep – and look at the smile on his face."

"We can't just leave him there," said Kirk.

"Hold on a minute," said Elizabeth. "I've an idea." She went over to the buffet table and picked up a pile of white paper napkins. Then she returned to Christoph and placed them around the outline of his body. By the time she had finished, an exclusion zone had been created around him, making him look like a corpse in a crime scene.

Once this was completed, Elizabeth stood and watched as the crowd started to settle once more. People were eating pizza and chatting to each other. Coats were offered to the cold, seats to those who needed them.

"Reminds me of the war…" said Mr Melford.

"Bad news, I'm afraid."

Elizabeth turned around; it was Enrico. Behind him were Franco and the five deserters who had claimed their places in the escape vehicle.

"I've just been trying to turn the Land Rover around…"

"And?"

"It's got stuck in the ditch."

"Okay." She looked at the boy. "So…?"

"Honest. It's proper stuck."

"What's stuck?" asked Hector Oliphant, having taken temporary leave from guarding the crèche.

"Land Rover. It's got stuck in the ditch. It was an accident."

"You sure? Come on, show me."

Hector followed son number one to the marquee entrance. He peeked outside and recoiled when he saw it was tipping it down again.

"Honest," said the soaked lad. "It's good and proper stuck. We'll need a tractor to pull it out."

"I believe you," said Hector. "The only person with a tractor is locked in the crèche in a drunken stupor with a bull and a donkey."

"Farmer Garlic won't be going anywhere for a while," said Elizabeth, who had followed them. "Hopefully it will stop raining soon, and one of us can give you a lift when we all leave."

"Nobody will be leaving…," said Franco.

"…for a while…" said Enrico.

"Silly bastard drove it into the ditch," said Franco.

"No need be rude!" said Enrico.

Elizabeth turned to Franco.

"So why exactly is that a problem for the rest of us?"

"It's at the entrance as you turn in. Nobody will be able to get out, get onto the track." said Franco.

"I see." Elizabeth stood for a moment, then she turned to face them and smiled. "Come inside - join us. Best not mention it around just yet," she whispered before returning to the stage and addressing the crowd once more.

"And now, if you don't mind, we shall continue with the final part of our play," she said. She winked at Sydney. "We'll go from your final speech."

Sydney repositioned herself on the stage and stood there until everyone was quiet.

"And so we left the EU... or did we?"

A group of six children came onto the stage carrying a long table, which they placed in the centre. More children arrived carrying chairs and when all the furniture was well placed they sat down. The children sitting on the floor got up and joined them at the tables.

Somerset stepped forward stepped into his character as the Ghost of Brexit Yet-to-Come once more and walked across the stage. He stared first at the children and then at the audience, a nod and he turned and disappeared into the shadows at the side of the stage.

"Our government must expand our infrastructure," Sydney said addressing the audience. "We must build longer tables. There must be compassion, integrity and respect. Respect for workers' rights. Care for the vulnerable and help for the needy. We need to build more houses and schools, fund our police force and the NHS properly for integration to work." She paused as several audience members clapped.

"In the past we have had all of these things," said Riku from his place at the table. "Why should they be taken away from us?"

All the children stood up and turned to the audience. Riku stepped forward.

"We the children of Bedwell Ash hope you have enjoyed our play," he said.

The audience cheered, some clapped, some whistled loudly. Proud parents beamed.

"Now we would like to ask something in return." Sydney nodded to the volunteers and they spread themselves around the marquee and started to hand out slips of paper.

"What's all this, then?" Roman Winters shouted out.

"The volunteers are now handing out polling cards," Elizabeth replied. "We're having our own referendum and we would like to ask you to vote again for us here today. Please tick your chosen option and place the cards in the boxes around the marquee."

"But this is wrong!" shouted Evelyn. "There are three options on here."

"Yes," said Elizabeth. "There is now a 'Change' option. Because that is what many people believe the referendum vote was - a vote for change."

"She could be right." Caleb stood up and addressed the audience. "I would have voted change if there had been a change option. Sadly, it was an option denied to us, denied to you, me, everybody."

"So let's pretend there had been a change option," Elizabeth shouted out. "And see what happens."

Polling papers were handed out, boxes were ticked and the slips were posted into cardboard boxes painted royal blue for the occasion.

The children sitting around the table got up and came to the front of the stage. The rest of the children came onto the stage and crowded behind them. A cheer went up amongst the crowd until Elizabeth held up her hand and everybody hushed. She turned to the young actors.

"Thank you to the children for giving up your time and putting on such a splendid performance. And thank you to Judy for helping."

More clapping, then Elizabeth turned to the audience once more.

"We'll count the polling cards later," she said.

"Is it time for the disco yet?" shouted Alice Grubb. "Can't wait to throw a few shapes."

"Nearly," said Elizabeth. "Just one more thing we need to do. Peter Dawson, our king for the day, will you please step forward."

PeeTurD stood up from his throne and made his way slowly towards Elizabeth, his cloak dragging behind him, his crown at an angle on his head and a look of puzzlement on his face.

Elizabeth waited until he was next to her and then turned to the crowd.

"Mr Martin North, are you here?"

"He is," a woman's voice shouted.

"Mr Glyn Shepherd, are you here?"

"I am," a voice shouted from the crowd.

"Could I please ask both of you to stand up?"

In amongst the crowd a dark-haired man looking uncomfortable in a shirt and jeans and a red-faced man with thinning red hair and a grey suit with no tie stood up. Elizabeth turned to face them.

"First of all, thank you both for coming."

"I take it it was you who sent the tickets?" said Glyn Shepherd.

"You got free tickets too?" said Martin North.

"I sent free tickets to both of you," said Elizabeth. "Now, you two gentlemen don't know it but you have something, or I suppose I should say someone, in common."

"We do?" The two men looked at each other.

"Yes, you both know our king for the day," Elizabeth turned to face him as she spoke. "Peter Dawson."

"What's going on?" asked PeeTurD.

Elizabeth turned to him.

"I accuse you... or should I say, j'accuse you, Peter Dawson."

"Me, what have I done? What are you on about?" PeeTurD's fists clenched.

Rafael glared at Elizabeth and from his place amongst the crowd headed for the stage.

"She doesn't mean it. Honestly..." he shouted. "She's been reading Emile Zola... she gets carried away sometimes..."

Elizabeth ignored her husband and instead continued to stare at PeeTurD.

"I accuse you Peter Dawson of stealing your brother's inheritance."

"Now watch it." PeeTurD stared back at her, still tight-fisted.

"She doesn't mean it. She's at that funny age." Rafael shouted as he reached the stage.

This time Elizabeth turned and glared at her husband.

"Shut up! I do mean it." Then she turned to PeeTurD again. "When your father died, you…"

"I looked after my mother, that's what I did."

"You looked after her money, and with the help of these two unwitting gentlemen you stole…"

"You, you… you fucking bitch!"

And then the fight started.

AFTER THE STORM

" Cats can be very stupid sometimes." Rafael was sitting with his wife and family at the top table. He looked around the grand hall of the Millennium Community Hub packed with family and friends and villagers pleased that he had everybody's attention.

"I do hope you're not referring to my Clementine," Crispin shouted from his seat three place settings along.

"What are you talking about? Cats are clever… really clever animals!" Evelyn Smith (now guardian of seven cats) shouted out. She was sitting a couple of tables in with her family and Markus Mark and his family.

"Raffy darling, have you been drinking?" Ava asked. "The doctor told you not to drink while you're on the drugs."

"Of course I've been bloody drinking! Why wouldn't I? It's my…" Rafael looked down at Elizabeth sitting beside him, "…our… party. And thank you, Ava, I'm off the painkillers now."

"I was just saying," said Ava.

"Okay, let me explain myself," Rafael said. "We have two cats, Dingle and Toc. Now, in our house cats are not allowed in the bedroom."

"Ahh, poor kitties," Crispin shouted out.

"Sometimes Dingle sneaks in with me." Sydney turned to confide to Ruby.

"Does she indeed?" Elizabeth pretended to be angrier than she actually was. "We'll see about that."

"Busted," said Ruby to her sibling.

"You have a cruel streak in you, Elizabeth," Crispin shouted and then, after a brief pause when the nearest sound to a laugh was Georgina Soros gurgling at her mother from her high chair, he added, "I'm joking!"

"They sleep downstairs," said Elizabeth. "They're quite comfortable."

"Anyway," Rafael continued, "a few weeks ago Dingle came into the bedroom, jumped onto the bed and lay down beside me. A few minutes later Toc came in."

"Did they! Where was I?" Elizabeth interrupted her husband.

"You were at your mother's, dear," he said. "Now please, can I continue?"

Elizabeth picked up her half empty wine glass and gulped down the white wine, then picked up the nearest bottle – a dry red - and poured herself a refill.

"Thank you," said Rafael. "Dingle and Toc knew they were not allowed into the bedroom. But they also knew Elizabeth was not there to tell them off."

"Huuuh!" said Elizabeth.

"But surely," said Crispin, "they knew there was nobody there to scold them so they took advantage of the situation. That makes them clever."

"Bear with me," Rafael replied. "They both lay there, sleeping contentedly, and then Dingle started to purr gently. This set Toc off and she started as well. Hearing Toc purr made Dingle purr even more loudly, which made Toc purr more loudly, and pretty soon it was like a couple of freight trains were passing through my bedroom."

"You should get dogs!" Markus Mark shouted. "And you wouldn't have that problem!"

Rafael laughed.

"My point is this. Cats, like us, just want to be happy. They want to be fed, watered and have somewhere comfortable to go." He looked around the packed hall; everyone who had been invited was there.

"You're wrong Dad, money is what makes a lot of people happy – and their pursuit of it no matter what the costs - I think you've just disproved your own theory," said Ruby. She turned to baby Georgina and tickled her tummy. "Silly grandad."

Baby Georgina returned a toothless grin, melting the hearts of those around her.

"I think she needs some fresh air," said Lars, looking up from his phone for the first time. "I know I do."

He got up, unharnessed his daughter and lifted her out of the all-wooden chair.

"What's up with him?" asked Elizabeth as he headed to the exit with his daughter.

"Something going on at work… take no notice," said Ruby.

The women returned their attention to Rafael.

"Well," he said. "Yes Ruby, thank you for the correction. Most... and I stress MOST of us just want to be happy, but sadly for some of us our pursuit of happiness is driven by greed and a lack of integrity. Anyway, getting back to our cats, they had a 'who can purr the loudest contest' and let me tell you none of us got much sleep that night."

"Sounds pretty stupid to me," Caleb shouted over from the next table. "What do you think, son?"

"Cats are stupid," said Jethro from across the table. "Dogs are much cleverer."

"Bear with me," said Rafael. "The point I'm trying to make is this. One stupid act doesn't make them stupid animals."

"Of course it does!" shouted Kirk Scott. "It's a stupid thing to do, so it makes them stupid."

"Okay, let me put it to you this way." Rafael turned to face him. "Who here has ever put the wrong fuel in their car?"

Three hands went up: Evelyn Smith, Jill Jones and Stefan Schmidt. Several red faces, including Kirk Scott, suggested additional evidence of guilt.

"It's something that a lot of people do," Rafael continued. "And I think we'd all agree, it's a stupid thing to do." He looked around the room again. "But should we really label somebody who makes a mistake like that as a stupid person? Of course not. Now if the same person does it three or four times then, yes, that person is stupid and deserves the stupid label."

He turned to Elizabeth.

"My wife…" He spoke with a little hesitation, watching her blush as soon as he mentioned her. "My beautiful, intelligent, well-meaning wife…"

"Me… he means me," said Elizabeth.

"My wife did something stupid." Rafael paused as a cheer took over the room.

"Me again," said Elizabeth pointing to herself.

"But she is not a stupid person."

There was a quieter cheer of agreement this time.

"She did what she did without my knowledge."

"You would have tried to stop me."

"True," he said. "But she did it with the best of intentions."

"You sit down, rest your leg, let me explain myself," said Elizabeth, standing up.

Rafael leant on his walking stick and sat down, looking up at his wife.

"First of all," she said, "I'd like to start off by apologising for the way things turned out. Particularly you know… what happened… at the end."

"I need an ambulance now."

The air ambulance arrived within forty-five minutes. By the time the flashing lights of three police cars and two ambulances appeared on the tracks over an hour later peace had been re-established within the marquee and the air ambulance had long gone.

PeeTurD started it. He approached Elizabeth and threw a punch. Elizabeth managed to sidestep but his fist still caught her on the cheek.

"I thought it was only pregnant women you beat up on?" she shouted after the glancing blow.

PeeTurD let out a yell in an effort to intimidate this woman who wasn't scared of him. He stepped forward again with his right fist ready to position another blow, but as he pulled his arm back Jan Kowolski got hold of it and attempted to twist it backwards and bring him to the floor. Unfortunately, it was at the same moment as Rafael attempted to rugby tackle the aggressor, and so when PeeTurD fell - like a toxic Laburnam tree - it was on top of Rafael.

Roman, Barry and Kirk then threw themselves on top of the two of them in an effort to restrict PeeTurD's movements.

As soon as the first punch had hit Elizabeth, Hector and several other adults had closed ranks around the children. Hector reasoned during a lightning mental risk assessment it would be safer for them to be in the company of a bull, a donkey and a drunken farmer – all of whom appeared passive - than it was to stay where they were. By the time the affray was in full motion the little ones had all been hustled into the crèche.

"Will everybody please keep calm," Hector had shouted to the crowd while attempting to get a signal to call 999 on his mobile. Some listened, others stood and watched. Several of the men and Alice Grubb ran forward to get involved in the affray.

"This is turning out to be quite fun," said Mr Melford from his mobility scooter on the sidelines. "Go on, give him a kick from me, nicked half me savings he did," he had shouted as he watched the men pile on top of PeeTurD and Rafael.

It was only when the writhing stopped, and after Roman, Barry and Kirk removed themselves from a now subdued PeeTurD and smiled congratulations to each other on a fight well fought, that they heard the screaming from PeeTurD's underside.

"Help... my leg..."

And they realised Rafael was hurt.

"I'm sorry for the way it turned out." Elizabeth looked at her husband with his still on the mend leg but she was also referring to Roman's cracked rib, Barry's kicked-in groin and Kirk Scott's lost tooth and bruised knee.

"You were just lucky the police didn't get involved," shouted a voice from the crowd, "and press charges."

"Against who?" Elizabeth turned to look at who had made the remark. It was Paul Hollyoak. "Not me, all I did was organise an event badly."

"You put people in danger..."

"Oh please, it would have been fine if PeeTurD hadn't kicked off. People were starting to enjoy themselves... I think..."

"Well, Elizabeth," Jan shouted from his table near the window, "I thought most of it was fun."

"The way you stood up to that bully," shouted Evelyn. "And look what he did to you."

"No shame that one," Markus Mark shouted agreement.

Elizabeth touched her now healed cheek and smiled.

"It was worth it," she said.

"I would like to add one last thing," Rafael stood up again. "While I was in hospital I did a lot of thinking… about our NHS."

"Did you?" said Elizabeth. "You never said."

"As everyone knows our National Health Service is seriously underfunded."

At that moment Lars returned to the table with baby Georgina.

"Her nappy needs changing," he said, handing the child over to Ruby.

Ruby looked at her husband. She got up and picked the bag up that was hooked over the back of her chair.

"Thanks," she said as she headed for the exit.

Elizabeth leant over to where Lars had sat back down.

"Nobody could accuse you of being a hands-on father." She spoke quietly so that Rafael would not hear before turning to her husband and saying in a louder voice, "So what were you thinking about the NHS?"

"It was about another revenue stream for them. Let's face it. It was PeeTurD's fault that I was in hospital, so why shouldn't he pay? I mean, why not make those people who are convicted of inflicting harm on others pay the costs of NHS care for their victims? And yes, if they are children make their parents pay. Let them know there are consequences to their actions, only once they're convicted of course."

"Mum, sorry I'm so late, the train…"

Elizabeth turned; it was Rory. She stood up to hug her son.

"Rory, I'm so glad you've made it."

"Wouldn't have missed this for the world."

"I've missed you so much."

"With all that you've been up to, I'm surprised you had the time." He leant over to his father. "Good to see you, Dad. Bloody hell, bet that was painful."

"Rory! Rory! Over here!" Rory looked over at the next table to where his friends Ahmet, George and Moses were sitting. Moses jumped up, arms outstretched, preferring a bear hug to a handshake.

"How are you, mate? It's so good to see you."

"And you, and don't worry, I forgive you..."

"Forgive him? What's he done this time?" said Rafael.

"Dad, you really don't want to know."

"As a matter of fact, I do," said Rafael. "Especially when I see my wife sitting next to me reddening up as if she's got a fever."

"It's nothing," said Elizabeth. "He just helped, that's all."

"Helped what?"

"You know, at the fete..."

"Oh that! Yes, I saw you." Rafael smiled at the lad. "You did the lighting and sound. You did a sterling job."

"And from what I heard you did a whole lot more," said Rory. "I heard about your new-found theatrical friends."

"It's true. I can't deny it," said Moses.

Somewhere inside Rafael's brain a virtual light clicked on.

"You! The gatecrashers! You arranged the whole bloody thing!"

"A few friends of mine from the theatre!" said Moses.

"I can't deny it. It was my idea!" said Elizabeth.

"They weren't ravers at all," said Rafael, his face aghast. "You planted them."

"Only to prove a point," said Elizabeth.

"Well I never!" said Rafael.

"But it's all behind us now." Elizabeth pushed back her chair to stand up and wave to the DJ on the far side of the room. "So how about we let the dancing commence."

"Excuse me... excuse us..." It was Freddy, sitting just along the table with Demelza. "Please may I say something?"

"As long as it's quick," said Rafael.

"As long as you're sober," said Elizabeth, holding her hand up to attract the DJ's attention.

"It will be quick and let me assure you I am sober." He smiled through his newly grown bushy grey moustache.

"Go on then," said Elizabeth as the music stopped. She stood up and shouted. "Excuse me, everyone, my father – I think you all know him - would like to say a word."

Freddy stood up and looked around.

"First of all, please let me apologise for my behaviour at the fete." He looked down at Demelza sitting next to him. Elizabeth noticed she smiled encouragement.

"I'm sorry, Elizabeth, for adding extra stress to your day and I'm sorry, Demelza, for embarrassing you as I did."

"Oy, what about me?" It was Isobel sitting further down the table. "You embarrassed me and crapped up my day too, you know."

"Sorry to you, too, Isobel." He turned once more to face everyone. "And sorry to all of you. It was insane... a mental, mad thing to do."

"You can say that again!" said Elizabeth under her breath.

Freddy turned to his daughter.

"Now I don't want to steal your thunder or anything..." he hesitated before continuing. "But I'm really pleased to tell you that following your example..."

"What example?" Rafael leant forward to try and see him better.

"Your example of this... you know, renewing your marriage vows..."

"Good God!" Elizabeth looked at her husband. "I think I know what's coming."

"Well, my friend, my soul mate, my beautiful lover of many years... the mother of my two beautiful girls has accepted my proposal and we're going to get married."

"Holy shit you're not!" said Isobel.

"Mum?" said Elizabeth. "Is this for real?"

"It's what I want," said Demelza with a smile. "It's what I've always wanted."

"Blimey," said Elizabeth.

"Congratulations!" said Rafael.

"Mum, are you sure you've thought this through?"

"Of course not, dear," said Demelza with a smile. "Why on earth would I do that?"

"Okay," said Rafael. "And now for some DANCING!"

"Not you." He caught his wife's arm as she got up. "I need to speak to you."

Elizabeth sat back down, looked at her husband and then picked up the glass of wine in front of her.

"What's up?"

"You know when I asked you if you were having an affair with Crispin and you said that I was a fool."

Elizabeth stopped drinking but did not immediately remove the glass from her lips, it hovered there, for a moment. When she did put down the glass, the movement was slow, as were her words.

"What about it?"

"What did you mean?"

"Nothing…"

"You meant something. What am I missing?"

"It's not for me to say…"

"Fair enough. But presumably you can nod a response to a question?"

"Maybe."

"Bob?"

Elizabeth nodded her head ever so slightly.

"And Crispin…"

Another nod, but this time no eye contact.

"They're lovers, aren't they?"

"I wouldn't say lovers, exactly," said Elizabeth. "They have sex… been at it for years, I think."

"But what about Ava, does she know?"

"Of course she does…"

"And…"

"And what?"

"Doesn't she mind?"

"Apparently not. She knows Crispin loves her."

"How long have you known?"

"A while."

"Blimey!"

"Blimey what?" All smiles, Ava danced towards Elizabeth. "Raffy darling, can I pinch your wife? Crispin won't dance with me."

"He knows…" said Elizabeth.

"Knows what?" Ava stopped dancing.

"About Crispin and Bob."

"Oh, that!" Ava started to dance away again. "Phew, for a moment I thought it was something serious."

"But don't you mind?" said Rafael.

"Of course not, why should I? It's just a sex thing... he loves me."

"But why has he never told me?"

"He has tried, on several occasions, honestly. But he didn't think you'd cope with it..."

"Not cope with it? That's ridiculous."

Crispin approached with a smile and a full glass of red wine.

"I say..." he said. "Who cope with what?"

The music continued and on the dance floor so did the dancing. At the table Rafael, Elizabeth, Ava and Crispin looked at each other.

"Who cope with what?" Crispin repeated.

"You... you didn't think I'd cope if I knew about you and... and... Bob."

For a moment, Crispin blushed.

"How long have we known each other?" said Rafael. "Well, thank you very much."

"Oh don't be upset!" said Crispin pulling up a chair next to him. "It's just that..."

"I'm listening."

"You're so bloody judgemental. There, I've said it. I didn't tell you because I didn't want your opinion or views on it, or to listen to you telling me it was a bad thing to do."

"Elizabeth, what on earth possessed you..."

They were the last words that Rafael said to his wife before they took him away in the air ambulance. She wanted to go with him but there wasn't enough room so she was left stranded in the marquee. Hector took complete control until the police took over.

PeeTurD was sitting on his splintered gold sprayed chair, head in hands. He stood up and shouted when he saw the boys in blue.

"At fucking last! Will you arrest this lot? Look what they did to me!" He pointed to his eye which was swelling nicely.

"I see," said a baby-faced policeman. "I'll need to take statements."

Elizabeth stepped forward.

"He did this to me," she said. "I can give you a statement if you like."

Rafael looked at his friend.

"Crispin," said Rafael. "I'm sorry you felt like that."

"No sweat, forgotten," said Crispin. He turned to Elizabeth.

"So tell me. How on earth did you persuade that arse PeeTurD to come along in the first place?"

"His face when he was arrested. It was a picture." Elizabeth chuckled to herself.

"He's lucky you're not pressing charges," said Rafael."Come on, out with it. What did you say to him?"

Elizabeth looked at her husband and smiled.

"Well, you know he wants to build two houses at the front of his manor?"

"I had heard…"

"I merely pointed out…" she paused. "That the parish council may look at his planning application more favourably if he participated in village life more. I suppose it was a bit of a bribe."

"Bloody hell, and he believed you…"

"Of course he did, he's someone who doesn't understand rules or right from wrong, so why wouldn't he?"

"Bit naughty though… does Hector know?"

Elizabeth shook her head.

"Don't be daft, he'd have a fit!" She paused before adding, "I might have also mentioned that I knew he'd been avoiding his taxes for years and that if he didn't come along I'd contact HMRC."

"What! You're lucky you only ended up with a bruised cheek." Rafael looked at his wife. "So, how did you know that?"

"I didn't."

"What!"

"Lucky guess, I suppose…"

"Tell me you're joking."

"I did base my views on the fact that anybody who could steal from family and friends would probably not have a problem with avoiding paying their share of taxes."

"Bloody hell! You're lucky you're still alive."

"I know…"

"I think the sooner we put this whole business to rest the better." Rafael looked at his wife as he spoke.

"I couldn't agree more."

"You know, I think I'll get a CCTV system at home… in case of repercussions."

"Don't be silly, he's a bully. He targets the weak and the vulnerable, not people who stand up to him."

"I know. Poor Kevin, any news there?"

"I spoke to him yesterday the solicitors have been in touch. It looks as if he is going to get at least some of his inheritance."

"So it was worth it?"

"Yes," Elizabeth nodded. "Apart from your broken leg, of course. I'm so sorry about that."

"I'm on the mend," said Rafael. "We're on the mend…"

"Oh shit!" said Elizabeth.

"What? What on earth's up with you?"

"I've another announcement. I forgot… … you know."

From his seat Rafael waved his walking stick at the DJ; the music stopped mid-song this time, along with the dancing, the chatting and the laughter.

"Sorry for the interruption, all." Rafael shouted. "But Elizabeth has another short announcement to make."

Everybody turned to face Elizabeth. She stood up and smiled.

"As you may remember during our event, we had our own mini EU referendum."

"I remember," shouted Alice Grubb. "And you added a third option to the paper."

"That's right," said Elizabeth. "Remain, Leave, or Change."

"So what was the result?" a voice shouted from the dance floor.

"Okay, before I give the results to you there is just something I would like to say."

"Keep it quick," Rafael hissed at her. "It's getting late."

"I would just like to say this. It's interesting, the elderly are accused of not wanting change, well I would suggest that change is exactly what they do want..."

"Elizabeth..." Rafael hissed a warning. "No speeches."

She looked at her husband, placed her hand on his shoulder then looked around the room, all eyes on her.

"I feel sorry for young people today, they have been brought up to accept zero hour contracts, to accept that they have minimal employment rights, to accept that they will be lucky ever to be able to afford to buy a home of their own, accept that our police and NHS are underfunded and that human slavery actually exists here, amongst us." She paused to look around, pleased that she had everyone's attention. "But many of us here know it doesn't have to be like that."

Rafael clapped his hands, several other people joined in.

"Good point," he said. "Now will you please announce the result of the vote?"

Elizabeth smiled at her husband.

"Anyway, I am pleased to announce that I have the results here and it was an overwhelming – I hope you hear that – an overwhelming vote for change. And I would suggest to you all that if there had been a change option on our original ballot paper then that would have been the referendum result, and..."

"That's enough now." Rafael leant over and put his hand on hers. "Quit while you're ahead."

She turned and smiled at him and then sat down.

And so the party continued, people laughed, they chatted and they danced together. There was plenty of food, more than enough alcohol and the number or state of the toilets did not cause concern. Elizabeth danced the night away, with Crispin, with Ava and with Sydney, watched by Rafael.

Just after 11:30pm Elizabeth returned to her husband at the table. He gripped her hand and pulled her towards him.

"You okay?" he asked.

"I'm exhausted."

"Do you want to leave?"

Elizabeth shook her head.

"No," she said. "I'm happy to stay."

ABOUT THE AUTHOR

S.A.Lama has been a writer of non-fiction for nearly twenty years. This is her first fiction novel. Her next novel 'A Dedicated Professional' is due to be published in August 2019.

Printed in Great Britain
by Amazon